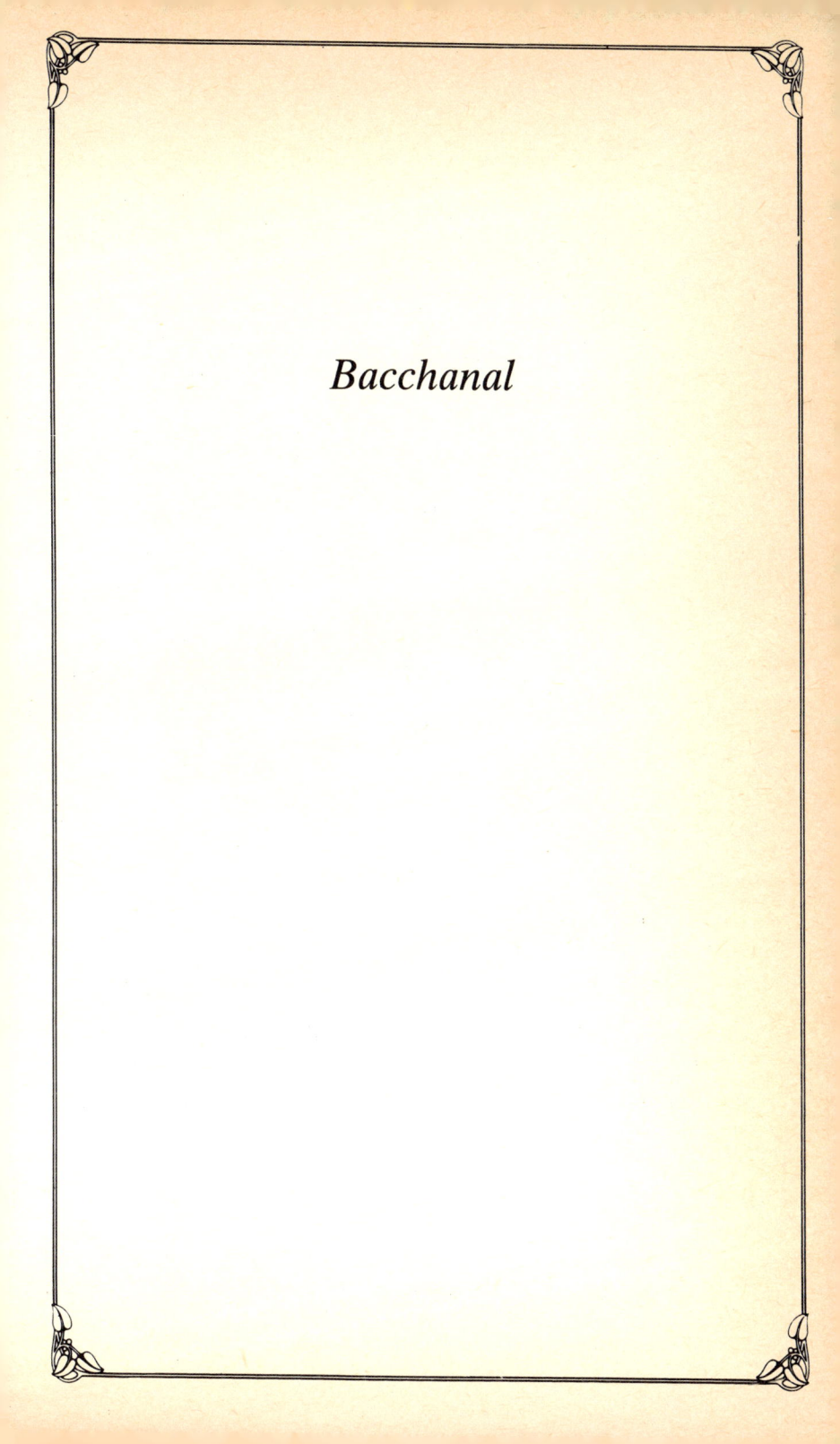

Bacchanal

By the same author

THE ALCHEMIST
(In Introduction 7)

PZYCHE

TANTALUS

Bacchanal

A NOVEL BY
Amanda Hemingway

Hamish Hamilton   London

For Maggie

I would like to thank the following people for their assistance: my cousin, Hanna Karsberg; Claire Toeman: Robert Fox; and most of all Michael White.

First published in Great Britain 1987
by Hamish Hamilton Ltd
27 Wrights Lane London W8 5TZ

Copyright © Amanda Hemingway

British Library in Cataloguing in Publication Data

Hemingway, Amanda
    Bacchanal.
    I. Title
    823'.914[F]   PR6058.E4918/

    ISBN 0-241-12079-9

Phototypeset by Sunrise Setting
Torquay Devon
Printed in Great Britain by
Billing and Sons Ltd, Worcester

'Life is like one of those wild parties we used to have in our first year, a sort of contemporary bacchanal where everyone has to drink and dance and smoke and screw – until they drop.'

Dominic Francis Hardinge:
Climax and Anticlimax

Part One

'Sex is a little death: Death is the big orgasm.'

Dominic Francis Hardinge:
Tumours

Chapter One

Some psychiatrists might have claimed that Dominic Hardinge's obsession with the total destruction of humanity stemmed from the fact that he was raped when he was twelve years old.

Unfortunately for those who would certainly have enjoyed dissecting his subconscious, he never confided in any of them – not even the famous Dr Hieronymous Glauber, a close personal friend and for years the recipient of Dominic's inmost hangups. Dr Glauber heard all about the conventional traumas of an adopted child, the insecurities of a public school adolescence, the Unpleasant Incident on the Yorkshire moors, the monk who fondled him in the chapel choir, the friend of his aunt who exposed her breasts to him, and a number of other stories which became increasingly detailed and colourful the more they appeared to reveal. The couch was comfortable, the audience attentive, and under such circumstances Dominic loved to talk about himself: the self he had invented, the self he wished to believe in, the self he wished other people to see. Perhaps that was why Dr Glauber never heard about the rape. In the event, very few people did. The witness – there *was* a witness – spoke of it to only one person, long after, and by that time two of the three responsible for the deed were already dead. Bryan Solloway died of heart failure and disillusionment five years after The Group broke up and six months after Johnny Sachs, loaded up to the eyeballs with whisky and barbiturates, drove his Ferrari into a petrol tanker on the M1 and exploded into eternity, taking with him not only the driver of the tanker but also the pursuing police car, a Mini which happened to get in the way and a sizeable chunk of roadworks. Like James Dean, like Marilyn Monroe, like Jimi Hendrix, Marc Bolan, Keith Moon, Johnny Sachs passed into legend. The few human remains proved so difficult to identify that bits of P.C. Trevor Wilkins, one Joe Broadhead, long distance lorry driver, and Miss Alison Broome of Chipping Ongar doubtless shared in Johnny's superstar funeral even as they had been allowed to share in his superstar death. Rafe Dunston, the only one of the three rapists to survive into the Eighties, had buried the whole incident long ago in the depths of his sub-conscience and had no intention of digging it up. Perhaps, even to Dominic, it became in the end relatively unimportant, a symptom and not a cause of the despair which is the disease of a generation. We are the ones who have learnt from history, at last. We have seen (usually on television) the failure of all political ideals, the withering of all religions. The threat of nuclear holocaust hangs above us like a vast spectral umbrella. We are over-educated, over-sensitive, over-protected, illiterate, brutalised, mechanised, liberated, unprejudiced, unfree. Despair, like herpes, is the fashion. Dominic Hardinge suffered from both. The story that he did not tell Dr Glauber remains a great psychological question mark, a finger pointing nowhere – or nowhere much. Only four people are left who even know that it happened: the witness, two others, and Cathie Lavalle, formerly Cathie Virgo Holdings, formerly Cathie Sachs. Like Rafe – like Bryan, like Johnny – she never learned the victim's identity. And, like them, she never talked about it.

Johnny Sachs told his wife about the rape on their wedding night. He told her for very much the same reason as he had married her: to hurt her. She was young and soft and pretty, gazing at him with innocent kitten's eyes and just a hint of gentle nervousness: ideally equipped to be hurt. If you buy a kitten for the purpose of torturing it the R.S.P.C.A. are quite likely to find out and deal with you accordingly, but young wives do not come under their jurisdiction. Cathie had been agreeably spoiled for all the seventeen years of her life and she expected a constant supply of love and affection the way most people expect the sun to rise in the morning. She had no strength of character, no temper or temperament, no native spite, no guts – nothing which might have saved her. She was very nearly a virgin. By the time she became Cathie Virgo and later Mrs Edmond Lavalle she was a harder, glossier, more sophisticated product, a woman with a lot of make-up exquisitely applied and very little face underneath. She had grown greedy, not for love (love had gone sour on her) but for the good things which she had once taken for granted. An instinct for survival, almost the only instinct she possessed, had taught her to suffer and to be sly. The kitten had turned into a cat who would purr at its owner's kicks or caresses for the sake of a saucer of cream. But when she married Johnny Sachs – for love, of course – she was still young and nervous and hopeful, a perfect victim. Too weak to fight back, too stupid to run away. Johnny knew very well what she would become, eventually: he had a gift of perspicacity which was both unnecessary and unwanted; he used it, like a third ear, to hear secrets, hating himself. He knew she would suffer and she would not leave; she might even still be around to cry at his funeral. (She did.) Later in their marriage he sensed she had eluded him, when he could not tell if her pain was real or simulated, a sop for his pleasure. Quite possibly she could not tell either. But on their wedding night, at least, her pain was real.

He told her about the rape with a sort of cold satisfaction, not gloating, not boasting, merely reading the sentence. This is me, this is the man you have married. Life. He piled detail on detail until her disbelief was drowned in horror and she shivered in the over-heated bedroom. He unpicked her personality, thread by thread, like a destructive child with a piece of embroidery; the stitches would never set straight again. Afterwards, he made love to her (if love is the word), forcing himself into her anus, thinking of the boy's white twitching buttocks, his useless childish muscles. Johnny's drug-soaked body had little inclination for sex these days and less ability, but this once he climaxed easily, and lay, at long last, filled, emptied, exhausted, totally and blissfully blank.

Johnny Sachs was not naturally cruel. He was a superstar, a media product, larger-than-life and less than human, five foot eight that looked like six foot, pig-eyed, wide-lipped, thick-nosed, irresistibly ugly-handsome, a brutal stage presence in erotic sweat stains and skin-tight jeans. He was rude to grovelling interviewers, coarse to sophisticated women, domineering with his colleagues. They all came back for more, particularly the interviewers. How he might have treated his friends no one knew, since the few he had had were long gone, a whole lifestyle away, gone with the bitchy inadequate schoolboy embarrassed by his own sexuality (that was a joke) and dreaming an impossible dream of stardom. The dream came true, in the way such dreams do, and turned into a nightmare. Sometimes, it seemed to him that they were eating him alive, drinking the sweat that rolled down his chest, the blood that dripped from his nerves: the audiences, the media, the women, even those he should have been close to, had he dared; Bryan Solloway (his manager), the other members of The Group. He feared and loathed and despised them, even as he feared and loathed and despised himself. In the end, he sacked Bryan and The Group broke up. The boys got other jobs; some of them were good. Bryan drank too much. Alone, Johnny spent or gambled a million pounds, made two million. He was the rock-and-roll supergod whom nothing could topple. If he sang 'Bangers and Mash' loud enough and often enough it would reach the top of the charts and get him another gold disc. Offstage, he fled in terror from the hungry, lascivious, blood-drinking public and tried to numb what was left of his unnecessary mind with alcohol and drugs. He bought huge houses to hide in, swimming-pools to drown in, islands on which he could be marooned. There was no one left to hate, no one left to hurt, but himself. So he got married.

In the brooding intimacy of his own thoughts, Johnny Sachs might have believed that he loved his wife. Through her pain, he lashed himself to new suffering; through her tears, he knew what it was to be able to weep. What else is that, if not love? But it is difficult for someone who has no love for himself truly to love another human being. Total self-love excludes all others, but total self-loathing excludes all self, and in the truest kind of love there is a place for the self and the beloved and all the rest of the world, down to the smallest of small seeds in the forest, or the least of little cells swimming in the sea. Too late, Johnny realised that she was not wholly his creature: she had withdrawn from him in a way he could not define, behind the whimperings and the increasingly easy tears. Sometimes he hit her, usually in the face, but it did not make him feel any stronger or closer to her. If he had known about love, he would have understood. Cathie had simply expunged all love from her heart. She had married him in a wild glory of adolescent passion, and one morning she woke up to find the glory had blown away as though it had never been. She saw that he was thirty-eight, that he had a hangover, that he gave her no pleasure in bed. She saw that his eyelids were swollen into fat red creases and underscored with shadows, and his lips slobbered in his sleep. She touched his cheek and it was rough as grit; his breath smelt like the wrong end of a Listerine advertisement. She might have felt sorry for him if she had not been so busy feeling sorry for herself. Awake, he turned over, groaned, mumbled something about coffee. She got up and went into the kitchen, fiddled about with the machine. She did not leave. It was easier to wait.

When Johnny Sachs died, no one was particularly sorry (except the families of P.C. Wilkins, Joe Broadhead, and Alison Broome. Q.E.D.). The masses revelled in their grief with all the healthy satisfaction of a tribe which has sacrificed its god and can now safely immortalise him for ever. Bryan Solloway drank half a bottle of Scotch, played an old record ('Ragged Robin', one of The Group's earliest hits), and seemed to feel a sudden sagging in his ventricles. Rafe Dunston told everyone how great Johnny was, what mates they had been, and tried not to look relieved. Alisdair Saunders, younger brother of Charlie, one-time drummer of The Group, read the scrawled headline outside a newsagent's, went into a cafe, bought a cup of coffee which he did not drink, lit a cigarette. And Dominic Hardinge, who did not know that his life and Johnny's had ever touched, let alone overlapped and invaded, discussed it with his schoolfellows, spoke with judicious wisdom of the loss to the music business and the great days of The Group. It was a good way to die, Dominic insisted, going out in style like a Viking warrior: a glorious way to die. Better than waiting around for cancer or senility or World War Three. What about the others? someone pointed out, glancing at the fleeting references to P.C. Wilkins etc. It was hard luck on them. Dominic admitted it, but without conviction.

At the funeral Cathie Sachs found it was easy to manage a few tears. They welled out without disturbing her mascara and trickled, one at a time, down her cheek, to be carefully dabbed away by her mother. She was not sure quite why the tears came so easily, only that this was what everyone expected of her. Cathie had always done what was expected of her; she was very well brought up. In her expensive black with her hair brushed forward to hide the slight bruise on her temple, relic of their last fight, she gave a suitable impression of pathos and fragility. She was still very young. (It was rumoured Jonas Virgo saw her there for the first time, on the Nine O'Clock News, caught by the camera in the act of releasing a teardrop.) Johnny had been notoriously unfaithful – more notoriety than fact, due to his frequent bouts of impotence – but that did not matter now. No one expected a megastar to be content with one of anything, particularly women. Huge floral tributes smothered the coffin as more stars and superstars vied with one another in ostentation. All her life, Cathie was to remember the stink of them. She felt faint. Everyone said she 'bore up nobly'. Afterwards, back at the house, she threw herself on the wide empty bed and cried and cried with the intensity of her relief – not elegant occasional tears but huge childish sobs, with red eyes and running make-up, swollen lips and leaky nose.

Her mother stroked her hair and murmured vague words of comfort, overcome by the spectacle of her daughter's grief. But even now Cathie would not tell her the truth. She had wanted to marry Johnny more than anything in the world, and it was impossible, quite impossible, to admit that she had been wrong, to face the warm impetuous gush of maternal sympathy and understanding. She could have left Johnny for her mother at any time during the past two years, but she had chosen to stay, to maintain the façade, to wait for she knew not what. And in the end Fate had been kind and arranged everything for her: Johnny was dead, her marriage safe. She had learned a few lessons and now her life would be as it was before. Or very nearly. For she, Cathie, was not the same any more. She did not want the same things as the Cathie who had once wanted to marry Johnny Sachs. Even the parental love in which she had sunned herself for so long now seemed stifling and uncomfortable. Her mother's gentleness galled her; her sympathy horrified; innocence grated; tenderness bored. Johnny had taught her so much about love. She had grown up and been corrupted in spite of herself, too weak to resist, and now her heart was empty and loveless for ever. She got up, no longer able to endure her mother's caresses, and went into the bathroom, locking the door between them.

So ended Johnny Sachs, rock idol, megastar, superstud, unregretting and unregretted, unloving and unloved. He would have laughed at the funeral if he had been there. There was a moment during the service when Cathie remembered the story of the rape and wondered, as she had often wondered before, if it was true or merely an ugly boast, intended only to shock and hurt. She did not really think it was true. Bryan Solloway, too, remembered the rape, and drank the other half of the bottle of whisky, thus shortening his life and the time he had left for remorse. Rafe Dunston remembered the rape, lying between his wife's thighs, and, as always, his erection wilted like an ice-cream cornet in a heatwave. And Dominic Hardinge, reading an account of the funeral in the newspaper, smoking an illicit cigarette and listening to the distant ululation of the school choir, did not remember the rape at all.

Chapter Two

Alisdair Saunders was barely seventeen when he witnessed the rape. He was still at school, at least in theory, studying for his A levels with little enthusiasm, handing in his essays grudgingly and late, determined to stop the aimless drift into further education by total and obstinate failure rather than outright rebellion. He was fond of his parents, but he thought them stupid, after the manner of their generation, stupid and shortsighted. 'Don't *tell* me, son,' his father used to say, with reference to almost anything, '*show* me.' Alisdair, carefully absorbing the parental dictum, decided to show him that his plans for the future, specifically Alisdair's future, were simply not feasible. Alisdair thought most of his family stupid, one way and another, including his two sisters and particularly his eldest brother, who worked in a merchant bank. Not that he disapproved of making money. It was just that he did not want that *kind* of money – safe, regular, nine-to-five, mortgage-and-marriage money. He wanted lots of money, exciting money, glamorous, dangerous, easy come easy go, bright lights and late nights money. Money that was *fun*. Like Charlie's money (his parents were still bewildered by Charlie). Like Johnny's money . . . Not that Alisdair was a musician: he had no delusions about that. But he could tinker with fuses, set up equipment, answer fan mail, find things which had been mislaid, produce cold beer when required. He was not afraid to take responsibility for his own errors or other people's. He was shrewd, for all his youthful daydreams, he had a talent for organisation, a nose for success. (Hadn't Johnny himself said so?) One day, he would be the manager of a group like The Group – not a tired, seedy, disheartened manager like Bryan Solloway but someone ambitious and dynamic, respected by all who worked with him. He would arrange new and still more glittering tours for them, vamp and re-vamp their public image, share in their profits, their girls, their lives. Alisdair knew without even having to think about it that Bryan Solloway would not be around for ever. He had seen Johnny ragging Bryan often enough, taunting him with a specious contempt he never showed Alisdair. In ten years – in eight – there might just be a chance for a younger (a much younger) man. If he had imagination and flair – and the right experience. It was a dream which Alisdair had never yet dared to dream, but it was there, ready-made, on the edge of his mind, waiting for the right moment to creep out into the star-bedazzled world of his secret hopes. He had no intention of frittering away that dream at university. He wanted to learn his business, from the bottom up. When he left school, there would be a job – some kind of a job – with The Group, he was sure. Johnny would never let him down.

And then came the rape.

It was because of the rape that Alisdair passed his A levels. It was because of the rape that he went to Cambridge, worked when necessary, smoked less dope, acquired a First. It was because of the rape that he gave up drink for a week and barbiturates for ever. It was because of the rape that he did not go to visit Elaine Gisborne, the night her parents were away. It was because of the rape that – like Cathie Sachs/Virgo/Lavalle – he began to have a vague distorted inkling of what Life was All About.

He didn't recall very much about the early stages of the party. It was in a house, a big country house with a pretentious name, Something Court: not quite a manor (there were other houses on either side, discreetly hidden behind trees) but very nearly. It was near a village but he couldn't remember the name of that either. The house belonged to a friend of Johnny's, not a real friend but the kind you acquire in the music business, easy come easy go, like the money. He was, of course, extremely rich. He had laid on – for Johnny's benefit – lakes of beer and champagne, floor-shaking music, mind-bending lights, dope, peanuts, lavatories, girls. There was a rolling of joints and a popping of pills. Later, several of the girls took their clothes off, but nobody noticed. It was not a very good party. Alisdair was not invited to the 'good' parties; Charlie said he was too young. But this time: 'It won't be much good,' Johnny said. 'Let the kid come.' Alisdair didn't mind Johnny calling him 'the kid', or 'baby', 'infant', 'brat', or even just 'Ally'. He didn't mind when Johnny flipped a careless order over his shoulder: 'Get me a beer', 'Do this', 'Fetch that', without bothering to add pleases and thank yous. He didn't mind (much) when Johnny told him to piss off. In the right mood, after all, Johnny would offer him a swig from a beer can, tell him anecdotes of the girls he had had (or even – precious confession – the ones he hadn't), pass him a joint like one of the gang. Charlie didn't really like it, but Johnny didn't give a damn about what Charlie liked. He didn't give a damn about anything. He was a loner, a maverick, a king. Sometimes, he even used to get a kick out of bugging people, showing them how little he cared. Like when Charlie protested about Alisdair. 'He's got it all wrong, Ally,' Johnny told him later. 'He wants to do the Big Brother act, protect you from life. But it won't work. Growing up is something you have to do on your own. Most of us fuck it, anyway. It's called freedom of the individual. Here, try this.'

Alisdair drew on the joint with a credible assumption of coolth. It was (he thought) far stronger than the stuff he was used to.

'Well done,' said Johnny. 'You know what that is? Camel dung and sulphur powder. If you can smoke that and stay cool, you can do anything.'

Alisdair tried to think of a suitable response, something

that would make him sound even cooler; but he couldn't.

'Don't talk much, do you?' Johnny remarked presently. 'Smart kid. I like people who don't talk much. It means I can rest my eardrums between concerts. One day, I'll find a bird who knows when to shut up.'

'Are there any?' murmured Alisdair, hoping he sounded knowledgeable.

Johnny grinned. 'Probably. Birds come in all types: blonde, dark, lively, shy, front, back, what the hell. Some talk, some don't. The trouble is, when you've had a lot, they all get to seem the same. That's the worst of life. You want to sing: you sing. You want to screw: you screw. The money comes rolling in and the lights go spinning round and you can sing and screw everyone. Only afterwards, there's nothing. No real friends, no real sex. You dreamed a dream and it came true and now you've nothing left to dream about. Catch twenty-two. You dope and you drink to stop yourself thinking, but it doesn't do any good. There's still that same space between your ears where your dream used to be. You can't fill it up. You can't ever fill it up. In the end, you die.' He picked up the joint, which was burning away untouched between Alisdair's fingers. 'You know why they call this stuff shit? Because it's shits who need it. Shit for shits. Dope is shit and alcohol – alcohol is urine. I eat excreta, like a maggot.' Suddenly, he looked at Alisdair, his eyes focusing on the boy's face with an almost savage intensity. 'What do you think of me now, brat? Have I shattered all your pretty illusions? That *would* please Big Brother, wouldn't it?'

'I think –' Alisdair hesitated, both shocked and warmed by so much unprecedented confidence, unaware that Johnny considered him too young, too negligible, too uncritical not to trust. 'I think,' he ended, lamely, 'you aren't very happy.'

'Not happy!' Johnny almost laughed. 'Well done, infant. Top marks. You ought to be a psychoanalyst. I – am – not – happy. Try again.'

Briefly, Alisdair remembered his own unspecified dream. Despite the mockery, he felt warm right through now, warm to his very core. Warm enough to be reckless, to stake all his hopes on a moment of truth. 'I think,' he began again, tentatively, valiantly, 'you must be rather a fool.'

There was a pause.

'Better,' Johnny said at last, brusquely. 'Much better. The world is full of fools. If you ever say that again I'll hang your balls around your neck before you've even learnt what to do with them. Understand?' And then, abruptly, his anger sloughed off and his expression grew remote and bitter again. Alisdair watched him drawing on the joint: frown, inhale, unfrown. Exhale. Smoke. He found he was shaking slightly, though not from fear.

'Are you still there?' said Johnny. 'Shit. Have another drag. Where were we?'

'The world,' Alisdair repeated cautiously, 'is full of fools.'

'Bugger that. You've got to hang on to what you believe in. It won't do you any good, but hang on just the same. It isn't the belief that matters: it's the hanging. I know – I let go. And that,' he added, absently, 'is the best advice I've ever given anyone. In fact, it's probably the only advice I've ever given anyone.' Inhale, pause, exhale. 'Tomorrow, I'll tell you something different.'

Tomorrow, he told Alisdair to piss off. But the next day, or the next, he would feel like talking – the rare self-indulgence of being listened to and (he carelessly assumed) believed, no matter how deep the shallows of his cynicism, how chill the waters of his soul. As for Alisdair, he tried very hard to remember everything Johnny said. He did not necessarily mean to live by it, but he wanted to remember. He wanted to say to Johnny, years later: I remember, you told me once . . . And Johnny would smile or frown and say: 'Did I? Did I?'

For himself, he never said much in return. Nothing of his distant ambitions, little of his immediate plans. He had learnt already that the less you say, the less you expose your own inadequacy and ignorance, your latent morality, your embarrassing youth. At the party, as at most parties, he talked little and drank lots. He took one or two brightly-coloured pills, dragged on every passing joint. He was desperately blasé. It was difficult to appear blasé when you were barely seventeen, under six foot, skin and bone and not much muscle, but (to begin with) he succeeded very well. Possibly because no one else was really interested in how old, or how blasé, he was. All they saw was just another hanger-on, long hair over his shoulders, long fringe over his eyes. By daylight, the hair was a fairish mouse, the eyes deeply blue, the true speedwell blue of princesses' eyes in children's stories. Perhaps it was those eyes which gave him an uncanny look of innocence – the peculiar innocence of a street urchin caught stealing apples who has managed to eat the evidence before falling into the clutches of the law. His other features, too, were immature and faintly Puckish; rounded cheeks, idiotically snub nose, pointed pixie chin. There was no sign (as yet) of Charlie's heavier jaw or Ian's stern bankeresque profile. Alisdair looked like one of his sisters – Catriona, the pretty one – which was all very well for a sister but definitely trying for a teenage youth. Once, to his humiliation, he had overheard a girl he admired saying he had a 'cheeky' smile. After that, he tried not to smile too often. Smiling was another giveaway. Like most adolescents, he attempted to plaster on a quick veneer of sophistication in order to conceal acutely felt but largely indefinable deficiencies. He did not want anyone at that party to realise how little he was used to such an assortment of vices.

His supercool deserted him abruptly about halfway through the evening. He had been indifferent to his environment for some considerable time but now he was conscious of it again in a wealth of unpleasant detail. He was scrambling across a revolving floor heaped with prone and semi-prone bodies in the direction of the downstairs loo. It was locked. He banged on the door, but it remained locked, firmly and definitely locked, like a dungeon or a personal safe or a loo at a party when someone is banging on the door. In the adjacent bathroom, his host's wife was making love in the sunk bath with one of the rangier roadies. Somehow, he got out into the garden. The cooler air temporarily revived him; he was aware of formal flowerbeds, neat small shrubs, marble steps, exquisite urns. Beyond, a stretch of lawn as smooth and shaven as a single pile carpet. Dimly, he realised that he could not possibly desecrate that lawn: it would be a social solecism far worse than throwing up on the synthetic fur rugs inside. Panic gripped him. Behind, a door opened, lights, music, voices spilled onto the terrace. Alisdair bolted.

   Some while later, when the worst was (he hoped) over, he found himself lying half under a hedge, presumably at the bottom of the garden. The shrubs here were larger and wilder than those close to the house and there was no sign of the immaculate lawn. He wondered if he was lying on rabbit droppings; there were almost certainly rabbit droppings in this part of the garden. Presently he tried to move, but even the preliminary exertion of tensing his arm muscles made his insides reel. He lay still. There was a gap under the hedge through which he could see into a sort of lane or bridlepath; another hedge on the far side – a thicker, darker, more positive hedge than the one bordering the garden – which blotted out even the faint grey glimmer of the night. There were people in the lane. He couldn't see them at all well but gradually his eyes grew accustomed and he made out three men gathered round something or someone on the ground. He didn't realise what they were doing, at first. There were giggles – high-pitched, drunken giggles – sounds of grunting and of heaving. And then his mind cleared, or the moon came out, and suddenly he saw with horrible clarity what was going on. They were raping a boy.

   He knew at once that it was a rape although the figure on the ground did not appear to resist. He felt the pain and terror and despair that emanated from it like a return of the nausea in his own stomach. Not more than a couple of yards away he saw a small hand clenched on a tuft of grass; no other details were visible in the muddle of crumpled clothes and sprawled limbs except a brief glimpse of exposed buttocks as one of the men moved aside. The bare flesh looked milky and luminescent in the moonlight. The faces of the men were in darkness but they were so close he could hear their breathing (or was it his own?), smell their sweat and their semen and the whiff of stale beer. It was all so horrible he could not quite believe it was real. He did not absorb or remember much of what they said but he knew their voices as we know the voices of friends in a nightmare. That strange emasculated giggle: Rafe Dunston, the guitarist – he always giggled when he was smashed. The deeper, slurred, drink-sodden accents of Bryan

Solloway. And the third voice, still more familiar, a voice that remained raggedly coherent despite alcohol and dope and obscene lust, a famous unmistakable voice that (as one columnist put it) hummed like a vibrator, drawled like a chainsaw – Johnny.

Alisdair knew he ought to do something. He ought to intervene, stop it, scream, shout, get help, the police, an ambulance. But sickness and horror seemed to have welded him to the ground. He felt as if he was a part of the earth, not camouflaged but invisible, non-existent. The creeping mosses, tangled shrubs, the very roots of the grass had grown over him and through him, and now there was nothing left but a pair of eyes, watching, blinking, from under the hedge. He thought he would have to watch for ever. Broken phrases came to him – noises – a disjointed commentary: 'Rafe can't get it up – yes I can – giggle – pant – giggle – told you – useless bloody drunk – get in there – hiccup – can't make it – take it easy; he's beginning to enjoy it – baby's beginning to enjoy it – of course he is – it's an education for him isn't it? – *education*! – fuck – so keep on educating – ' Alisdair did not know how long it was before they decided they had had enough. Five minutes, ten, an hour, a night. He thought the figure on the ground had been sobbing quietly for some time. One of the men pulled him to his feet; another seemed to be fastening his clothes. The third man was just sitting in the lane, rocking gently from side to side, giggling. The boy stumbled when they released him but they dragged him up again. 'Run along, baby. Thanks for the fun. Run, baby. Run . . .' Somehow, he began to run off down the lane. Alisdair imagined he heard him fall again, only a few yards away, but he wasn't certain. The three men made off in the other direction, presumably back to the party, the giggler sagging between the shoulders of the other two. After a while, Alisdair moved.

He looked at his watch. The luminous dial told him it was still not yet midnight. He thought of the party, pursuing its inexorable course somewhere at the other end of the garden. He thought of the next day, and the next, and the next. He thought of dying, and of having to live. He was a flea on the face of the Universe, a mote of dust in God's eye. He did not

[17]

think about God much because God, he knew, wasn't thinking about him. God did not see the sparrow fall any more. He was too busy watching T.V. Alisdair retched emptily into the grass, scarcely able to raise his head. He could never remember if he actually lost consciousness. Later, when he was able, he began to get up.

After a week or two, when he knew the police wouldn't come, he tried to tell himself it had all been some kind of a dream. A hallucination – a 'bad trip'. The following morning he had woken in the back of the Range Rover with his head on a pile of coats. He had gone into the house and seen his hostess asleep in the sunk bath and the downstairs loo still irrevocably engaged. He had tried not to look round too obviously for Rafe and Bryan and Johnny. Rafe was on the sofa trying to drink from a bottle of flat beer: his face was white and ill and the beer bottle shook in his hand. But that, surely, was just a hangover. Bryan Solloway was propped against the wall, still unconscious. (He did not come round until they were halfway back to London.) Johnny was in the kitchen eating Weetabix without milk and talking in a series of staccato grunts. 'Hi kid. Siddown. Shitty party. Shitty coffee. Shit.' Alisdair could never decide if the eyes behind the bloated eyelids were a little colder and more watchful than usual. He waited for something to happen, but it didn't. They left around lunchtime, as soon as someone could be found who was fit to drive the Range Rover. Alisdair got in the car with Charlie.

'Johnny chuck you out?' his brother said.

'No.'

Charlie didn't ask any more questions. He never said much. His wife Nita said he talked with his drums and claimed he had proposed to her by tapping with a fork on an empty champagne glass. Alisdair never thought of confiding in him but he was very grateful that he was there. He had forgotten, in the exclusive limelight of Johnny's personality, how fond he was of Charlie. They drove on in a comfortable silence.

* * *

After that, Alisdair avoided Johnny. He thought at first that it might be difficult, that Johnny himself might notice and ask awkward questions – questions which he, Alisdair, did not want to have to answer. But Johnny didn't notice. Presumably someone else brought his coffee, nipped out for a hot dog, found his dark glasses or misplaced newspaper. And when he wanted to talk, he would talk to the wall, or the chair, or Peter Galley's electric organ, banging out a discord now and then by way of a response. Probably (Alisdair thought) he never even registered the difference. Alisdair was beginning to understand just how important he had been to Johnny, just how viable his former ambitions really were. The shame he felt for that particular folly – the dream so private he had scarcely dared to dream it to himself – worked into him like a splinter, always there, always hurting, always invisible. At times, it seemed to him impossible that no one else could see it. Supposing Johnny had somehow divined his thoughts, had been laughing at him, despising him all along?

Even now, he did not appreciate how little interest Johnny had ever felt in him or any other human being. Johnny, the ultimate egoist, was interested solely, bitterly, destructively in himself. In the emptiness of his own spirit, the darkness of his own mind, Alisdair, with the self-centredness of the very young, still found it incredible that his suffering could be so unworthy of attention, even of contempt. Looking in the mirror each morning, as he razed optimistically at an almost hairless chin, he searched his face for some sign of his painfully acquired adulthood. Over the last few weeks (he felt) his rounded cheeks should have sunken in, his eyes grown colder and somehow greyer, his mouth hard. But his face had not changed. Only, if he gazed for long enough, he would begin to discern at the back of those eyes a faint shadow of bewilderment and hurt, and the lips would look no longer set but clenched as though against anger or tears. Once or twice, waking in the night, he thought that it would be a relief to cry. But he would not add to the tale of his stupidity and cowardice with either tears or relief. If only it was as easy for him to forget Johnny as it evidently was for Johnny to forget him. *Catch twenty-two. You dope and you drink to stop yourself thinking, but it doesn't do any good. There's still that same space between your ears where your dream used to be. You can't fill it up. You can't ever fill it up.* I'll find things to do, Alisdair promised himself. Things better than stirring up mob hysteria with cheap lyrics. Nobody's ever going to call me Ally again, or kid, or brat. Nobody's ever going to talk to me again as if I was a wall or a chair. I don't need a dream. What's the use of a dream anyway? Life isn't about dreams. Life is about reality. Life is about dodging the slings and arrows, and getting on top where you'll be safe. Nothing else matters.

Nine months later The Group broke up. Alisdair never saw Johnny again. Charlie coasted for a while; he'd saved money, invested, unlike some of the others; he could afford to look around. Rafe Dunston drifted from job to job, unable to settle down. Peter Galley took up the Moog synthesiser. The other guitarist, Billy Neele, went into his father's business and became a butcher. Bryan Solloway dropped out of sight until Alisdair read of his death five years later. A brief, insignificant paragraph. Alisdair, with five years' perspective on that long-forgotten dream, felt sorry for him and obscurely guilty, as though it was in some way his fault. He hadn't felt sorry when he read about Johnny. He hadn't felt pleased, either. It wasn't God's justice which had done for Johnny – or the devil's revenge. It was Johnny himself. Alisdair had tried hating him, once, but it didn't work. Johnny, he reflected, was like a plague or a tornado, something that blew across your life leaving emptiness and wreckage in its wake. But you could not blame the plague or the wind. He did not blame Johnny. Occasionally, when he could not prevent it, he blamed himself – for listening to Johnny in the first place, drinking in his barren philosophy, like the sucker he was; for remembering it, even now, word for word; for being young and credulous and not very wise; for lying in the dirt, doing nothing, while three men raped a boy. He saw himself as a fool and a coward, and no amount of success, no cultivated cynicism, would ever take away the bitterness of the aftertaste.

Sometimes he wondered what had happened to the boy – the Boy, as he always called him in his own mind. It was difficult to decide exactly how young he had been: maybe an immature teenager, maybe less. Alisdair remembered very vividly the smallness of that clutching hand, the impression of skinny childish limbs, the bare diminutive buttocks. What kind of a home had he returned to, where they did not notice the tearstains on his face, the slime of grass and earth and sex on his clothes? What kind of a child was he, not to have run weeping to the first sympathetic adult? It was almost as if the Boy had never existed save in Johnny's imagination, but such was the power of that brooding, empty mind that some wretched puny spirit had been born, for an hour, a night, to serve his lust. He had been born, had been victimised, and had vanished into the dark on stumbling, unspirit-like feet. Alisdair could almost believe it until he remembered the stumble, and the sense of despair and anguish which had been transmitted to him, in some indescribable way, from the figure on the ground.

He spent a lot of time speculating about the Boy. There was a period, nearly a year after the rape, when it became almost an obsession. He even dreamed of the incident once – a vaguely surrealist dream in which buttocks figured prominently – and woke to find he had wet the bed . . . After that, he acquired a horror of homosexuality which he always feared was tinged with a sort of loathly fascination. All the normal eighteen-year-old worries about sex became terribly magnified and distorted, until in the end he was afraid even to think about it, lest some perverted fantasy should creep into his brain. He began to avoid children, specifically his two nephews, of whom he had previously been mildly fond. He agonised over the sensual pleasure he had so often experienced in rough-and-tumbles with them. He even contemplated suicide, in a detached kind of way, the night he stood up Elaine Gisborne. He was a little in love with her at the time, or so he thought. Several people were. She was a skimpy girl, not very tall, bra-less, flat-chested, with coarse, coppery-brown hair and a plain, pale, freckled face which somehow managed to be piquant. Her eyes were too small and her lips too thin. She was said to be sensational in bed. Alisdair had wanted to make love to her for some while, at least in theory.

He hadn't made love to anyone since the rape. The night her parents went away ('Let's do it properly,' she had said. 'In Mummy and Daddy's bed. I hate floors.') he had set out to walk to her house. He passed the front door on the far side of the road, shrinking from the watching windows, and went on towards the railway. Behind drawn curtains in the other houses, he imagined other people, happy, normal people, having happy, normal sex. He wanted so much to be happy and normal. He distrusted his own desires, his sensuality, his fixation on the Boy, his longing for Elaine Gisborne's milk-white androgynous body. Standing on the railway bridge, he wondered about climbing the wall and jumping onto the line in front of the approaching train. But the train had stopped for the signal and there was a policeman not twenty yards off, already watching him suspiciously. Suddenly, he knew that if he didn't move on the policeman would come up and speak to him, might even guess his intention. Alisdair could already envisage the conversation.

'Now then, sonny, wot's all this 'ere? Not thinking of doing anything *silly*, are we?'

'Actually, I was just going to commit suicide.'

'Suicide, eh? We can't have that. You're a young lad with your life before you; you don't want to go killing yourself.'

'You don't understand. What else can I do? You see – I'm afraid I'm a pervert. I don't want to be, but I can't help it. Maybe a homosexual; maybe – something worse. I don't *know*. I get so frightened every time I think about it . . . it's all right for someone like Quentin Crisp, but I don't *want* to be a homo. I've always liked girls. I can't bear it, I tell you. I just can't bear it –' Inside Alisdair's mind, the conversation petered out. Even to an adolescent suffering from an excess of bottled-up emotion, it had begun to sound faintly ludicrous. The policeman was coming towards him now and Alisdair thrust his hands into his pockets, murmured an aloof 'Good evening' and walked purposefully off down the street.

Away from the bridge, his pace slackened. As he passed Elaine's house again he saw the lights were still on in the living room, a yellow glint between drawn curtains, like a sly invitation. Perhaps she was there waiting for him. Perhaps she had someone else already. In any case he knew he would never be able to explain. Not to a girl. Particularly not to a girl who was sensational in bed. He closed his lips in the expression that was already becoming familiar to him, hugged himself tighter into his combat jacket, and made his way slowly home.

In his first year at Cambridge Alisdair gradually overcame his inhibitions. Waking one morning after a particularly alcoholic party, he found a girl in his bed who told him he had enjoyed himself the previous night. He did not take her out again but he found the incident made it easier when it came to a Girton blonde called Clare, a bosomy mathematician called Frances, an American historian (Elsa), a zoological brunette (Jan), two or three linguists, a seductive lecturess. He never stayed very long with any particular girl. Sometimes, he wanted to, but it seemed safer to move on, insulated by a bitter cynicism, a careful detachment, from anything which might injure his fragile ego or his uncertain heart. There were still moments he did not like to remember. One girl – the lecturess – wanted him to take her from behind, but he would not. 'You aren't very imaginative, are you?' she had said, teasingly. He didn't go back to her again. The historian, who was into psychology on the side, told him he had homosexual tendencies, because he liked being underneath. Left alone, it was fatally easy to start analysing his tastes, his pleasures, his inclinations until he had no taste or pleasure or inclination left. Far simpler merely to shrug his shoulders and walk away – a proceeding that somehow carried more dignity than running, though it came to the same thing in the end. He got very good at walking away, during his time at Cambridge: away from self-revelation, from pain, from trust, from the generosity of others. He knew little of real desire or sexual fulfilment, and, avoiding them, he began to believe them imaginary, an idealistic delusion in the minds of a handful of writers and poets. Cynicism spread thinly over every facet of his persona, excepting only his ambition to succeed; he had forgotten that the true cynic does not strive for success because he knows that, like everything else, it is a waste of time. He was determined, like the miller in the song, to care for nobody, and to have nobody care for him.

Occasionally he had lapses, when he loved his family or was kind to children and dogs. Such moments – when he remembered them – always embarrassed him. His persistently youthful features became overlaid by what he hoped was a faintly sardonic expression; his blue eyes were dissipated, sometimes bloodshot; his mouth a little twisted by too many smiles unsmiled, too many gentle words unsaid. By the time he left college his waist had thickened slightly and he had acquired an adequate amount of muscle. Some of his hair had been cut off but the straight fringe still covered his eyes. He looked young, tough, prematurely disillusioned, not very happy, not very sure of himself. The fears which had haunted his late teens were now so much a part of him he never wondered what they were doing there. Only rarely, when something reminded him – Johnny's death, or Bryan's – would he think about the rape. As he had promised himself – or was it Johnny he had promised? – he had other things to think about.

Chapter Three

Francis Preston told Dominic he was an adopted child three years after his mother died. Nobody knew, least of all Francis himself, why he had waited so long to impart this information. Dominic did not tell his uncle-by-adoption that he had known anyway, since the day after his arrival at the Prestons' Cambridge home, when he had overheard the daily telling the milkman that it was 'very, very sad, but of course, it's not as if she was his *own* mother'. At the time, the words barely registered. Later – months or weeks later – when he began to think about it, he found his subconscious had assimilated the idea without any particular surprise or shock. He was an adopted child. Pieces of his life which had never quite fitted together seemed to fit together. 'Your mother always wanted children,' Francis explained, fiddling with his spectacles in the way he did when he was nervous. 'Unfortunately, she was unable . . . and of course, by then she was too old anyway. She saw lots of doctors – dear me, yes. Lots of doctors. Specialists, you know. And she tried some pills – little green pills – and a health spa. I forget which health spa. The water was supposed to have healing properties. She prayed a lot, too, at one time. To the Virgin, of course. I often wondered, myself, if that was quite the right person to approach, under the circumstances. So difficult to know with saints. She was a good Catholic, your mother: a woman of great faith. I'm afraid I'm not such a good Catholic myself. One has doubts. Anyway, God – or whoever – didn't see fit to give her what she wanted. So then she tried the pills, and the health spa. She was a great one for trying things. I sometimes felt if she had thought to try . . . however, your father – poor Geoffrey – was not a very forceful man. Not forceful at all . . . It was after the health spa that she decided to adopt. She said it came to her while she was drinking the waters, like a message direct from Heaven. Maybe the prayers and the pills and everything had finally made an impression on Someone. You were called Francis after me, you know. I don't know why she chose Dominic. No, I don't know that.' His mind appeared to fasten on this relatively minor point in a manner that would have been familiar to his students, who had frequently spent an entire tutorial discussing the poor quality of modern print-spacing, or why this particular edition of Chaucer had a *brown* cover, when the previous one had been *blue*. Dominic waited, thinking his own thoughts.

Presently, he asked: 'Does it make any difference?' and, with a touch of irony which entirely missed his auditor: 'Do you think I should stop calling you Uncle?'

'No, no, dear boy, of course not. At least – I don't know. After all, I'm *not* your uncle. And it is so very important to be accurate about details. Dear me, how difficult all this is. Perhaps you should just call me Francis.'

'I think,' Dominic said firmly, 'I would prefer to go on calling you Uncle.'

'Well of course, if you would *prefer* . . .'

Dominic escaped.

Downstairs, in the kitchen, he found his aunt Zoë making quince jam and Theresa, his elder cousin, reading a battered copy of *Private Eye*. He sat down in a vacant chair, swinging one thin leg over the arm. 'Aunt Zoë,' he said, 'should you mind desperately if I go on calling you Aunt?'

Zoë Preston pushed one of many stray locks rather stickily back from her face and surveyed him with an expression of great seriousness. She did not say anything. She often felt, with Dominic, that he was mocking people just a little more than was natural or kindly, and she was determined never to encourage him. Not that it was his fault, she told herself, for the hundredth time. He had been through a very traumatic experience. Surely it was quite plausible for a sensitive boy to develop a slightly unpleasant mental kink as a sort of defence mechanism. He would almost certainly grow out of it.

'Uncle Francis,' Dominic continued, 'sorry, I mean Francis – has just told me I'm adopted. He feels I should be more accurate over details.'

'What!' Theresa glanced up, startled. '*Told* you you're adopted? That's too much, even for Daddy. We've always known you were adopted. So what?'

'You shouldn't make fun of your uncle, Dom,' Zoë said gently. Her voice was always gentle, a low, soft note that had a soothing effect on babies and animals and angry people. 'He's very fond of you. That's why he gets into those little tangles about things that sometimes seem rather irrelevant. It's because –' she paused, perhaps for emphasis – 'because he's so afraid of hurting you. He says it's very easy to hurt people without even meaning to and it worries him terribly.'

'Yes, but –' Theresa brushed this aside '– why did he want to make a big performance of telling Dom something he knows already? It's like a scene from a film.' She went into pantomime. 'Study. Dim light. Ageing relative removes his spectacles. "My boy," he says – did he?'

'I think so,' said Dominic. 'Once.'

'There you are.' Theresa made a graphic gesture of despair. All her gestures were graphic. She was eighteen and had theatrical ambitions. 'What will it be next? My God – you don't suppose he'll want to tell me the Facts of Life, do you?'

'No, no, dear,' Zoë murmured, with her furtive, mischievous smile. 'He thinks I'll do that.'

Theresa gave her mother what was known in the family as a Look. 'What did you say to him?' she asked Dominic. 'Did you explain that you already knew?'

Dominic glanced swiftly at her from under his eyelashes. He had very long lashes which he used, not quite unconsciously, to conceal the expression in his eyes. It was a trick which gave him, at times, a misleadingly sleepy air. 'What makes you so sure I knew?' he said. 'Have we ever discussed it?'

'Well –' Theresa hesitated, seized by sudden doubt. In fact they had discussed it, once, but – as Dominic had guessed – in the anguish of the moment his cousin could not remember. She said in a much smaller voice: 'Surely you knew?'

Zoë considered him thoughtfully from her position beside the basin, where she was washing spoons. 'He knew,' she said.

Dominic tapped the kitchen table, twice, with his swinging foot. 'As it happens,' he said, 'yes, I did know.'

Theresa's plain, rather sharp face (Becky-Sharp-face, she called it), as graphic in feature as any of her gestures, showed a fleeting illumination of relief. 'Not that it matters,' she went on with would-be nonchalance. 'It's not as if you can remember your real parents at all. Aunt Joan was just the same as a proper mother.'

'Not quite,' Zoë temporised unexpectedly. 'Not that I would say anything against her. She was a fine person and a very strong character. But parents who adopt a child sometimes tend to be a little – overprotective.'

'You mean, I was spoiled,' Dominic said with a flickering smile.

'That too.'

'Did you love her *very* much?' Theresa asked shyly (for her). 'You hardly ever talk about her.'

Dominic made a twitching movement with his thin shoulders which might have represented a shrug. 'I suppose I must have done. When I was a child she was the hugest, most real person in the world. She sort of filled it up. I don't remember my father – my adoptive father – well at all. Just my mother and me. She loved me and I loved her and we didn't need anybody else.' Inexplicably, he shivered. 'And then she died. At the time, I didn't really understand how I felt, but I think I've worked it out now. You see, death is the end – of everything. The big full-stop. When my mother died, she stopped loving me. And I – stopped loving her. It was that simple. Death is always simple, really, only people like to pretend.'

'Don't!' Theresa, for all her assumption of toughness, was sincerely distressed. 'I know you don't mean it, but it sounds so horrid. Even if she was a bit possessive – '

'*Nil nisi bonum*?' said Dominic knowledgeably. 'I didn't think you approved of all that, Terry. She would have eaten me alive. I'm quite glad I haven't got a mother, now. I wonder if I was a foundling?'

'I'm sure you were,' Zoë said comfortingly. 'In a handbag, you know, on Victoria Station. At least, I think it was Victoria.'

Dominic grinned. 'Yes, but that poor bastard found his family in the end, didn't he? Sorry, Aunt Zoë. Poor bugger.'

Zoë said, a little sorrowfully, 'You think you're so clever, don't you?'

Dominic never learned anything about his actual parentage. Sometimes, he would tell people in confidence (Dr Hieronymous Glauber, for instance) that his mother was a prostitute and his father a Romanian sailor, that he was the son of a man (unnamed) who had been hanged for murder, or even – his favourite – that he was the bastard offspring of a cleric and a notorious actress. It was extraordinary how many personal confidantes succumbed to the charm of this last story; indeed, Dominic told it with such conviction that he almost ended by believing it himself. In fact he was, as he had wished (or thought he wished) a foundling, discovered not in a handbag on Victoria Station but in a shoebox on the doorstep of an orphanage run by nuns. A premature baby, according to the doctor, less than a week old and weighing barely six pounds, his chances of survival were considered remote. It was February, not an ideal time of year for leaving a baby on a doorstep, and only the devotion of the nuns – and their misguided prayers – maintained his tenuous hold on life. The doctor spoke of his 'will to live', and the unexpected strength and determination concealed in that fragile little body. It was a curiously ironic beginning for someone who was to propound, in his work, that the whole of human existence was an obscenity.

The nuns tried to find out more about his origins, but without success: his appearance corresponded with no recorded birth in the area and the rather inexpert knot in his umbilical cord suggested amateur handling. The only real clue was the shoebox itself, which came from Rayne. For over a month after Francis inadvertently released this detail Dominic lay awake at night, speculating fruitlessly on the possibilities it opened up. Finally, he concluded that the likeliest solution was that his mother had been an assistant in a shoe shop. There were no other indications. No documents, no memorabilia, no shawl of antique embroidery wrapping his undersized limbs. 'The stork didn't bother to deliver to my parents,' he told a girlfriend once. 'He just dropped me off at the nearest sorting office. I dare say he was working to rule.' With him in the shoebox (and largely out of it) was a woollen blanket, none too clean, and a quantity of tissue paper, as though the shoes had been removed and the baby set in their place in a great hurry and with a certain lack of dignity. There was an air of pre-party distraction about the gesture: oh-put-the-baby-in-there-how-do-you-like-my-new-shoes-darling. Dominic found the presence of tissue paper far more significant than the Rayne label on the shoebox. It showed, for one thing, that it was a shoebox *which had contained shoes*. After Francis told him about it Dominic spent another month of sleepless nights deciding that his mother might not have been a shop assistant after all. Despite his teenage espousal of Left Wing causes and his adult conviction that all men were equal and equally unfit to inherit the earth, he never quite forgot that he was brought up to be an intellectual.

Meanwhile for all practical purposes his mother was Joan Hardinge, who descended on the orphanage when he was barely a year old and bore him off, charmed (doubtless) by the length of his eyelashes and the sweet helpless smile which he still used, in later life, whenever he had done something particularly uncivilised. It was the nuns who had christened him Dominic: Joan kept it, possibly for its Catholic flavour, only adding the Francis and the Hardinge. Originally, the Francis was for St Francis of Assisi – like many unimaginative people, Joan was attracted by sentiment in religion – but her brother, on being introduced to the baby, acquired a misconception which neither she nor her sister-in-law ever attempted to put right. ('You named it after me,' said Francis. 'How very charming of you. Most unusual.') Joan, indeed, hardly noticed; she was too absorbed in the jealous and miraculous possession of her first child. 'If she had carried him,' Zoë said afterwards, 'if she had actually borne him – suffered, you know – she might have been more humble. As it was, I sometimes think she believed he arrived not only by immaculate conception but also by celestial special delivery.'

A strong-minded, domineering woman, with her square unmade-up face, square masculine body, square feet in sensible square shoes, Joan Hardinge had long wanted or needed something sweet and helpless on which to lavish the hitherto untapped resources of her affection. Her husband, a country solicitor, was helpless but not particularly sweet; after the arrival of the baby he seemed to fade, withering slowly, like a plant no one talks to any more, until his unobtrusive death some six years later. Dominic remembered little of him save a huge bouquet of funeral flowers malingering in the drawing-room for what seemed like weeks after. The sickly infant whose hold on life had proved so tenacious grew up sweet and helpless perforce, as though he knew what was required of him. Teased at school, he never fought back, being shy of physical encounters – even friendly ones. His mother was doting but not demonstrative and although time had made her more caressing he never grew accustomed to her awkward kisses or the touch of her large square hands. When he was made unhappy, he turned to her for protection, both warmed and disturbed by the excess of her response, her full-sail descent on irresponsible teachers and the parents of erring children.

Later, he learned to manage his own revenges, hiding books, bitching, spreading stories which his partial belief made peculiarly convincing. 'Unfortunately,' one form-master wrote in his end-of-term report, 'Dominic seems unable to differentiate between fact and fiction.' He retreated from the claustrophobic atmosphere of maternal love into a world of the imagination which was, at times, more vivid to him than any reality. He knew without having to think about it that his mother's imaginative faculty was limited: his world was therefore entirely private to him and in it he was entirely free. In the event, it was some while before any of his imagination found its way out into his school work; he hugged it to himself, secretively, and it was not until he was ten or eleven that teachers began to comment on the originality of his essays. Joan was so avid to share in every aspect of his life that, superficially candid and confiding, he kept the most important part of his personality hidden from her. Whether such ambiguities in his nature were inborn or cultivated no one ever knew, least of all himself. His upbringing – or his gods – had made him both diffident and arrogant, timorous and sly, bitterly sensitive, self-conscious, cruel, delicate, tense. He had impulses of sweetness and genuine warmth, brief sparks that flared and vanished, but, as a well-known director said of him long after, his good qualities came only in flashes, whereas his bad qualities were always with him. Perhaps they were with him before he was born, the inevitable heritage from a mother who could discard her premature offspring carelessly in a shoebox without even removing the tissue paper first. If that was what had actually happened. Much of Dominic's early life was composed of such ifs.

The village where he grew up was called Gresham. It was a small, expensive village in the South of England which has since become, if not smaller, still more expensive, with a village green, cricket, two or three picturesque pubs, a fringe growth of cheaper cottages, a perfunctory modern estate. The Hardinges' home stood on the edge of the green. It was less modern than some and less expensive than most, with thick whitewashed walls and the kind of latticed windows which Joan called 'quaint'. It had once had an outside loo. The little garden was full of roses, not just Peace and Masquerade and Frau Drouschke but nameless old-fashioned roses as shapely as flowers in porcelain and smelling of some long-lost Victorian spring when maidens were maidens (some of them) and dresses were flounced and young men, as always, were desperately trying to be young men. Geoffrey had grown the roses, but few people remembered that. Joan herself frequently took credit for them without even a passing nudge from her normally alert and dutiful conscience. (Her conscience seemed to have a blind spot where her late husband was concerned.)

'As a child,' Dominic said once in an interview, 'I lived in a whitewashed cottage with roses. Almost olde worlde, I give you my word. The kind of place that should be inhabited *only* by a sweet white-haired old lady, with cats. I had nowhere to grow but up.' In fact Dominic, like some of the roses, grew sideways, avoiding obstructions. He went to primary school in another, slightly larger village a short bus-ride away and thence to grammar school in the nearest town. He was unpopular not only with his classmates but also with the teachers, some of whom suspected him of cheating, an imputation which was untrue but not wholly unmerited. During lessons, he wasted time, distracting his neighbours, reading under the desk lid, or writing childishly obscene limericks which did nothing to endear him to those members of staff they immortalised. In exams, however, he invariably did well, partly because exam conditions meant there were no distractions and boredom forced him to concentrate, and partly because he had (when he chose to use it) an effortless memory for facts. One unhappy French teacher, unaware of this, went so far as to carry the accusation of cheating to Dominic's mother, in a moment of misplaced excitability during a particularly memorable Parents' Evening. The teacher was only saved from horrifying retribution when Joan's subsequent fury induced a mild heart attack, which gave everyone time to cool down and apologise. The French teacher left voluntarily two terms later in a whirl of unsettled dignity and Joan, emerging from a brief stay in hospital, was instructed by her doctor to lose weight. But – as with so many large, strong-willed women – her will was noticeably affected by such things as cream cakes and Yorkshire pudding, and despite much discussion and carrot juice she never grew visibly thinner. Dominic, both smug and insecure, continued – except in free essay – to waste his own and everyone else's time at school, and Joan's square, substantial body continued to overwork her insubstantial heart. Yet such was her solidity, her complacency, her superficial stoicism that when she died abruptly less than a year later, her doctor was the only one who was not surprised.

'Extraordinary how these women seem to think it doesn't matter what they eat in private as long as they diet in public,' he had commented. She had been baking scones (and eating them) that same night.

'She overdid it,' Francis said at the funeral, sighing. 'She never spared herself. Such energy; such drive. She never spared anybody. So sad, really. In the prime of life.' (She was fifty-two.) 'Dreadful for the boy. The whole business – absolutely dreadful. We must do everything we can to make him welcome. He needs to feel wanted – loved. You'll see to it, won't you, dear?'

Unexpectedly, Zoë found herself thinking: He must have had enough love to last a lifetime. All she said was: 'I'll do my best.'

Dominic was standing just in front of her and a little to her left, so that if she leaned forward slightly she could see his profile. In spite of their proximity he looked strangely alone, isolated by his youth, his terrible broken stillness, as deaf and blind children are isolated among their fellows. His eyes were dry, his face blank: a white, hollow, brittle mask with no thought behind it. His very stance looked awkward, somehow painful. Yet he had been a graceful baby, she remembered, a graceful child. She had a sudden feeling that at the touch of a fingertip he might disintegrate, falling to pieces like a cracked toy – and that it might be a good thing, he might be able to cry and scream and pour out all the pain that he had blocked inside. Or it might be a bad thing, a slight, disastrous gesture that would push him over some indefinable line into insanity. She could not know. His mother must have been the centre of his universe; she would have seen to that. For the very young, Zoë reflected, death was the ultimate betrayal, the final and total act of abandonment. Perhaps that was how Dominic saw it. Perhaps he felt, not only confusion and grief, but fury, resentment, bitterness, guilt. Too many emotions and too strong for that frail physique to bear. Briefly, she fancied that it was emotion which had warped his body, even as heat can warp metal. He half turned towards her, and for a moment she saw the look in his eyes: a cool, lonely, distant look. Infinitely distant.

'Poor child,' she murmured, with a depth of pity which she did not understand. 'Poor, poor child.'

On the night of the party at Wellesley Court Dominic had been to visit a friend. He acquired friends from time to time despite his general unpopularity, subservient, admiring sort of friends who were dazzled by his quick tongue and precocious wit. They never lasted very long. Dominic did not seem to possess the knack of inspiring true friendship. Perhaps he did not know he needed it. This particular 'friend' was of no permanent significance in Dominic's life except as a minor catalyst; it was in his company that Dominic stayed out too late, missed the last bus home, and set off to walk the mile or so back to the village, alone and in the dark.

Afterwards, he could never recall exactly how they had spent the evening, or what it was that had delayed him. His mother did not like him to come home late, especially on his own, although the countryside was considered relatively safe and he would (as he had once tentatively reminded her) be thirteen the following year. Possibly the boys had been studying the magazines which Dominic, in a great show of bravado, had bought with several weeks' pocket money from a back street newsagent (Joan thought he had spent the money on sweets). Some of the pictures had given him an unpleasant feeling of excitement, not unmixed with nausea, a sensation which he found both loathsome and curiously fascinating. But that might have been another time. Possibly they played records, even records by The Group. Dominic admired The Group, or said he did, when he was trying to act like a teenager. He did not know the members of The Group were at a party nearby. He did not know about the party at all until he heard the roar of the music breaking like distant waves on the night. He had chosen to go via the lane because the road, at that point, became a tree-lined avenue, with high, closed gateways and no verges, where (his mother said) you could easily get knocked down by a car, if you walked along there after dark. On the surface, at least, he still did what his mother said. It was a habit. The lane was a little frightening by night: a place of bewildering shadows, thin fingers of moonlight, soft imagined snufflings, velvet-soft silence. But for Dominic, even as a child, fear was a stimulant. It both weakened and compelled him. Perhaps, if he had been different, none of it would have happened. If the night had been less dark, the road less unfriendly, the world less jaded. But people remain as they are made, and the world turns quickly and changes slowly. What followed was apparently the result of a string of random chances, but there was a certain blind inevitability about the actions and interactions of the persons concerned which belied that. Perhaps it would have happened anyway – it would have happened to *Dominic*, at some stage in his life – whatever the chances. It was his own particular karma. Passing the first house, surrounded by a high wall which reared grey and daunting above him, he heard the music. Even at that range the sound reassured him: music meant parties, lights, people, things to drive away the nightshadows. To his right the wall became a fence, the fence a hedge, and then he was looking over a low wooden gateway into the gardens of Wellesley Court.

  He did not notice very much about the immediate foreground: vague forms, shrubs maybe, patchy darkness, the glimpse of a path. His gaze was focused on the row of lighted windows above the terrace, scarlet-curtained windows translucent with light, where now and then a dark shape was pressed against the curtains and then withdrawn. He saw the terrace below the windows and the tracery of a parapet and a person who came out onto the terrace, possibly to piss in an urn. The roar of the music had condensed into a recognisable beat which grew suddenly louder with the opening of a door; he did not hear anything else. He wasn't frightened now, not even alone, in the dark. He felt the party was so close he could reach out and touch it.

  He did not see them until they were right beside him. Even then, he could have run away. They were in the garden, on the wrong side of the gate; he was in the lane. They were large and clumsy and drunk, stumbling in the darkness; he was small and quick and light on his feet. But he did not move. His hands clung to the gate like weed to a rock: a cold moist grip. When they opened it, catching him by the arms, plucking his fingers carelessly from the wood, he did not try to break away. Their unseen faces were terrible in the gloom; their looming shoulders the shoulders of giants. They smelt of alcohol and of something else which he did not recognise: a heavy, sweetish, exotic sort of smell. One of them cupped his face in a hand far larger and harder than his mother's, turning it up to the moon. His cheeks were squeezed against the bone. 'A nymph!' The famous, molten-asphalt voice remained strange and dreadful to him, though he had heard it often before on record. 'A nymph of the woods! No: a nymphet.'

One of the others said: 'It's a boy.'

'I can see that!' For a moment, the fingers tightened painfully, gouging into his face. He felt as if he were made of wax. 'A boy. A pretty boy. What do you call a boy-nymph? Ariel? Where the bee fucks, there fuck I. I like that.'

'For God's sake!' A third voice, as drunk as the other two but more conscious. 'It's only some kid. What do we want with a kid? Let him go.'

'Let him go.' It was almost a croon. Above him, Dominic saw – or thought he saw – the dark features shift, as though in some imagined travesty of a smile. He sensed anger, cruelty, strength as an animal might sense them, instinctively; and every nerve in his body shrank. 'A kid. A pretty boy. What do we want with a pretty boy?' And then the night was blotted out as the face came down on his, and his lips opened, and something huge and thick and course as leather was thrust into his mouth. It was several seconds before he realised it was a tongue. The hand that had gripped his cheeks held him by the nape of his neck; the other hand seized his crotch. He thought he was going to wet himself. In the background, he heard someone laughing, heh-heh-heh-heh, like the yapping of some small dog. Then the tongue released him, abruptly, and he was gasping for air like a fish.

'A virgin . . . I think.' The voice that went with the tongue was slurred now, but not from beer. 'A virginal nymph. A virginal fuck. It's a long time since I had a virginal fuck. How about it, pretty boy? How would you like a little education?'

If he had resisted, even then, it might have been all right. If he had answered or screamed. But his vocal chords were numb, and his limbs folded beneath him as though they were filled with water. Under the big untender hands he felt soft and frightened and submissive.

'For Christ's sake, Johnny –' (afterwards, Dominic forgot the name) '– you must be out of your bloody skull!' The third man again, evidently trying vainly to sober himself and everyone else. 'Let's go back to the party. There are plenty of girls – '

'Slags. Fucking ugly slags at a fucking awful party. Why don't you feel him, you bugger? Feel him *here*. I'm so hard it's beautiful. I haven't had a hard-on like this for half the cunts in London. D'you think I'm going to waste it?'

He didn't cry out, even when they pushed him onto the ground. His face was pressed into the grass; grass filled his mouth. Somewhere up above him he could still hear that strange high little laugh as regular as gunfire. They had dragged his clothes down about his knees and he was horribly conscious of his nakedness, of those parts exposed which his mother had taught him should always be covered up, shameful parts which at school were only mentioned with giggles and half-understood obscenities. Hard fingers explored the cleft between his buttocks; hands touched him, clawed him, kneaded him, splaying his thighs, opening him to the cold impersonal breath of the night and the hot pressure of alien flesh. Still he did not understand what they were going to do. Nothing in the cheap porn magazines, none of his secret speculations or infrequent experiments with his own genitals had educated him for this. His very innocence reduced him. In the last analysis, his mother and all her works had shielded him too well. He tried to brace himself for pain, without knowing how it would come. Something that felt like another finger – a huge, swollen, boneless finger – was pushed against him, groping as though without touch or feeling for a keyhole in his body. And then the pain began, as he had known it would, only worse, far worse than he could ever have imagined, tearing at his anus, invading him, stabbing and stabbing into his vitals like a great spear. He did not scream; his voice was driven out of him. He yawned hideously, stretching his lips against his teeth, tasting dirt. He thought that if the pain went on he would not be able to bear it, he would faint or die, but it went on and he did not faint, he did not die. It filled him, flooded him, devoured him: he was crushed into the ground as though beneath the heel of an unthinking giant. Later – he did not know how much later – there was a moment when he realised the stabbing had ceased; the pain was still there, but it was a latent pain, almost a respite. There was something wet and bubbling between his buttocks; for a few seconds he thought he must have lost control of his bowels, but he was already too far gone in humiliation to care. Presently, remembering the dribblings which had resulted from his own sexual ventures, he realised what it must be. It seemed somehow incredible to him that this could be the same bodily function. And then the weight against his legs shifted as one man withdrew and another took his place, and the pain was renewed. He lost count of how often it happened. He lost count of time, of thought. Gradually, his body grew accustomed to the pain, accepting it, embracing it, surrendering. He was scarcely conscious of the silent sobs that racked his chest or the tears that oozed steadily down his face. He had no feeling left, no humiliation or fear. He had never had any anger. His spirit retreated into a tiny corner of his mind and did nothing. Nirvana. It was some while before he realised it was over.

   He couldn't stand. They pulled him to his feet, but his knees gave. They pulled him up again, tugging at his clothes. He felt semen running down his thighs inside his trousers and he found himself wondering, stupidly, what his mother would say. She always made a fuss about dirty clothes. Suddenly – though he knew it was too late, too late to be of any use, too late to expiate this last hour from his life – his longing for her was acute and physical. He wanted to be *home*, safe, warmed and protected by the strength of her avenging presence. Somehow, he managed to stay on his feet. A voice mocked him, meaninglessly; a hand jabbed at his back. And then he was running, running, driven on by the panic which should have seized him at the start, down the lane and over the fields towards the village. Afterwards, that part of the night was lost in a blur. He remembered falling – once, twice, twenty times – forcing himself up again, going on, somehow, anyhow, with that wild urgency pursuing him and pulling him forward. He remembered the huge pain of his violated body, bruises, scratches, stitch in his side, breathing that tore at his lungs, tears that dried on his face and bubbled again from his eyes. When he came to the first houses he slunk past them, furtive with shame, shrinking from lighted windows or the opening of a door. Once, he saw someone approaching from the other direction, but he hid in a gateway and waited until the solitary walker had gone past. And then he was there, fumbling with the door handle – he had no key but it was left on the latch for him – dragging himself into the hallway, too weak to stand upright, pausing in sudden, inexplicable terror at the sound of his mother's voice.

'Dominic? Is that you, Dominic? Where on earth have you been?' He found he had begun to tremble all over, so that his hands shook visibly and his teeth knocked together. The door to the living room was in front of him, a little ajar, but he could not go in. He could not go in. 'Dominic!'

She did not speak when she saw him. She had been baking scones, eating one of them for something to do while she waited. Her hand, clutching the scone, was frozen halfway to her mouth. Her mouth was open as though just about to take a bite. The high colour from years of country living, from fresh air and a strong temper and too much good food, drained slowly out of her broad square face, leaving it like an image in pale clay. He could not recall having seen her look pale before. He was horribly aware of his tell-tale dishevelment, the earth on his face and the blood on his hands, the clammy streaks down the inside of his legs, the stale unmistakable smell of semen.

'Dominic!' she said at last, her voice hushed and changed. 'My Dominic!'

He started to cry again, though he thought he had cried himself out, gently at first and later with a terrible violence, clinging to her skirt and burying his face between her knees. She tried to lift him up and take him in her arms, but he would not look at her and she could not disentangle his clutching fingers from the skirt. When he was much older, he wondered if perhaps she had not immediately realised his condition. Her marital relations (he thought), if they had existed, must have been brief and hygienic; it might have taken her a while to recognise that smell. She plucked at his clothes in vague distress, murmuring automatically: 'You must get changed, Dominic. Put on your pyjamas. Look at your shirt – your jumper. I'll never get them clean.' Like the beginning of an advertisement for soap powder. And then her hands touched his trousers, felt the stickiness that was not blood or grime, the ugly unfamiliar stains. Slowly, very slowly, she whispered: 'What – have – they – done – to – you? *What have they done?*'

The horror in her voice – bourgeois horror, he told himself, years later, the horror of sex or violence in any form – made him stop crying. He stammered out a few words but he could not bring himself to say it. Not the truth. The whole truth. 'What have they done?' she repeated, stonily, without inflection. It was no longer a question but a sentence, implacable and harsh. Her hands gripped his shoulders: the fingers dug in so that he was reminded suddenly of other fingers, bigger and stronger and more cruel, digging into his face. He shuddered painfully, but she did not notice: she had felt his body shaken with sobbing and trembling ever since he came in. For the first and last time in her life she was calling on God, not in prayer, but in anger and disillusionment, as other, lesser mortals have called on God since they first created Him. All-wise, All-merciful, how could You let this happen? Where were You? Why didn't You stop it? Father – Heavenly Father – why did You fail Your daughter? How have I sinned, to be punished like this? Through a child, an innocent child. *My* child. (Whoso shall offend one of these little ones . . .)

But if there was an answer, she did not hear it. Her God had let her down, and she would not listen for His excuses. She had closed her ears against Him for ever. A rage rose in her such as she had never known, a cold rushing fury, ice-cold, death-cold, turning her to stone. She felt as strong as the earth, as relentless as the sea. She would stride across the fields like a giantess, find the monsters who had violated her darling – her son and her darling – strangle them with her own bare hands, dash their brains out, trample them into the mud from which they came. Let them hide where they would, she would find them. Morning would not come again, until she had found them. The Night, if need be, would stretch on for ever. She sat in the chair like a rock, deaf and blind with her fury. Her hands on Dominic's shoulders were the hands of a rock. He called her, suddenly frightened by her still face, but she did not hear. She tried to rise, but her limbs were stone and her body dragged on her like a great weight. There was a cramp in her chest from the weight of her body. She thought, fleetingly: I should have tried harder to diet; but there was no time now for thoughts, no time for anything. With one last, terrible effort she sought to stand up, to free herself from the weight which held her. The cramp became a knife which turned under her ribs. And then it was gone. She sat like a rock, unmoving. Her hands bore down on the shoulders of her child with a heavy mechanical pressure. He whimpered a little, clinging round her legs: but they were as immovable as pillars.

Gradually her stillness crept into him, draining him of further tears. At last he looked up again. Her face was as rigid and unforgiving as he had seen it look sometimes when he was a little younger, and returned from school weeping because he had been teased. But there was nothing behind the rigidity any more. No warm and frightening love, no passion of vengeance. Nothing at all. He noticed that the red colour in her cheeks was broken into tiny veins and patches, and between them the skin looked grey. Her eyes were fixed, unseeing. He stared at her for a long time while the full comprehension of that nothingness registered on his benumbed mind. She had gone. This was the moment when he needed her as he had never needed her in his life before, and she could not help him. She would not ever help him again. He was quite alone.

A fit of shivering took him and he pressed his cheek against her knee, hugging the pillars of her legs like a supplicant. Her skirt had ridden up and after a while he found he was looking at a varicose vein in her thigh: the sight embarrassed him horribly and he tried to get up, but her hands weighed down on him. He moved them from his shoulders with an effort and laid them in her lap. For some time he stayed there, kneeling in front of her, still holding on to one hand, not in love or grief but in despair. The small clock on the mantelpiece ticked briskly and quietly; the grandfather clock in the hall ticked slow and loud. Joan had been too busy fretting at Dominic's lateness to remember to wind it up, and little by little the ticking slackened and then stopped. The mantelpiece clock went on alone. Tick-tick-tick. Time. Life. He was alive and the clock was alive but everything else in the room was dead. He lifted his mother's wrist and saw that her watch was still going, the second hand creeping inexorably round its rectangular face. It seemed like a kind of affront that his mother's watch should outlive her, and he took it off, very carefully, winding it and overwinding it until it stopped. Then he fastened it round her wrist again. He ought to do something, he knew. What were you supposed to do, when people died? His mother had always done everything. He supposed he could dial nine nine nine, ask for the police or an ambulance; but there was no point now. There was no point in doing anything. Half an hour later – an hour later – he decided she was getting cold. He stood up, stiffly, because his legs were cramped, and went upstairs to fetch a blanket. At the top of the stairs, he was sick. The sick spattered the wall and his clothes, reminding him how dirty he was. His mother hated dirty clothes. He took off his trousers and pullover and shirt and put them in a basin with some detergent. Then he remembered his pants must be stained and he took them off too. He found some clean pants and a dressing gown and fetched a cloth to wipe the wall. It was difficult because he felt weak and sick still and he had to keep pausing to rest. In the end, he left the cloth on the floor, pulled the quilt off his mother's bed and took it downstairs. He was almost surprised to find her still sitting there. Her back was as straight, as unyielding in death as it had been in life. He tucked the quilt round her as best he could and sat down at her feet again.

Presently, it occurred to him that if he switched off the light her face, half hidden by the darkness, might seem less set and terrible, her eyes might even close and cease to stare. (He thought the dead always closed their eyes.) He got up again, extinguished the light, returned to his place at her feet. He was cold now, as cold as the corpse, or so he fancied, and shivering lightly again. The pain from his various injuries had deadened into a sort of dull constant throb which he barely noticed. Later, he knew he must have slept a little, although he could not see a clock, because the patch of night between the half-drawn curtains had changed from black to blue, and he could hear birdsong. Soon, he thought, someone would come. Something would happen. The milkman would ring and call, or the postman. A neighbour would peer through the window. A policeman would bang on the door. If no one came, he might stay there for days and days. He knew he would never be able to do anything himself. He had changed his clothes and fetched the quilt: those were the important things. Other people would do the rest. Eventually, men in white coats (or so he pictured them) would put his mother on a stretcher and cover her in a sheet and take her away for ever. He had no idea what would happen to him. He did not even try to think about it. His entire existence was broken into pieces and he could not imagine it ever being whole again.

The patch of blue beyond the window slowly lightened into grey. There was no sun. In the street outside, he heard a car revving up, passing footsteps. The murmur of traffic carried faintly from the main road on the far side of the village. The milkman came and went, then the post. He lifted his head a little at the rattle of the letterbox, but that was all. 'He was there all night,' they said afterwards. 'All night and nearly all day. If Betty Penrose hadn't gone round after tea to see about the cake for the Conservative Bring-and-Buy goodness knows how long he'd have been there. She said he was all huddled up at his mother's feet in a dressing gown and he didn't even look up when they came in. Even P.C. Gillam was shocked, and policemen see so much of that kind of thing, don't they? Of course, Joan absolutely doted on him, poor little boy. A terrible, terrible experience for a child. The doctor says it could affect him for the rest of his life. Apparently, he wouldn't speak or cry, not even when the relations came. A brother and his wife. He's going to live with them. Betty stayed with him until they arrived and she says it was simply pathetic the way he just sat there, trembling like a leaf, not saying anything. She tried to make him eat but it was no use. One can only hope the family will be able to do something. Honestly, it's heart-breaking to think of it. That poor little boy . . .'

The evening drew on. Dominic sat beside his mother holding her leaden hand and waiting, waiting. Hour succeeded hour and still no one came. Once, the hand moved, the muscles clenching automatically so that her fingers closed upon his. But he was past shock, past fear. If anything, the gesture seemed like a little miracle, a distant response to his loneliness and his need of her. He spoke to her then: 'Mother' – he had never called her Mummy – but she did not answer. Later, when the clock on the mantelpiece told him it was gone midday, he wondered if anyone would come at all.

It was after six and beginning to grow dark when he heard Mrs Penrose's Italian leather heels tapping up the path to the door.

Part Two

'There are two hells: Life and Death. You start in one and finish in the other. No alternatives. Above all, there is no such place as Heaven. That is the great delusion.'

Dominic Francis Hardinge:
Memoirs of a Nihilist

Chapter Four

Zoë Preston found Dominic's clothes hanging over the bath where Mrs Penrose had left them. The knees had been torn out of his trousers, she noticed, but she did not think it at all strange since her own two daughters, when they were a little younger, had frequently torn the knees out of their trousers. It was an occupational hazard of childhood.

'I'm afraid he was a little sick,' Betty Penrose had explained. 'I found his clothes in the basin; he must have put them in to soak. Children do the most extraordinary things, don't they? Of course, poor Joan definitely belonged to the cleanliness-is-next-to-godliness school of thought. I don't know any other boy of his age who would have bothered.'

'He was in shock,' Zoë said. 'Perhaps that had something to do with it.' The desire to carry on as usual, she thought. To do what his mother would have expected. Had she been alive, he would probably never have made the gesture: it wouldn't have been necessary. Zoë had always considered him an odd child, though she had not been certain if his oddness was native to him or merely an extension of Joan's. He had fulfilled so perfectly the dream Joan had made for herself, the pretty (too pretty?) boy with the slightly wistful smile and winning manners, always childish, always vulnerable, always devoted to her. But he isn't really a child, Zoë thought, he's nearly thirteen. I wonder what he *thinks*? He was sitting downstairs, waiting, patient and very quiet. He looked a little pale but otherwise quite normal. Only he shouldn't have looked normal, under the circumstances. He shouldn't have remembered to be so polite. He'll break down in a day or two, Zoë told herself. He'll be very quiet for a bit and then suddenly he'll break down. But he didn't.

They spent the night in a hotel; Zoë wouldn't stay in the cottage. 'I can't sleep in *her* bed,' she said to Francis, 'it would be indecent. Besides, we ought to get Dominic away from here.' She wasn't usually so fanciful, but it seemed to her that the whole place smelt of death, the cold, stuffy, scent-less smell of an unopened sepulchre. A smell of nothing. In the hall, the grandfather clock had stopped, and the uneaten scones, on a plate in the kitchen, were dry and hard as though baked in papier mâché. No mice had appeared to steal the crumbs: presumably Joan, in death as in life, would not tolerate mice. Even her watch had stopped. The doctor gave it to Zoë, who, rather absent-mindedly, tried to rewind it; but it must have jammed. 'I won't stay here,' she reiterated when Dominic was out of earshot. 'It feels as though – as though she's been dead for a long, long time. Not just twenty-four hours but years. She's been sitting there, dead, like something mummified, and Dominic's been alone in this room for years. I'm sorry; I'm being very silly, aren't I? I make it all sound like a horror film. Only poor Joan was rather like a mummy – an Egyptian one, not a motherly one. What do you suppose would have happened if no one had found them?' And then: 'Please let's go, Francis.'

At the hotel, Dominic slept on a small bed in their room. The doctor gave him a sleeping pill and Zoë found him a hot-water bottle. He did not seem to have nightmares. 'He should be all right,' the doctor said (contrary to popular opinion). 'Children are very resilient. Don't believe in all this something-nasty-in-the-woodshed stuff myself. Pity he's so highly strung, though. Too sensitive. Could have done with some more friends his own age to toughen him up a bit. Didn't mix much.'

'He'll have his cousins from now on,' Zoë said, making a mental note: We must warn them not to talk about it. She thought with a sudden painful warmth of Theresa, curled up on a sofa with Freud boastfully analysing her own neuroses, of Sandy, 'dressed up' in one of Zoë's nightdresses, carefully tinting her eyelids with felt-tip pen. Both so – no, not normal, who wanted their children to be *normal*? – but natural, open, unaffected. She tried to picture Dominic in their company, learning to relax, teasing and being teased, laughing, crying, growing up. But Dominic's pale, shrunken face remained pale and shrunken no matter what expressions she sought to superimpose on it. I'm tired, Zoë told herself. That's all it is. She opened the bedroom door and saw Dominic lying on his back in the little bed, straight and still. It was impossible to tell whether he slept or not. Ordinarily Zoë would have tip-toed over to see, kissed him goodnight. But she could not quite bring herself to do it. Not with Dominic. Had Joan, she wondered, kissed him goodnight? She tried to imagine such a kiss from the lips which she had last seen parted in death: a cold, mechanical gesture, a stiff plaster-cast of a kiss . . . She closed the door softly and went to talk to Francis about something else.

Zoë did not really want to send Dominic to boarding school. She had always felt that sending your children to boarding school was a way of opting out of parenthood, avoiding the responsibilities (and the pleasures) that you should have anticipated with pregnancy. Theresa and Alexandra did not board. Dominic, of course, was not her child, but she wanted very much to feel towards him as his own mother might have felt, or, failing that, to behave as if that was how she felt towards him. But the months went by and he remained silent, unapproachable, lashing out occasionally with ineffectual spite and then withdrawing abruptly into his own secret, empty world. It was difficult not to be over-solicitous, not to try too hard, to leave him (as she had promised herself she would) to come to her of his own accord.

She was not to know that Dominic, contrasting the

apparent carelessness of her attitude with Joan's, thought it sprang from indifference rather than sensitivity. (He had so little experience of sensitivity.) In any case, he had no desire to turn to anyone; not even Theresa, whom he would have quite liked if she hadn't been three years older than him, extremely bossy (or so he thought), and a girl. When Francis told him he was to go to Ampleforth he accepted it without comment, as he had accepted the move to Cambridge, his new family, their tentative plans for his welcome – as a prisoner accepts the name of the gaol where he will serve his next five years. If he had protested, Zoë would have taken his part; but he did not protest, and, as Zoë said to Francis: 'Perhaps he will be better off with boys of his own age. The staff there must be very experienced, too. Perhaps they will be able to do something for him that I can't.' Dominic did not want to go to boarding school, but then, he had not wanted to come to Cambridge; indeed, he was not conscious of *wanting* anything any more. He was the Cat that Walked by Itself: all places were alike to him. But the Cat had been free; Dominic was not free.

Most of the time, he went from day to day like a robot, unfeeling, obedient to the dictates of others. He thought a lot about death. The Prestons took him and Theresa (Sandy was considered too young) to a production of *Measure for Measure*, and when they got home he looked up Claudio's speech in the *Complete Works* and lay awake all night brooding on it. Was *that*, he wondered, where his mother had gone? There had been times when he had thought of death as a warm, dark place where he could sleep and be safe. Now, suddenly it was a frozen inferno where he would be stripped of his body and exposed to all the torment of the elements, trapped in regions of thick-ribbed ice, tossed by viewless winds. He visualised his mother's strong spirit, torn from its anchor of flesh and bone, whirled helpless and shrieking through all the dark paths of the upper air. Outside, a wind had picked up – a Cambridge wind which had come galloping across the fens and now blew, always in the wrong direction, down every street in the city. Windows clattered; doors shook. Dominic listened, without wanting to, for his mother's voice; but there were so many voices in the gale that her once strident and forceful tones were altogether lost. So that was Death: a scream that no one heard, a gaggle of spirits, clutching at the last shreds of their humanity, sucked up irresistibly into the great vacuum of the universe. And for the first time he saw the universe as a huge impersonal machine, Godless, uncaring, rolling on its predestined course driven by vast scientific forces, in which the whole of mankind was little more than a momentary check, a speck of dust in the works, soon to be crushed, sucked up, spewed out for ever. Years after, he knew it was that night when he first realised there was no God, nothing to believe in, nothing to live for. He was caught between two hells with no way out. He could live, as he had lived since the rape, without emotion or purpose. Or he could die, and his little spirit, caught up in the storm, would be blown into mindlessness in an instant of eternity, his last conscious thought shattered on a knot of cloud and the fragments spun through the stratosphere like sparks, until the dark swallowed them, and they went out. The vision was terrible enough at thirteen; Dominic did not know that it would never wholly leave him. He switched on the light, but it made strange, wicked shadows which moved inexplicably in the draught. In the end, he switched it off again and hid under the bedclothes, shivering with assorted terrors, until daylight brought some alleviation, and he could sleep.

The best thing about Dominic's first term at Ampleforth was coming home. Suddenly, Cambridge had begun to seem like 'home': he greeted Theresa (who was far less bossy than some of the other boys at school and nowhere near as good with her fists) with something like enthusiasm and surprised Zoë by returning her hug with a brief, convulsive embrace. At the time, she thought they were making progress, but he never repeated the gesture and as so often with Dominic she felt she would have to go back to the beginning and start again. He even tolerated Sandy, at least for the first few days, inadvertently causing her to fall violently in love with him.

She was a pretty child two years his junior, less intelligent and less forceful than her elder sister, and already given to falling violently in love, usually with remote unattainables such as film stars, pop-singers, and her physics teacher. Like Jassy Radlett she was saving up to run away to Hollywood (in her case to marry Davy Jones), but unlike Jassy Sandy's pocket money was invariably dissipated on bubblegum and *Jackie* and a secret store of make-up which Zoë pretended not to know about, so the savings did not amount to much. Her mother was not particularly disturbed by the film stars or even the physics teacher but she admitted to herself, after a few days of watching Sandy trail round in the wake of her no longer tolerant cousin, pale at his teasing, and lose her appetite when he sat down to dinner, that she would be relieved when Dominic went back to school. He seemed to be happy there, becoming more approachable (or so she reasoned, remembering that unexpected embrace), and with his frequent absences Sandy would probably forget her unrequited passion before he grew old enough to want to reciprocate, even as she invariably forgot some actor whose T.V. series went off the screen for a time. A night of tears, a day of sulks, and there would be someone else. Zoë was a realist and she knew both her daughters would start experimenting with sex sooner or later (probably sooner), but she did not really want them to start at home. Dominic, she noticed, despite a certain superficial interest in Britt Ekland and Raquel Welch, seemed totally devoid of sexuality.

Thinking it over after the holidays, when Sandy had reverted to Davy Jones, she was troubled. 'What do you want?' she asked herself, both irritated and amused by her own inconsistency. 'There's nothing you can do, anyway. Except leave him alone. He's probably just immature. They say boys *do* mature later than girls, after all. And even if he *was* interested in sex, he wouldn't talk about it. Not to me. Nor Francis.' Her thoughts broke off and she was left with the sensation of helplessness, of having failed in some way, which Dominic frequently inspired in her. It was a sensation which was to become still more familiar in the future.

Dominic confided his hatred of school only to Theresa, and even then he would not say much. 'Is it the religion?' she asked him. 'All those monks must be really out to indoctrinate you.' They had discussed their views on religion several times.

Dominic shook his head brusquely, and then turned the gesture into a shrug. 'It's not that. I'm just not one of the chaps, don't you know. I have no Team Spirit and I can't bear rugger. I don't like punching people on the nose – or getting punched, for that matter. Worst of all, I've got brains. The hulking, muscular sons of the landed gentry can't stand anything to do with brains. They hate me, and I hate them. The perfect balance, you might think. Only there are a lot more of them.'

'They can't *all* be like that,' Theresa said unhappily, trying to be encouraging. 'There must be *some* boys who are – well, intelligent and everything.'

'Oh – *some*.' Dominic grimaced, not very pleasantly, at her sympathetic face. 'At least I run fast. That's one thing about being skinny and long-legged.' (He was growing taller.) 'I can run faster than any of them.' And then: 'Don't worry about it. I wish I hadn't told you now. I can't endure people worrying over me.'

Like your mother? Theresa thought; but she was old enough not to say it. 'I can't help it,' she explained as lightly as she could. 'You're my cousin. Coz, dearest coz, sweetest coz . . .'

'What's that from?'

'I don't know. Probably Shakespeare: it usually is. The Elizabethans were very into cousinship. I daresay, since there were less people then, it was easier to be related. Dom – you will be all right, won't you?'

Suddenly, he looked irritable. 'Of course I will.'

She smiled quickly and uncomfortably. 'Keep running.'

It was not until the fifth and sixth forms that Dominic began to feel at ease in school life. For a long time after his mother died he had been unable to concentrate at all, even during exams, and his normally reliable memory had tended to lapse without warning into total blankness. Fortunately, the teaching staff at Ampleforth were, for the most part, patient and perceptive. He managed good O level results without any excessive effort and his confidence improved almost in spite of himself. His writing talent attracted attention and even began to give him a certain status among his classmates: he wrote plays, one of which was performed to visiting parents, verses that a century ago would have been called 'scurrilous', repeatable and unrepeatable lyrics, teaming up with the son of a well-known conductor who did the music. (His partnership with Ricky Verelst was the nearest he came to making a real friend at school.) On Sports Days, he won a race or two, earning a doubtful acknowledgement from his games master. In private, he was working on a novel called *The Fall of the City Beautiful*, under the combined influence of Tolkien and George Orwell – an improbable combination which produced a would-be allegorical fantasy of a perfect Atlantean civilisation destroyed by corruption and revolt, not necessarily in that order. Almost everyone was killed, and the all-powerful deity who had been in direct communication with the High Priest turned his face away from catastrophe, saying in effect: 'I can do nothing. I do not exist.' Happily, the novel was never finished. Theresa read the first few chapters and thought it was 'wonderful, of course, but what does it all *mean*?'

'Well,' said Dominic, trying belatedly to arrange his ideas, 'it's about people destroying themselves. And Fate, you know. And Doom. And the hopelessness of everything. I thought I'd end it back on the hillside above the ruined city, with the bees humming around the flowers like when Nenhereth was there. The bees were all right, you see. So were the flowers. It was the people who were all wrong.'

'*I* see,' said Theresa, who didn't. 'You mean it's symbolic. It sounds terrific, Dom, but – you don't mind? – I like your plays best.' (She was doing a drama course at Guildhall.) 'Would you write a play with something in it for *me*?'

It became a secret joke between them, a sort of cousinly pact. Theresa was going to be an actress and Dominic was going to be a playwright and together they would take the West End by storm. 'Dominic Hardinge's sensational new play, *The Double-Decker Bus*, tears off the veneer of middle-class respectability to reveal the passion and corruption seething beneath . . . Miss Preston's performance as Meghan is profound, moving, and irresistibly true.' In those days it was Theresa, older and more self-assured, who dominated the relationship; there was nothing, nothing at all to prepare her for the moment when another Dominic – an elegant, dissipated, successful Dominic – would say to her, not with anger or regret, but with a cold and ruthless detachment: 'I'm sorry, coz. I can't recommend you for the part. You're simply not good enough.'

When talking about his schooldays, Dominic always portrayed himself as a temperamental, erratically brilliant boy, undersized, quick-witted and quick-footed, abhorred by the undiscerning masses and never long out of trouble. A rebel, a practising coward, an embryonic genius, a demon in the classroom, an angel in the choir. 'I was caviare to the general,' he would say, at his most flippant. 'Honestly. They all loathed me.' But it was only in the sixth form that he became a noticeable member of the school community, loathed or otherwise. Before that, he was just a silent, almost sullen boy, usually too listless to misbehave, whose occasional flashes of spite and temper were just enough to make him unpopular without giving him any actual notoriety. The sexual harassment which he later described in such detail to Dr Glauber was actually so infrequent as to pass (at the time) virtually unremarked. The only incident of any significance was when another boy accused Dominic of 'watching' him in the shower. The accusation somehow found its way to Dominic's housemaster, who took him on one side for a Little Talk. Dominic went first scarlet and then white, so white that the housemaster was afraid he was going to faint, and cut the Talk unusually short. After that no more was said of the matter, but Dominic's classwork fell below his normal standard for over a month. Curiously enough, this incident never reached Dr Glauber's sympathetic ears.

In June 1974 Dominic passed his A levels without revision, working furiously on *The Fall of the City Beautiful* during study periods. In July he burnt the unfinished novel with a sort of sacrificial ceremony on a bonfire in the Prestons' garden and went hitch-hiking round Europe with Ricky Verelst and some of his friends. He took with him a new, blank notebook which he attempted to fill with very impersonal, artificial, intensely symbolic poetry which was not supposed to rhyme or have any recognisable rhythm – although from time to time his instincts betrayed him.

The skies cave in (he wrote) *over nagasaki*
for a fraction of eternity
God unveiled the Light of His face
and turned men blind
clouds belched upward
like a Jovean fart made visible
the universe hesitated

next year
trees did not flower
nor dragons hatch
the God Who made trees flowers dragons
did not notice
He too was blinded
in His own Light

He did nothing
he had ceased
to exist

Theresa, the only person to be shown any of the poetry, inadvertently destroyed it. 'It's very fashionable, isn't it?' she said. 'When I was in the sixth form everyone was trying to write poetry like that.' Dominic wondered about burning the poetry too but this time no bonfire came to hand and in the end he contented himself with hiding it away at the back of a bottom drawer. In October, he started at St John's College, Cambridge.

A well-known English author and editor once said that it was not only unnecessary but potentially disastrous for any would-be writer to study literature at university. Fortunately, Dominic did very little studying. He attended the occasional lecture and submitted the occasional essay, but most of his energy went into writing for various magazines and dramatic groups, supporting (and discarding) an assortment of causes, Flashing for Rag Week – equipped with a collecting-box and an artificial phallus many sizes larger than the norm – and opposing almost everything from zoological experiments on stick-insects to the misuse of college premises (e.g. the chapel at King's) for religious services. His atheism was so fervent that at times the deity he denied seemed more real to him than to many believers, an Enemy who loomed over the universe, huge and threatening, while Dominic, a small and solitary rebel, shook his pen in useless defiance. It was a pose that evidently appealed to him: in the end, he gave up supporting things altogether and concentrated solely on opposition. His magazine articles were signed 'The Nihilist' after a suggestion from Ricky Verelst (Ricky was at Oxford but spent frequent weekends with his Cambridge ex-schoolmates). His politics, though theoretically socialist, consisted more of condemning the Right than vindicating the Left – indeed, on occasion he would forget himself and condemn the Left as well. He staged sit-ins on rugger pitches in the rugby season and on cricket pitches in the cricket season. The sit-ins were never about vital issues, but he disapproved of both rugger and cricket. At rare intervals he got riotously drunk or mind-bendingly stoned, driving himself deliberately to nausea-point as though to see how it felt, and what other people did it for. The next day he would endure his hangover as if it were some kind of religious flagellation, but if he saw any visions he did not mention it.

He dressed almost exclusively in black: black brushed-denim jeans, black jumble-sale evening suits, black shirts washed and rewashed until the creases and the seams had turned pale, a gash of scarlet from an old scarf which (he said) he had bought from a tramp for half a bottle of gin. A disgruntled English tutor and close friend of Francis once commented: 'At least he *looks* like Hamlet, even if he can't be brought to study him. He even behaves like the bastard on occasion. When the wind is nor' nor' easterly, I often wonder if he knows a fork from a chainsaw.' At one stage, just to confuse his tutors (or so they claimed) Dominic changed his course, reverting three weeks later when he discovered the Faculty of Oriental Studies expected him to do some serious work. His writing – despite intermittent sessions with

D. H. Lawrence, T. S. Eliot, F. R. Leavis – remained almost impervious to outside influence. He was subject to stylistic fads but the thought behind the style did not change, nor would it ever do so. In all his later plays there was the same adolescent gesture of rebellion and despair, the same hopeless, childish protest: 'Life isn't fair!', the same cold voice echoing: 'Life isn't fair.' No matter what the age of the characters, the playwright did not age, or mature, or learn. There are dark, lonely places in the human soul, abysses where the self shrinks to a tiny spark, lingering tremulously amidst desolation. Dominic had got into the dark places and now he could not get out. Perhaps he had chosen to stay there, shutting the door on his imagination, one night when he was thirteen, afraid of the bright treacherous promise of hope and courage and belief. Whatever the reason, his ideas were fixed; acclaim would only make him a little harsher, more cynical, more certain that what he had to offer was the only Truth. 'The public,' he said, in an interview for the *New Statesman*, 'likes to hear about Doom, particularly its own Doom. That makes it so much more real. They like it in the theatre, in the cinema, in the living-room over tea. If you could condense it and put it in tins they would go out and buy it.' Dominic did very well out of Doom.

Meanwhile, he was beginning to experiment with sex. It was time, he knew. At school, in the quasi-religious, all-male environment, there had been a lot of talk and very little action. At college, there was still more talk and a great demand for action. Women (he discovered) must not only be done but must be seen to be done. Dominic's college friends all seemed to think he would have very little difficulty with women. Yet despite his uncertain arrogance and a growing inner conviction of special talent he remained curiously unconcerned with his physical assets. He had grown taller without putting on any more weight and his thinness made him look somehow taut and stretched, as though he had burnt up his calories bringing the good news from Ghent to Aix or sitting up all night in search of the philosopher's stone. In fact, he frequently sat up to write, though never to study. There were hollows under his cheekbones and tiny dents drawing down the corners of his mouth, making him look vulnerable, child-like, reluctantly adult. He was always being pursued by maternal types. (He used to say he always had been.) His hair was of a curious grey-fairness – later, he had white-blond streaks put in – cut short on top but with long tendrils straggling down his neck. His eyes, behind their veiling of lashes, were pale, almost without colour, thin arteries of green spreading out from the pupil like impurities in crystal. His hands were too small and too slender: 'Artist's hands,' Theresa said; child's hands, Zoë thought. Even callouses and inkstains only made them look whiter and more sensitive, the hands of a schoolboy who works too hard and doesn't play football. He was nearly always inkstained since his pens never functioned properly for long; he could kill a Parker in three months. Writing about sex, which he did fluently and with ease, he knew he was missing something important if not essential: imagination was straightforward enough but he flinched from reality. Not that he remembered, or not often; he had pulled down a blind on memory, a long time ago – darkness, pain, Nirvana had become fragments of a dim and distant nightmare which he would not revisit. His youthful vigil by his mother's body was the true cause of his fluctuating moods and increasingly self-indulgent traumas. Only rarely would there be a lifting of the blind, a glimpse into the dark (or was it light?) beyond, and he would shrink away in panic or some other fear, willing himself to unremember. He was not afraid of women but he was afraid of homosexuals. He had fits of strange naiveté, as though somewhere in his mind there was a blind spot, an unawareness of the outside world; in one such moment of abstraction he fell into conversation with a fellow student at a party, apparently oblivious to his homosexual tendencies. They left the party together. Later, when Dominic reached home alone, he was shaking as though with terror.

It was after that he began going out with Sandy.

Why Sandy? Theresa asked him afterwards, not once but – with her usual persistence – four or five times. Dominic only shrugged, varying the depth and brevity of his shrug but not improving on it. When it happened, it had seemed somehow inevitable, going out with Sandy. She was there, she was convenient, she looked good – he had heard other men comment favourably on her in the past. She liked him, or seemed to. He took her to *Citizen Kane* at the film society and *Slaughterhouse 5* at the Arts Cinema ('I like Kurt Vonnegut; he's so meaningless'), to an upper-class party at Magdelen and a bad taste party at Caius, to the theatre, the Mitre, the Anchor, one or two concerts, and a reading of haikus translated from the Japanese. He kissed her and found it pleasant: her kisses were firm and assured and she did not salivate too much. She bit him with her small sharp teeth – like the baby-teeth of a puppy – leaving marks on his neck which were much admired by his fellow students. His uncle looked with approval on a cousinly intimacy and asked him if he had hurt himself at golf (Francis was a keen if unpredictable player who had once knocked his opponent out cold with an errant golfball). Theresa, away touring with a children's theatre, wrote from some unpronounceable Welsh outpost, but her letters were always hurried and rarely to the point. As for Zoë, she said nothing to Francis and little to Dominic, only her manner to him became even more gentle than usual – always a sign of some unwelcome emotion carefully repressed.

After the poetry reading he took Sandy back to his room and they drank cheap white wine and listened to Yes on the stereo. Dominic found himself hearing more of the music than he wanted to. Her breasts were round and soft; when he squeezed them they gave under his fingers like air moving about in an inflatable cushion. Presently, her right hand slid down between his legs. At the time, he thought her touch instinctive; later, he thought it practised.

'I've always been in love with you,' she said, as though she had read the line in a book, 'ever since I was a little girl.'

'I know,' Dominic said absently. 'I thought you were a bloody nuisance.' He began to undress her, quickly, feeling suddenly that it was important to take hold of the moment, the urge – the impulse – before it abandoned him. Under her briefs there was a pad of hair, not silky like the hair on her head but prickly and soft. Her thighs opened for him and they were white and very slim, without muscle. In between, the entrance to her body was like the tip of a tiny pink tongue poking out between wet pink lips. A great coldness took him – not repulsion, not fear, but a blood-draining, heart-stilling cold like a physical loss. He pressed himself against her for a few seconds, striving for warmth, for stimulus, for the flickering return of desire – for gentleness in pain, for reassurance in desolation. But only for a few seconds. Then he rolled away from her and lay still. He did not speak. He was afraid he had already given enough of himself away. After a while, Sandy got up and dressed.

'I – I suppose I'd better go,' she said, 'hadn't I?' She had seen no pain, only failure. She wanted to say something kind but she was too embarrassed and Dominic's face looked remote and unencouraging. When she had gone, he wondered if she would talk about it. At that moment, it did not seem very important.

'You mustn't worry so much,' Theresa said when he eventually told her. 'You weren't in love with her, were you? That's the whole point. Men are so stupid about sex. They think that if a girl's pretty and – and appreciative that's all that's necessary. And they boast amongst themselves and talk a load of macho bullshit and so the whole myth is self-perpetuating. Underneath, many of them are quite sensitive and pleasant human beings, really.' She smiled at him. 'Like you. You're an artist, so naturally you're hypersensitive. Sandy's a nice girl but she screws around a bit: she's at the age where she thinks it's clever. Anyhow, you don't love her – not in that way. It's not surprising you found it all just a big turn off.'

'Isn't it?' Dominic murmured, languishing in the glow of her misconceptions. And then, with real gratitude: 'I'm so *glad* you're here . . .'

Later, she whispered: 'It'll be all right with me, won't it? I mean, you do love me, after all.' He said yes in the half belief that it was true, and presently it *was* all right. She climbed on top of him and her body felt strong and sure and her warmth was enough for both of them. He could not see her in the dark and that was easier too. Afterwards, sighing his relief into the hollow of her shoulder, he did not know that she was the only girl with whom it would ever be perfectly 'all right'. He knew only that he had found a kind of peace. For a little while.

It was not a great affair. Theresa returned to London for the familiar weary round of auditions and they parted without regret, each knowing the other would always be there. The next time Theresa came home – or the time after that – she found Otis Friedland in her mother's kitchen with one tin of Lapsang Soochong and one of Earl Grey, trying to master the secret of making tea. He was in Cambridge to give a couple of lectures and Francis, with his unique natural flair for disaster (said by some to have been inherited by his daughter), had invited him to stay. It took Theresa twenty-four hours, one punt, two bottles of wine, curry, bed, and breakfast to realise that Otis Friedland was the Love of her Life. She gave up everything for him – everything, in this case, signifying a rather depressing shared flat in Balham and a so far undistinguished career in the West End theatre. And Dominic. 'I'll see you,' she told him. 'This is the Love of my Life. Isn't it wonderful?' Like a teenager going to a party, he thought. For the first time he felt older and wiser than her, and a little lonely. He had not felt really lonely since the fifth form at school.

They did not see each other again for several years. In New York, Theresa cleaned Otis Friedland's flat, cooked unappetising meals for him, tinkered with his car (he was a great believer in Women's Lib), wrote rave reviews of his poetry under various pseudonyms, carried and miscarried his child. When he eventually returned to his wife and six kids in Philadelphia she stayed on with a sympathetic girlfriend until the sympathy had long worn out, writing agonised letters to her former lover which were returned unopened, having a nervous breakdown, and refusing to communicate with her parents. After the sanatorium, she tried without success to get work as an actress, and finished up spending nearly a year in a hamburger joint, eating little, paying her debts, and saving her fare home.

'Why don't you ask your folks?' said the ex-sympathiser Jodie, who had taken up being bracing. 'They've got plenty of bread. D'you think they'd like it if they knew what you were doing – working your ass off in that dump and getting as skinny as a stick of spaghetti?'

'I'm a grown woman,' Theresa said shortly. 'I can manage. Besides –' with a hint of irony or merely histrionics '– I've got my pride.'

'Sure you've got your pride, baby, but what else have you got?' Jodie pointed out. 'Seems to me you're all set on being a martyr.'

'Look,' Theresa said, 'they offered to pay my fare home two years ago for my sister's wedding, and I wouldn't go. I said would they pay for Otis as well and they said no, so I said if he wasn't going, then I wasn't going. I was selfish and obstinate but after that I won't – I *won't* – ask them to pay for me now. Okay?'

Jodie sighed. 'You know best, babe. If you really think it matters.'

Theresa got off the 'plane at Gatwick in the late summer of 1981. It was a day of faint rain and no clear sun, a grey English day such as she had dreamed of for over a year. On the train to London she stared out of the window at the ugly little houses, the squat office blocks, the sky that seemed somehow lower with no soaring plateglass towers to hold it up – and she cried and cried. The other people in the compartment looked away in embarrassment. This was England. At the thought, Theresa cried even more.

She had been offered temporary sleeping space on the sofa at a friend's house. When she arrived they kissed, gushed, sat down amidst the debris of last night's dinner party, shared tea and cigarettes. Theresa tried to remember how she had behaved, in the days when she was trying to look like an aspiring actress. She smoked furiously. The friend talked. It was almost a reflex action to pick up a copy of *Time Out*, to flick through the pages as she used to when she wanted to know what was on, what was in, what was new. And there was

Dominic's face, gazing up at her, a little thinner perhaps, rather dreamy, but (she thought) scarcely older, scarcely changed. 'Dominic Hardinge, the brilliant young playwright whose highly controversial play . . .' She read the interview through twice, very quickly and then very slowly. The friend said: 'Darling, have you heard of him? He's supposed to be the latest genius. I saw the play last week and I must say I thought it was very –'

'He's my cousin,' said Theresa. 'I must call him. At once.'

At last, after endless 'phone calls, Dominic. His voice, aloof, surprised, altered by the telephone. His flat – very much a man's flat – expensive stereo, uncomfortable paintings, haphazard furniture. Books: Proust, Böll, Garcia Marques. Biographies of actors and politicians, poetry, plays, several different kinds of dictionary. Black cigarette-ends in the ashtrays. Whisky and gin on the sideboard. Tonic and rancid butter and caviare in the fridge. Stale bread. No health food. Dominic himself, looking not at all dreamy and tired around the eyes. 'You look thin. There might be something in the kitchen. We eat out most nights and I don't have breakfast . . .' Coffee. Gin with very little tonic. The stilted talk of long-lost friends trying to pretend talking is easy, nothing has changed. Trying to pretend. Music: Debussy, 'Dialogue with the Wind and the Sea'. The sound of uneven waves breaking on surrealistic shores. Questions: what plans? what projects? what next? And somehow, inevitably, her audition piece. From *Under Milk Wood*. She had tried it out – optimistically – in front of the bathroom mirror at her friend's house. She had felt confident. Now, her confidence was gone. She tried Shakespeare – Ophelia. She was too old for Ophelia. And then, Dominic's play . . .

Silence. Her voice had stopped, the record had stopped, even the traffic in the street below seemed to have stopped. His words fell into the silence like cool cool droplets of water. 'I'm sorry . . .' (sorry, sorry) '. . . You're simply not good enough.' She was already on her feet.

Afterwards, she thought he might have offered to take her for a meal, if she had waited. But he didn't offer and she didn't wait. She went out without speaking. She didn't slam the door. For once, her timing was perfect: the sound of traffic began again even as the door closed behind her. She ran down the stairs very quickly and out into the street. Into the road. If there had been a bus she might have run under a bus. But there wasn't a bus – only a leisurely Mercedes just pulling out. Breaks screamed. Theresa apologised. She wondered if Dominic had heard. She pictured him up in the flat, turning the record over, lighting a black cigarette, twisting his lip in the faint familiar grimace, half revulsion half pain . . .

She did not call him again and she had not left a number where he could call her. She tried the usual round of theatres and agents, looking for old contacts, new openings. She had never had much success and now she had none. The friend – Sue – pointed out delicately that she could not sleep on the sofa indefinitely. Why didn't she go home, darling? Bury the hatchet? What hatchet, Theresa thought. There had never been any hatchet. She was pregnant again, though she hadn't told anyone. She wasn't quite sure who the father was but she hoped it wasn't the Italian barman because he had had a very small prick and if the child was a boy she didn't want him to inherit a small prick. The pain began one day when she was getting off a bus. It was so bad she thought she was going to faint and then suddenly there she was, sitting on the pavement clutching her knees, with faces clustering all around her. Kind, anxious, helpless faces. Someone took her to the hospital and there was a white bed and nurses and questions, and pinpricks and morphia and eventually sleep. No more pain. No more baby. After so much morphia it was difficult to be sure if she was unhappy or not. Sue came to see her twice. It was Sue – she learned later – who had tried to call Dominic.

He came to the hospital on the second or third day after her miscarriage. The nurse said: 'Visitor for you, Miss Preston. Are you awake?' and she said she was although she didn't feel particularly wakeful. The nurse let him in and he sat down beside the bed. A young man. Youngish. About thirty, maybe, although he looked less at a first glance. Long out of date fringe, snub nose, slight tell-tale hardening about the mouth and chin. Eyes blurred from too much work or too much drink or both but still darkly and vividly blue. She had never really cared for blue eyes. A lack of pigment, she had always understood. How could you trust somebody who had no pigment? She tried to remember what colour eyes Otis had had, but could not. Grey possibly. Or a pale hazel. It was disconcerting, not being able to remember.

After a brief, uneasy hesitation, the young man said abruptly and obviously: 'I'm afraid you don't know who I am.'

'No.' Theresa tried to smile. 'I'm sorry; should I? I'm not very well, you see . . .' What a stupid remark, she thought. If she had been well she would not have been lying in a hospital bed, being visited by an unknown young man. An unknown young man . . . Once, that would have intrigued her. Perhaps drugs and pain had dulled her capacity for being intrigued.

'Of course you're not well. Perhaps I'd better explain.' This time, when he hesitated, he seemed to be thinking things out, choosing the right words. 'You see, your cousin's sharing my flat for a bit.' *His* flat. 'Dominic Hardinge. There was a message on the answering service. I thought – somebody ought to come and see you.'

She did not ask if Dominic had heard the message. She had a feeling it would be better not to. She said 'Oh' very quietly and then there was a silence which went on too long and began to be uncomfortable.

'Look, I should have brought you something,' he said at last. 'Grapes or chocolates or whatever. It was stupid of me – I didn't think. Is there anything you'd like me to get for you? Anything particular, I mean? Something to read . . .?'

'That's very kind of you,' Theresa said, rather surprised. She wondered if he meant it. He did not (she thought) look as if sincerity was one of his strong points. Besides, he lacked pigment . . .

'You tell me what you want,' he reiterated, 'and I'll bring it for you tomorrow.'

Perhaps he did mean it. 'I'd like a good book,' she said. 'Something really escapist.'

'Can do.' He seemed more at ease now. Suddenly, he smiled at her. It was a nicer sort of smile than she had expected. 'Fantasy or Victoriana?'

'Oh – Victoriana. *Wives and Daughters* would be heavenly. Or even Jane Austen if it isn't *Mansfield Park*.' She smiled too, rather tentatively. 'I think Fanny Price would give me a relapse.'

'I haven't read much Jane Austen,' he confessed. 'I couldn't really get on with her. To be honest, I prefer the modern writers . . . Anyway, I'll get *Wives and Daughters* for you.'

'Elizabeth Gaskell,' she murmured.

He grinned again. 'I didn't know,' he said, 'but I would have found out.'

The next day he came early, bringing the book and a huge bunch of flowers which one of the nurses arranged fussily in a vase that was entirely the wrong size for them. 'I brought you *Vile Bodies* as well,' he said. 'Something to make you laugh.'

They talked about books for a while and it was quite easy to continue not mentioning Dominic. And the more they talked, the easier it became. When the nurse brought her tea, Theresa asked for another cup. 'This is stupid,' she remarked. 'I don't even know your name.'

'Alisdair,' he said. 'Alisdair Saunders.'

When she came out of hospital he drove her down to Cambridge. 'Did you tell Dominic,' she asked him, 'about driving me home?' It was the only time she had ever spoken to him of Dominic.

'No' he said.

At home, she thought her father looked the same and then she thought he looked older. Zoë hugged her very tightly but didn't cry, or if she did, it was hidden by her new reading-glasses. Alisdair stayed for tea. 'You'll be all right now, won't you?' he said. He didn't seem to doubt it.

'Yes of course,' said Theresa. 'I have the constitution of a goat. Or whatever animal it is that's supposed to have a really resilient constitution.'

'I didn't just mean physically.'

'Oh, I'm not at all neurotic. I got *that* out of my system when

Otis left me. I'm not going to start all over again.' She produced a faint smile, self-consciously brave. She could still act off the stage if not on it, a sign – with Theresa – of returning spirits. 'I shouldn't think English sanatoriums would be half as comfortable as American ones. Anyway, neurotics are a very expensive luxury.'

'You know,' Alisdair commented, 'when you've thought about it for a bit you'll realise it was quite impossible for you ever to have loved someone with a name like Otis. Particularly a poet. I'll bet his poetry was bloody pretentious.'

'It was wonderful,' Theresa said, defensively. 'It sort of – *meant* something.'

'Did it?' Alisdair grinned. 'Well, that's . . . that's . . . I suppose that's . . . wonderful.'

'Have a piece of cake,' said Zoë.

Before Alisdair left, he asked Theresa, rather too diffidently, if she was going to try and go back on the stage. She shook her head. 'I know I *can* act,' she said, doggedly. 'It's just that I can't face that "scene" any more. All the bitching and back-stabbing and the awful professional claustrophobia. I want to get out into the *real* world. I think – I should like to do something for other people, for a change. You get so selfish, wrapped up in your own problems. And they aren't all that big really – not compared with people starving, or dying of cancer, or being imprisoned and tortured for what they believe. Do you understand?'

'Don't rush it,' he said, surprised to hear himself giving advice and knowing it was wasted. 'You've got lots of time.'

At the door, she asked him abruptly: 'Are you – something to do with the theatre as well?' He had never talked much about himself.

'Yes.'

She nodded. She had wondered, once or twice, if he worked with Dominic, if he was in some way dependent on him. It didn't matter. She would never have asked Alisdair for that kind of help, not now.

'When you come up to London,' he said, getting into the car, 'give me a call. I'll buy you dinner.'

'I will.' She felt herself smiling, like the heroine in the final moments of a film which doesn't, quite, end happily. 'Thanks. I mean, for everything.'

His face closed – tightened. 'No thanks necessary.' He drove off into the sunset – or in this case into a drab twilight of low cloud, promising rain – leaving her wondering who was really the hero, and what essential part of the action she had missed.

Chapter Five

Dominic graduated from Cambridge in 1977, gaining his degree more by luck than application. He preferred writing plays and poetry to literature essays – the plays being promising, the poetry derivative and mostly bad. His tutor saw the plays, dismissed the poetry, and waxed philosophical about the essays, doubtless reminding himself of the many geniuses who had shown no interest in regular study. In Dominic's final year a play of his entitled *After Brideshead*, performed by the A.D.C., attracted extensive critical attention. 'It is appropriate,' one Arts Page commented, 'that Hardinge should use a novel by Evelyn Waugh as a springboard for his ideas, since his style has much in common with Waugh's early work. There is the same subtle, sometimes painful satire, the same economy of word and thought. Hardinge, however, presents a view of life that is in the end totally devoid of hope or spiritual meaning, the bleak, frighteningly clear perception not of an atheist but of an anti-humanist. The characters live, the play lives, but the author himself is as cold as a machine.' (After the success of I.T.V.'s *Brideshead Revisited* Thames Television revived Dominic's play, to mixed reviews.) The story centres round Sebastian, dying of some unspecified disease resulting, presumably, from his alcoholism, who comes to young Lord Marchmain's new residence (in Brighton) in order to die more comfortably with his family round him. Or so it appears. Marchmain, now a widower, is pursuing the Swedish au pair. Cordelia has married a black African twenty years her junior. Then Julia and Charles arrive, by now also married (to each other), and the true facts about Rex Mottram's death begin to emerge . . . In short, it was a black comedy with a peculiarly unpleasant ending which, purists complained, was a long way from the spirit of the original novel. 'To the purist,' Dominic retorted, 'nothing is pure.' Anne Heywood of the Heywood Starr Agency saw the play while on a visit to her former tutor. 'Give me a call,' she told Dominic over a dinner at Fagin's for which she paid, 'when you've written something a little more mature.'

Dominic said: 'Maybe' and stuffed her business card carelessly into his wallet. He had heard of the Heywood Starr Agency. Of course he had. But he wanted to show her that he wasn't flattered, that he didn't have to accept her opinions on maturity of style. His wallet was old leather, worn around the seams, crammed with crumpled scraps of paper very few of which had any financial significance. He wanted her to see that her business card was just another piece of rubbish. He knew he had had too much to drink and was behaving irrationally, but he didn't care.

When she dropped him off at his college he was very drunk and looked, she thought, younger than his years, a wretched adolescent who could not handle wine or women or any other symptom of growing up. He propped himself against a wall and groped for a cigarette. 'Death,' he said. 'I want some death.' (The black cigarettes which he took up later he called Black Death.)

'Have one of mine,' offered Ms Heywood. 'Will you be all right?'

'Fine.' He took the cigarette without saying thank you, clicked his lighter several times, held the flame in an unsteady hand. Then he lurched off into the darkness and vanished.

'There goes one,' she thought, 'who doesn't care if he is alive or dead. Who believes in nothing, hopes for nothing. Oh well – probably an unhappy love affair. I daresay he'll grow out of it – if he *can* grow any more. I wonder if he'll ever send me another play. Maybe the need to write will be too strong for him. Artists often create in spite of, not because of, themselves. I wonder.' She started her car and drove off down the road. It was nearly three years before she heard from Dominic again.

After university, it was a while before he could make up his mind what to do. His decisions had always been made for him: as a child, by his mother; when she died, by Zoë and Francis. He had not always liked the decisions, but he had acquiesced in them, if only from an ingrown habit of docility. Zoë and Francis had sent him to boarding school and school had sent him to university and he had never had to worry about the next meal or the next day. He had only to do as he was told. Now, he felt it was time to make his own decisions. He knew he wanted to write but he was not quite sure how to go about it. Writers didn't (surely?) just sit down, pick up a pen, and get going. They had to have jobs first, menial jobs where they were bullied by small-minded bosses and their luncheon vouchers barely covered the cost of a stale pie-crust. ('Dear me,' Francis had said. 'So you want to be a writer. Well . . . I suppose you could get a job in publishing. I'll give Charles a call.') They lived in squalid little rooms crawling with cockroaches, scribbling away by candlelight. (He didn't want to live at home.) They closeted themselves in the Reading Room of the British Museum, or retired like hermits to rural solitude. They suffered and starved. It was all useful material. Sometimes, they went abroad. They rented garrets in Paris, palaces in Venice, villas in Greece, tents in the Sahara. They fell in love with French whores and cabaret girls and contessas and odalisques, and then they wrote books about it. On the whole, Dominic decided he liked the idea of foreign travel better than that of a 'job in publishing'. He had his mother's money left in trust for him until he was twenty-one. He could do teaching, or translation (from French, anyway), or even journalism. Besides, he wanted to get away. There was a girl at college, a quiet, earnest girl with an unexpectedly beautiful mouth. He had come in her mouth several times when he was thinking of other things. But he didn't like the things he thought of or the expression on her face afterwards. He went to Paris.

In Paris he didn't teach, or translate, or journalise. He lived in a moderately comfortable second floor garret in the Quartier Latin, writing a sort of diary, intended for publication, entitled *Memoirs of a Nihilist*. He made an assortment of friends, mostly English and American. He drank a lot of cheap wine and ate a lot of cheap cous-cous. He had an association (scarcely a relationship) with a girl who told him she was an 'actrice' and whom he fondly believed was a prostitute until she finally admitted she worked for the post office. In the spring, he went south, to Florence, Venice, Rome, in search (so he claimed) of Life and Art. Occasionally Zoë received postcards from him, commenting on the state of Europe in brief phrases that were not always quite as witty as he intended. 'All the great Italians are dead,' he wrote from Pompeii. 'On the surface there is a living, breeding scum of trattorias and Gucci handbags. Underneath, paintings of dead people by dead artists, hanging in palaces as dead as tombs. Some places are so dead they have had to be dug up.' Zoë smiled when she read it, though Francis looked mildly shocked. 'He doesn't seem to really appreciate any of it,' he commented a little querulously. 'It's almost as if he *enjoys* hating everything.'

'Of course he does,' Zoë said.

He ended up in Greece, staying in a decrepit villa overgrown with what he assumed was bougainvillea and spending most of his time in a local bar. He drank a great deal of ouzo and talked about inspiration, usually with antique peasants whose limited command of English made them a silent and admiring audience. Unlike Lawrence Durrell, John Fowles, Herodotus, Homer (to name but a few) he did very little writing. In due course, his money ran out, and he sent another postcard to Zoë requesting the fare home.

Back in England, Dominic moved to London. He tried to get work as a journalist but decided his style was not suited to the medium and so took a job as a waiter instead. Francis made protesting murmurs but fortunately they never got beyond Zoë. Dominic shared a flat with a friend he had met in

Italy, a director called Ben Gamble some five or six years older than him. Ben worked in fringe theatre and had already been described by the press as 'breaking new ground', although this had not as yet led to any engagements in the West End. It was a while before Dominic realised he was gay. Strangely, despite his horror of sexual deviance, he liked the company of gays and found them easy to talk to. Ben had never made a pass at him and Dominic had closed his mind, perhaps deliberately, against any whispers of doubt. Afterwards, he claimed that if he had not found Ben in bed with a pick-up one morning he might not have realised.

'You should have told me,' he said, when the pick-up had gone, banging the coffee mugs to aggravate Ben's headache.

'Why? You never told me you were a het.'

'It's not the same.'

'Okay: it's not the same. I'm sorry, Dom. I thought you knew.'

'I didn't know.' Dominic's insistence sounded, even to himself, a little overdone. 'You deceived me – you *meant* to deceive me.'

Ben came into the kitchen, putting on his shirt. Though not tall he was heavy-shouldered, the muscles showing in his bare chest like a da Vinci drawing, a triangle of course black hair between his breasts. His face betrayed his Sephardic descent: thick nose, sullen jaw, small deepset eyes. An ugly, strong, masculine face. When he saw Dominic flinch from him he stopped in the doorway, leaning against the frame.

'Look, Dom, I've said I'm sorry. If you want to leave, that's up to you.' His mouth twisted. 'I won't touch you, anyway. I haven't yet, have I? If I'd known you would feel like this, I'd have got things straight at the beginning. I'm afraid I misunderstood. I thought you were – well, that way inclined, at least. My mistake. I am sorry – really sorry.'

'*Sorry*!' Dominic did not look at him, did not seem able to find any words.

'You're behaving,' Ben remarked, 'as if you were jealous.'

Dominic looked at him then. 'I'm leaving,' he said flatly, dropping a coffee mug. 'Now.' He slammed out of the room.

'Shit, Dom, I – ' But Dominic was out of earshot. 'I'm

sorry,' Ben repeated, to himself. He bent down and began to pick up the pieces of the broken mug. Two hours later, Dominic came back.

He didn't leave of course. Good flats were hard to come by and Ben could be a useful friend for a young playwright – or so Dominic told himself. (*Memoirs of a Nihilist* had petered out somewhere between Pompeii and Paxos and he had reverted to writing plays.) The knowledge that Ben was in love with him came upon him only gradually. It worried him, but more because he felt it *ought* to worry him than because he was genuinely troubled. In some bizarre fashion it even gratified his vanity. It was so comfortable to know that whatever he did, no matter how tiresome, Ben would always be there to support him, to believe in him, to be hurt. Sometimes Dominic would be consciously rather than unconsciously tiresome just to observe Ben's reaction. Much later, he grew afraid – of Ben's infinite patience, the tenderness in his eyes, the moments of nearness that bordered on intimacy. But that was later. To begin with, there was only the curious luxury of being cared for and required to give nothing in return. He was working on a new play which he read to Ben from time to time, listening to his criticisms with reluctance but making an occasional alteration. Predictably enough, it was about a graduate student who goes abroad in search of Life and Art, ending up in some nameless foreign city entangled with a number of undesirable people and being framed by his ex-prostitute girlfriend for a murder he did not commit. It was entitled *Climax and Anticlimax*. 'Why?' asked Ben. 'The significance,' said Dominic, obscurely, 'is sexual.' Progress on the play was slow. It was not as easy as he had imagined to do a menial but exhausting job and then return home to burn the midnight oil in a burst of creative energy. In the end, something had to go. Needless to say, it was the job.

He was sacked, or so he said, after an incident where a quantity of fricasséed veal finished up in a customer's lap instead of on the plate. 'It was a sudden impulse,' he told Ben, arriving home very late unable to remember where he had been or who had put him in the taxi. Ben, gentle and impersonal, helped him to bed. Dominic watched him blearily from under his eyelashes but did not resist. The next day he signed on. He got other jobs from time to time – as a barman, a meat-packer, an assistant cook in a vegetarian restaurant (until he cut his finger on a kitchen knife and bled all over the salad, turning would-be vegetarians into cannibals). When he had money, he spent it. When he was broke, he sponged off Ben. Once, he sold a short story, took Ben out to dinner, and then picked up a girl just to show that he could. He was unable to do anything with her afterwards, but Ben never knew that.

Increasingly, there were moments of panic, when Dominic saw his growing dependance as an insidious progression towards something closer and more deadly. He never actually formulated to himself the idea that he might sleep with Ben, but it was there at the back of his mind, like a secret cupboard, long shut and locked, where he tried the handle and yet feared to open the door. He began to think about leaving again, though this time he did not mention it. Ben's strong maleness repulsed him, the sombre features and quiet unshakeable control made him feel flimsy, violent, inadequate. Dominic both wanted him and loathed him, needed him and was terrified of learning to need. In the play the villain of the piece, a restaurateur with unspecified Mafia connections, began to resemble Ben in a vague way – like a reflection in a distorted mirror, accurate in features but squashed and misshapen out of all proportion. Ben did not comment; maybe he did not see. Out of a job, Dominic worked harder on the final scenes, crossing out, rewriting, typing up the manuscript on Ben's portable with two fingers. He became too absorbed for other problems; briefly the play took over. When it was eventually completed, late one night with no drink in the flat to celebrate and nothing but baked beans in the larder, he decided to contact Anne Heywood.

Climax and Anticlimax first appeared at the Attic in April 1980. The Attic (for those who do not know) is one of the more successful fringe theatres, situated over a pub called the Broom and Bucket and seating, at a pinch, over a hundred people, in circumstances of extreme discomfort. Ben was directing; he had frequently worked at the Attic. 'I wonder' he remarked once, after a row at rehearsal, 'what makes you write like that.' There were a good many rows at rehearsal. They usually followed the same pattern: Dominic raged, the actors shuddered, Ben grew irritable and tense. Afterwards, Dominic would lapse into irritability, Ben into thought.

'Like what?' Dominic was deliberately obtuse. 'I write with words. It is customary.'

'You know I didn't mean that. I was talking about your attitude to life – to people. I used to think you hated everything but it isn't like that. Reading a play you can only get a vague idea of its possibilities. Directing it – seeing it come alive – you begin to understand what it's about. You might have wanted to hate but couldn't manage it – you couldn't manage anything stronger than a sort of indifferent distaste. Almost as though humanity was an alien species which you had been forced to study against your will, noting down their more unpleasant habits for the benefit of some other civilisation. Your notes are always so accurate, so cold, so – uncaring. Sometimes, I feel you are trying to be angry or bitter but when it comes to the crunch you just can't summon up any emotion.' He smiled faintly. 'At least in the play.'

'That's nonsense.' Unexpectedly, Dominic sounded defensive. 'There are plenty of emotional scenes. Look at the murder.'

'The *characters* can be emotional, yes. But the play is always detached. So is the playwright. Even in life, I sometimes think you are trying too hard.'

'You go too deep for me,' Dominic sneered.

'Everything goes too deep for you.' As always, Ben ignored the sneer. 'You try to feel but you cannot, or you repress what you *do* feel because you are afraid of it. Either way, it must be painful.'

'Do you want to help?' The sneer had become a threat.

'I can't, can I?' Ben made it a generalisation. 'You wouldn't let anyone help. I only wondered,' he reiterated, almost incuriously, 'whether you were born like that, or whether it was thrust upon you.'

'I was born like that,' Dominic said. 'Of course.'

A week later he went back to Gresham.

He had not been back before – not since the night after his mother died when Zoë and Francis took him away. On the train going south, he told himself that he was changed now: a grown man (or nearly), a successful playwright (or nearly), half a lifetime away from the child who had once been humiliated and unmade. He would go back and look at the past as if it had happened to someone else, someone in a story, and so he would be able to understand it and put it behind him. It was time to lay the ghosts. He told himself that Ben's words had not troubled him; they had only shown him it was time. He had always known he would go back, some day. Everyone always went back. Failed suicides – or so he had read – revisit the place where they once jumped, one year, two years, ten years later, when they have rebuilt their lives and achieved success and happiness. They stand on the cliff edge looking down at the sea, and presently someone else comes running up to end it all, and they grasp his arm and say: 'No. You can't do it. Life is never that bad' and plunge forthwith into their autobiographies. Mechanically, Dominic began to make up a story about such a case, a man who was saved from death by some miracle or other and who climbed up from the nadir of despair to wealth and distinction and marital felicity. And at the last he comes back to the cliff-top, and looks down at the sea, and jumps. Dominic didn't know why he jumped but he knew that was how the story ended. There was something uncomfortable in the thought – ominous. But endings grow inevitably out of stories and cannot be changed, even when you do not like them. Dominic was a storyteller by profession; he knew that only too well.

The train drew into the station and Dominic got out. A little station exactly as he remembered and exactly like any other little station anywhere else in the country. He went through the exit and down the road into the village. Here, he was surprised to find himself noticing changes. A baker's which had become an Oxfam shop. A new supermarket – or was it just the old one with a face lift? A new boutique. The antique shops were the same, of course. And the gunsmith's with the same stuffed pheasant in the window, now getting rather moth-eaten (as a child, he had stared at it for hours). The shop where his mother had bought her clothes, with the same dress – or what looked like the same dress – on the display model; the same greengrocer's; the same token branch of Boots.

He came to the green, where some children were playing football. Beyond – with a sudden sinking in his midriff – his parents' cottage. The latticed windows were too dark to see inside; even the curtains might have been unaltered. His mother might have been in there, waiting, sitting bolt upright in the chair as she had sat all that terrible night, still refusing to speak to him. And suddenly he remembered her hand closing on his, a cold involuntary gesture . . .

A cat jumped onto the wall and began washing itself, breaking the spell. His mother would never have had a cat. She disapproved of pets on the grounds that they were unhygienic. Once, he had caught some tadpoles and tried to keep them hidden in a jamjar in his bedroom, but she had found them and thrown them away in disgust, saying they were dead already. He stroked the cat rather tentatively, afraid it would scratch him. In the little garden the roses looked uncared-for; hollyhocks grew up against the cottage wall. Joan had not liked hollyhocks either; she said they were too big: ugly flaunting flowers. Perhaps, Dominic thought, she felt there was no room for both herself and the hollyhocks in such a small area. She liked roses in rosebeds and tulips in vases and geraniums in pots. It occurred to him that he should have brought her some flowers. He found a florist's and then made his way to the cemetry. He had to ask a man mowing the grass where her grave was; he knew she lay beside his father but it was too long since he had been there and all graves looked alike to him. Row upon row of headstones standing up like labels on butcher's meat, carved with their meaningless sentimental phrases, meaningless names. Here lies . . . much loved . . . much mourned . . . Eliza Margaret . . . Walter James . . . Joan Elizabeth. The older stones leaned a little this way and that, as though tired of standing upright. Was she a relation? asked the man who was mowing the grass.

'My mother,' said Dominic.

The man looked sad, in a weary sort of way, as though other

young men had stopped him before now, asking like strangers for the graves of mothers and fathers, brothers, cousins, lovers. Dominic left the flowers and went.

Beyond the village he skirted a field which had once been pasture and was now neat furrows sprouting green with some crop or other. There was a barbed wire fence which he did not remember, a new gate, another field. And then over a stile into the lane. He stood for a moment, hesitating, half expecting some quickening of the pulse, some catching of the breath, a visitation of Fear rushing up out of the past to engulf him. But there were no terrors, no visitants. There was only the faint warmth of a day in early spring, a fat wild bee humming in the hedgerow, a yellow butterfly flapping ahead of him along the way he had once stumbled and fled. He followed the butterfly until it rose over the hedge and was swallowed up in a wide blue shimmer of sky. A little further on there was a low wooden gate, obviously little used now and largely overhung by some flowering shrub. A twelve-year-old child would scarcely have been able to see into the garden any more. Or be seen. Too late, he thought, wondering at the littleness of the chances on which huge and terrible events can depend. The height of a shrub. Under the hedge, weeds and grasses had encroached from the lane, closing any gaps, but he did not notice that. He leaned on the gate and looked into the garden, no longer expecting phantoms. There was a girl there, folding a garden chair: evidently she had been sitting on the grass. She was about twenty, maybe younger, with spiked blonde hair and a man's shirt hanging loose over Levi cords. When she saw Dominic watching over the shrub she hesitated, made as if to go in, then seemed to change her mind.

'Hello!' Having spoken and committed herself, she came towards him. 'I thought it would be nice enough to sit outside but it isn't really – the sun only *looks* hot. What's more, the wind keeps blowing my pages over. It's very irritating when you're trying to read the serial.' She had a magazine under one arm. From close to he saw the tips of her fringe were dyed a pale pink. She wore too much make-up carefully applied and the effect, inevitably, was to make her look far less sophisticated than she had doubtless intended. When she smiled, her teeth were small and perfect as cultured pearls. 'Do you live round here?' she asked. Her friendliness was not quite natural, the friendliness of a town girl in the country who has always heard how friendly country people are.

'I used to.' He paused. 'I live in London now.'

'*Do* you?' Dr Livingstone, she might have said, had she known the allusion. Her delight was patent. Evidently she thought Gresham the heart of the wilderness. 'So do we, really. Only Jack wanted to rent this place for weekends. I don't mind when we have guests but it's a bit flat on our own. Jack's out now,' she added in explanatory manner. 'He's gone to get the booze. We've got people coming tomorrow, thank God. Were you –' she hesitated '– were you looking for someone?'

Dominic shrugged evasively. 'Who owns the place now?'

'Oh, it still belongs to the Raikes – we rent it from Sheila. She divorced him, you know, after all the scandal – ran off with some guy who used to be a roadie with a pop group. One of the big groups back in the Sixties, ages ago. They had a villa in the South of France but she had to sell up. She wants to sell this place too but she can't – something to do with the terms of the divorce. I suppose he still owns half of it. Jack says she's broke.'

'What was the scandal?' Dominic asked idly.

'The court case, of course! Bribery and corruption. It was in all the papers. I didn't understand it properly, myself. It was all to do with Nevile Raikes taking some local councillor to Marbella or somewhere and then getting a contract to build warehouses next to the river. They said it upset the fishing, or perhaps it was a beauty spot. There was lots more than that, though. Jack says it goes to show how careful you have to be in business. Didn't you know about it? I thought – I mean, I assumed – they were friends of yours.'

She looked suddenly doubtful, like a child who has been indiscreet. Dominic said: 'Not really. How long have they owned this house?'

'I'm not sure. Fourteen – fifteen years. Why . . .?'

'I came to a party here once,' Dominic said slowly. 'A long time ago.'

'Oh, I *see*.' There was relief in her voice. She liked things explained, Dominic thought. Nice, simple explanations requiring no extra consideration. He hoped she would not begin to wonder how old he was or how long was a long time ago, but he did not think arithmetic was one of her strong points. 'They used to give a lot of parties, didn't they? Jack worked with Nevile Raikes for a bit, about seven or eight years ago, so he used to come here sometimes. Nevile had a lot of friends in the music business – I think he once financed some group or other. Or perhaps he was something to do with a record company. Anyway, Jack said he met this pop star here once – at a party, you know. I forget her name but –' she half smiled, deprecatingly ' – Jack says she used to be really famous.' Jack, it was evident, was at least twice as old as his wife. 'Are you in the music business too?'

He shook his head. 'I'm a playwright,' he admitted, oddly reluctant although he liked the sound of it. 'Dominic Hardinge.'

'I'm Karen Forder.' She held out her hand, a little shyly. He took it for a moment. It felt very small, even to him. Small and cold. *Che gelida manina* . . .

Now the introductions were over she assumed, very faintly, the manner of a hostess. A sort of parody of the tweeded county chatelaine who welcomes guests in the absence of her lord and master. She said: 'Would you like to see the garden?' with a little gesture that seemed to indicate herbaceous borders, compost heaps, greenfly. But he was quite sure she knew nothing about any of them.

'All right.' Of all the gardens in the world, that was one which he had never even dreamed of entering. It had remained in his mind as a view beyond a hedge: a vast dark lawn sloping up to a Palladian terrace, red-lit windows where shadow-figures moved to and fro. Now, inside the gate, he saw the lawn was shrunken, the stone parapet a contemporary imitation. Aubretia grew out of the urns. And through the windows he glimpsed William Morris wallpaper, a vase of dried flowers, the back of a sofa.

'Was it very different when you came here?' Karen Forder asked, unwittingly echoing his thoughts.

'Very.' He didn't want to look at the garden any more: it no longer interested him. Or the house. Instead, he looked at her. Now he was standing beside her he saw she was taller than he had imagined: perhaps he had been misled by her slightness, her narrow shoulders, small fingers. Her face was like a flower, an artificial flower made of silk and painted in pastel shades by the hand of an expert. He felt as if, at a single careless gesture, the colour would smudge, the silk crumple and tear. She offered him coffee and he accepted, suddenly frightened by her simplicity, her defencelessness, her trust. As she went up the steps ahead of him he noticed how impossibly thin she was. Not a thinness of angles and bones but a sort of sexless fairy intangibility. He pictured her naked, perched on some monstrous fungus, a white attenuated body unbroken by any bulges of breasts or genitals, hard little nipples that jutted like leaf buds, a gossamer patterning of ribs. Pink-tipped antennae sprouted from her forehead; spotted, membranous wings trailed behind her. For a minute, the fantasy creature which he had created became so real to him that he was aroused. A desire so rare and desperate that he wanted to take her, now, in this place where he had once been taken, entering her, humiliating her, tearing her even as he had been entered and humiliated and torn. As they went into the kitchen she turned round. Does she know? he wondered, looking into her eyes. Can't she tell? *She* is not a child. Is she really so innocent, so wholly unsuspecting?

'How do you like your coffee?'

And suddenly, studying her expression, he understood. She knew. She was a bored little girl who had seen a pretty toy, a new game. In her flower face he saw diffidence, eagerness, coquetry. All desire left him.

He said: 'I'll take it black' and sipped the coffee to be polite. He wanted to go, quickly, before he stumbled further into the trap, but she was chattering easily again, like a brook (he thought) babbling over a few stones with much noise and no depth. How clever he must be to have written a play. Should she come and see it? She went to the theatre sometimes with Jack. He was very cultured. (Like your capped pearly teeth, Dominic said to himself.) He liked musicals best . . .

'I'm afraid it's not a musical.'

The scorn in his voice evidently registered on her. She said, with a reversion to her former hesitancy: 'I'm sorry. I must be boring you . . .' If he had not been so self-absorbed he might have remembered how young she was.

'Of course not,' Dominic murmured without conviction. 'But I must go now. I have a train to catch.' A standard excuse. He had no idea of the train times back to London. Undoubtedly, nor had she.

'Of course.' They had become awkwardly polite, as couples do when one or other of them has made a pass – if only by inference – and been rejected. But she was too inexperienced to let it go like that. 'Did you want – I mean, were you just passing or – or did you wish to get in touch with someone? I can give you Sheila Raikes' address if you like. She lives in South Ken now. She's a good friend of ours.'

'Well . . .' Did he want to see Sheila Raikes? He had come, after all, to lay the ghosts. He looked round the room but he had never been there before and it meant nothing to him. The ghosts had moved on, into their own lives. Did he really want to know – could he *bear* to know – who they were, or where they had gone to? He had never really expected to find out anything. In fact, it was difficult to decide *what* he had expected . . .

Karen was already writing down the address. She still had the handwriting of a schoolgirl, rounded and childish. She said: 'I'll come and see your play. If I can.'

Dominic said goodbye.

Back in the lane, he didn't look round. He was sure she was staring after him, from behind a curtain, or behind a door: he could feel the eyes on his back. A thin cloud slid almost imperceptibly over the sun. He was suddenly conscious of the hedgerows, shutting him in, a quiver of birdsong, the insect-hum of distant traffic, the quiet. It was a long time since he had lived in the country and listened to that kind of quiet. He thought: the ghosts have moved on but the lane – the lane remembers. Grass that he had clung to, earth that he had tasted – footprints of Men that the ground still cherished. Under the springing weeds, the new green, the lane remembered. He saw the stile ahead of him and abruptly he broke into a run . . .

That night, when at last he slept, he was still running towards the stile. But he never got there.

Dominic always maintained (at least to himself) that it was Ben's fault he went to see Sheila Raikes. Ben being protective and somehow subtly domineering around the flat. Ben being patient and disagreeing with him at rehearsal. Ben in a dream of darkness, turning into a man with no name who put his tongue in Dominic's mouth.

Sheila Raikes' flat was in a basement in a square called Osborne Gardens. The gardens were in the middle, surrounded by an iron railing and a quantity of evergreen undergrowth. The houses were tall and elegant and painted the whiter shade of pale that only really elegant houses can carry off. The basement flat looked more than adequate for someone who was supposed to be broke.

'Have some tea,' said Sheila Raikes. 'Or Scotch.' She had Scotch.

Dominic, who didn't want tea and didn't like whisky, said he was all right, thank you.

'Gin?' suggested Mrs Raikes, looking at him as if her opinion of him, never high, had just dropped several points. And finally, hitting rock bottom: 'Beer?'

Dominic said he would have beer.

She fetched a can from the fridge and sat down in the chair opposite him, crossing her legs in a stylish way as though she knew they were still presentable. Evidently she was re-living the days of miniskirts and gauchos and had forgotten she was wearing a tracksuit. Once, Dominic thought, she must have been considered a beauty: her face had the impossibly high cheekbones which suffice for contemporary good looks although her other features were unremarkable. Her skin was brown and looked oddly speckled, like a used teabag; presumably the aftermath of too many summers in the Midi. He supposed she must be in her mid or late forties.

'Karen Forder gave me your address,' he explained. He

didn't say how he had met Karen Forder.

'Karen?' For a moment, Mrs Raikes looked vague. 'Oh – Jack's wife.' She was the kind of female who only remembers other women by their husbands. 'Pretty little thing. Dim. They say he found her in Woolworth's.'

Working, Dominic wondered, or for sale? The comment – doubtless intentionally – implied both. He said: 'I don't know her very well.'

'Not a lot there to know, I should imagine.' She took a mouthful of the whisky. 'Anyway, so what's this all about? You said on the 'phone that you're writing a play.'

'It's only an idea at this stage.' Dominic plunged into his story very quickly, half afraid of telling it, half afraid of losing his nerve. It was too close to the truth for comfort but he knew it had to be close to the truth if he was to find out anything at all. He was still not sure what he wanted to find. 'I lived in Gresham when I was a child. One night I remember going past your house when there was a party going on. I watched from over the hedge at the bottom of your garden. It made a great impression on me.' He stopped for a minute, wondering suddenly if she knew, if someone had told her, if he would see her face change – realise. Perhaps her husband . . . He felt sick inside. But there was nothing in her face beyond a mild enquiry, a touch of amusement. Possibly she was contemplating the tawdry glamour of her past lifestyle reflected in the eyes of a child. He went on: 'Thinking about it the other day, I thought I could write a play around a party like that. A group of people, middle-aged and disillusioned, looking back on the Sixties when they were young and hopeful. The people they were in love with at that particular party contrasted with their present boring marriages and awkward adolescent kids. You know the sort of thing.' Briefly nauseated by the concept, he added: 'It's for television, of course. My agent wants me to do something for television.' It sounded like an apology.

Mrs Raikes, however, appeared unaffected. 'Sure. Good idea. Now we're in the Eighties everyone's bound to go mad on Sixties nostalgia anyway. So how can I help?'

'I thought if I could use that actual party as a kind of basis to work on – if I could talk to some of the people who were there – '

'Hold on a minute. You're talking about this party – at our house – that you saw when you were a kid peeping over the hedge?'

'Yes. I know it's a long time ago – '

'A long time ago! We bought that house in '66. Over the next few years we had endless bloody parties – one every bloody weekend, or at least, it felt like it. My ex-husband was party-mad. I was just – mad, I suppose. How the hell am I supposed to remember one particular occasion? It may have made a great impression on you but I was probably under the table counting the hairs in the carpet. You, I suppose, can remember the exact date.'

'September,' Dominic said, ignoring her sarcasm. 'Autumn, anyway. I think it must have been September because it wasn't too cold. '68. I know: I was twelve.' Of course he remembered the exact date.

'Well, you may remember but I don't.' She lit a cigarette – her third since he arrived – forgetting to offer him one. Not discourtesy, he decided; merely something in the recollections he had conjured up – unwanted recollections? – which had disturbed her.

He tried again. 'Look, even if you can't remember one special party you must remember the – the *era*. You must remember who your friends were.'

'Friends!' She laughed mirthlessly. 'What friends? People who tagged around us because we had money and contacts. People we tagged around because they had money and contacts. Garbage who wanted to keep "in" with us. Garbage we wanted to keep "in" with. Oh yes, I remember them – some of them. Nevile had a nice line in business associates. Fat slobs who thought they were smart pulling off fancy deals under the counter. Much good they ever did him.'

'I heard he was involved in the pop scene.'

'He wanted to be. He put money into Phebus Records at one time. He was a sucker for rock stars – even if the stars didn't twinkle all that brightly. Any idiot with a guitar slung on his crotch was a hero to Nevile. Poor sod. I suppose he envied them, really. They used to come down to our place – drink our booze – smoke our grass – throw up on our floor. Then off the next day without so much as a thank you. They knew he was a sucker and they showed it. Why should they care? Most of them were too busy whoring their fame for the sake of a good time. God knows what's happened to them since. Got older, I suppose – like the rest of us. Serves them right.' She substituted a mirthless smile for her former mirthless laugh. 'I daresay their names wouldn't mean much to you, but some of them were big stars in their day. The Shades, the Peeping Toms, Aleister Crowley – that negress with the pink hair, Jeanie What's-her-name. *She*'s still around.'

'I've heard of them,' Dominic said. 'Old singles never die.'

'I was a sucker too – that's what you're thinking, isn't it? Well, I was. All those big names – it turned me on. Funny, really. Bloody hilarious.' She paused, drank her whisky, drew on her cigarette. 'That's how I met Alec. Must have been '68. Yes, '68. Might even have been September; I don't know. He was a roadie with The Group – you know, *The* Group. The one and only Group. The party was for them, of course. Nevile thought they were wonderful. I thought they were wonderful. I even thought their roadies were wonderful.' She made a face. 'Alec was a different kind of loser. Six months later The Group broke up and he was out of a job. He took an overdose once but they pumped it out of him. He had that kind of luck.'

'Is he still around?' Dominic asked, glancing involuntarily round the room as though expecting the luckless Alec to emerge from behind an arras.

'He comes and goes.' She sucked her cheeks in so her cheekbones jutted more than ever. 'Goes, mostly. He comes back when he wants a screw. He'd like a beautiful young thing but he can't afford one.' She went over to the mantelpiece and picked up a photograph which had been stuck behind an ornament.

'That's him. Not exactly a pin-up, is he?'

He wasn't. Hair that receded on top and made up for it lower down. A thin face, tapering towards the chin, which might once have looked tough. Dominic's eyes lifted automatically to the other photo on the mantelpiece. A sleek, good-looking man with a square jaw and a plump waistline. One arm round a much younger and blonder edition of Sheila Raikes. 'Nevile,' she said briefly. 'Am I giving you ideas for your play?'

'Maybe.' She was standing very close and suddenly he wondered if she, too, was going to make a pass at him. He was both repulsed and intrigued. But she moved away, almost as if she had thought about it and then changed her mind.

'Look, I'll make out a list for you. Anyone I can remember. It won't be the party you saw – just round about the right time. Give me a couple of days. I'll ask Alec. Doubt if he'll be much help but you never know.'

'Thanks,' Dominic said, a little surprised. He realised he did not sound particularly grateful and he wondered if he really *was* grateful. Perhaps what he had been hoping, subconsciously, was to come up against a brick wall – a nice, safe brick wall, large and solid and immoveable. No Through Road. Forget it.

'I'll make out a list,' Sheila Raikes was saying, 'and then you can go and see them, and listen to them maundering on, just like you've listened to me. And then you can put them in your play.' Once again the mirthless smile. 'It's a neat approach, darling. Everyone wants to be immortalised.'

Back at the flat, Dominic made himself some coffee. It was lunchtime, but he could not be bothered to have lunch. With his usual duality of feeling towards Ben, he was both annoyed and relieved to find him absent. Annoyed because he wanted someone to talk to, something to distract him from his own thoughts; relieved because he was afraid of talking, of confiding even a tiny fragment of the truth. It would be so easy to confide in Ben. Ben would be sympathetic, encouraging, would lead him gently from confidence into confidence, from truth into truth, looking at him with eyes that were too warm and too understanding. Knowing him. *Owning* him. Dominic shivered as though at a premonition. But Ben – presumably –

was at a rehearsal: out of the way. He would come home in the evening and ask Dominic why he hadn't been there, and Dominic would make some remark about how little pleasure it gave him to see a group of incompetent actors and an even more incompetent director ruining his play. He wouldn't necessarily mean it, but he knew he would say it. He disliked other people, he decided, only marginally less than he disliked himself.

He left his coffee to grow cold and put a record on the stereo. Most of the records belonged to Ben; Dominic had given his collection to the owner of a bar somewhere in Southern Italy in order to cover the drinks bill. Ben's taste varied from heavy rock – Pink Floyd, The Group, the Stones – to medieval chants and long albums of strange Oriental twanging noises. Thinking of Mrs Raikes, Dominic chose The Group. He lay down on the sofa listening to the voice of Johnny Sachs extolling the charms of a Black Titania and letting his mind drift. Sheila Raikes would forget about the list. He would never know who had been at that party. It was too long ago and the door was closed; he could not open it now. Weeks and months and years were piled against it like leaves; Time had stolen the key . . . *'I am going to spend my life,'* sang Johnny Sachs, *'forgetting you. Black Titania . . .'* Anyway, even if he found out anything – even if he found out everything – what could he do? Revenge? Nobody went in for revenge nowadays. They liked to read about it in books and see it on stage and screen but in real life it had been superseded by Justice and the Law and psychiatric therapy. People saw their sisters raped and their children strangled and they sat back and let the courts administer their vengeance. This is a civilised society. Effete. Spineless. He, Dominic Hardinge, was effete, spineless, as wretchedly civilised as everyone else. He had no capacity for revenge. Ben had said he tried to hate and failed – perhaps Ben was right. But he could not remember trying.

For a minute, he let himself linger, perilously, on the edge of recollection, feeling his thought float backwards towards the dark. And then it was too late. Memory rushed over him, immediate and horribly clear. Three men. Two – lesser figures, shadows, hardly real. One – the leader – a faceless giant with iron hands and leather tongue, moulding his body like a lump of clay. Abruptly, his mind spun away into the present – he saw himself walking into an office high above the city, facing a man who sat behind a desk plotting takeovers. A civilised office with wall-to-wall carpeting, futuristic telephones, an aerial view of the Post Office tower. And behind the desk, inside the business suit – the same man. The same hands on the desk-top. The face – the face he had never seen – with its leathern lips and cruel intelligent eyes. No, not hate. He could not hate. He lay on the sofa and shivered, dragging himself slowly back into reality. It was a while before he realised the record had stopped.

Sheila Raikes didn't forget about the list.

'I won't use it,' Dominic told himself. 'I don't want to know.' Some of the names had addresses attached. He called one of them on an afternoon when he had nothing else to do. A lawyer. Too busy. Another had emigrated to Scotland. The name of Marten de Witt came fifth or sixth on the list. The telephone number was ex-directory. Dominic went for a walk in Hyde Park and then decided to go and look at the house.

A foreign maid answered the door.

'You want to see Madame? Please? You have press card?'

Dominic explained that he was not a member of the press.

'Always the press want Madame. All morning. She is very tired. Maybe she see you. I go ask.'

It did not sound promising from any standpoint. The maid came back and ushered him through the hallway into a vast living room. A young woman was standing at the far end – a young woman or a girl. She could, he thought, have been twenty-five or thirty-five or even – due to the miracles of modern science – forty-five. She had long dark hair and a beautiful nondescript face, a face like a hundred other faces between the pages of a hundred glossy magazines. Perfect make-up. Expensive clothes. A slight air of gêne.

She said: 'I saw the *Star* this morning. And – I think – the *Mirror*. Are you –'

'I'm not a reporter.'

'Oh.' She looked surprised but not particularly curious.

'I'm afraid I –'

'I was hoping to see your husband.' Father? Lover? She was, he decided on closer inspection, too young for the time he was interested in.

'My *husband*?' For a moment, she sounded almost angry.

'Mr de Witt.'

'Oh.' Again the faint surprise. 'I'm sorry. A – a misunderstanding. I'm not Mrs de Witt.' She moved rather haphazardly away from him, pausing in front of a mirror with her back turned. Glancing at her reflection, he noticed that it was her own face she watched, not his. 'I suppose Marie – ' She hesitated, turned towards him ' – she's rather flustered today. I don't think I can be of any help to you. Marten – Mr de Witt – is just a friend. I don't know anything about his business affairs.'

'It isn't exactly business,' Dominic said. 'I'm a playwright. I was given his name by Sheila Raikes in connection with some research I'm doing. For a play,' he added, just to make matters totally clear.

She seemed not so much unintelligent as uninterested. Here was one, he thought, who had no desire to be immortalised. Possibly she was getting all the immortality she wanted from the *Mirror* and the *Daily Star*. He wondered who she was – he had a bad memory for faces, even famous ones. Perhaps just somebody's secretary or ex-wife who had picked up a little excess notoriety like nettle rash. He was briefly conscious of curiosity – the inevitable curiosity of the writer tempted by someone else's tale. But he had his own story to worry about.

She said again: 'I'm sorry: I can't help you. You'd better call him at work.'

'Do you have the number?'

She hadn't, of course.

'Perhaps a business card – ?'

She sent Marie to find one. She was, he felt suddenly, the woman of leisure enjoying ordering someone else to do something she could perfectly well have done for herself. The business card, when it arrived, revealed that Marten de Witt was the chairman of Phebus Records – something that Sheila

Raikes had not mentioned on her list. Dominic was not sure whether or not that fact was significant. On the whole, he thought not. He thanked the young woman without learning her name and the maid showed him to the door.

The next morning – without telling Ben, who read the *Guardian* – Dominic bought a copy of the *Daily Mirror*. Not vulgar curiosity, or so he told himself: merely a desire to tie up loose ends. He found what he wanted quite quickly. Tragic Catherine, said the article, had already managed to be twice widowed despite her youth and her third marriage was now heading for disaster. Her first husband, rock star Johnny Sachs whom she had married when she was a Mere Schoolgirl, had died (tragically) in a spectacular car accident while under the influence of alcohol and drugs. Her second husband, the business magnate Jonas Virgo (Virgo Holdings), had expired after three brief years of connubial bliss. This was rather less tragic since he was sixty-eight. And now, having at last ventured up the aisle again, this time with handsome young French actor Edmond Lavalle, she was facing a different kind of problem, though still, of course, tragic. 'I hope Edmond and I can work things out,' Catherine had said bravely. Edmond Lavalle was currently in the Antibes with his friend, handsome young fellow actor Paul Derigueur.

There was a photograph, presumably of Tragic Catherine although the black features and white face effectively blanked out identity. Under it, there was another print, more blur than photo, showing a couple standing in front of a sports car and surrounded by what looked like an unruly crowd. The girl must be Catherine again, though she was laughing and unrecognisable. The man was Johnny Sachs. 'Catherine Lavalle on the occasion of her first marriage . . .' Dominic knew a sudden *grey* feeling inside, a coldness that he did not understand – or did not want to understand. The secret nightmare which he had hoarded inside himself for so long seemed to change shape as he drew it towards the light, no longer an isolated incident but a speck of darkness at the centre of a web whose threads reached out into other lives, other worlds. He was afraid of too much light – afraid to see, to be seen. But his hand was on the thread and he could not let go. Johnny Sachs, The Group, Phebus Records . . . Marten de Witt. Karen Forder, Sheila Raikes, Catherine Lavalle . . . and again, Marten de Witt. A businessman, perhaps, with an office high above the city. Fantasy. He was a writer – he lived on fantasies. He had come to lay the ghosts, but the ghosts had been undisturbed for years. He was too close to calling them up again.

Chapter Six

Climax and Anticlimax opened to enthusiastic reviews, a catastrophic first-night party and a shattering row between Dominic and Ben. The party (opening scene of the row) took place after hours in the Broom and Bucket and included such features as the collapse of an actress who was hopelessly in love with Ben, the advanced melancholia of the stage manager (who was in love with the actress), and the breakage of an art nouveau mirror which upset the superstitious element in the company – i.e. most of it. Dominic and Ben started their row over the fragments of the mirror and finished it in an alley under the disinterested gaze of a scavenging cat and a couple of dustbins. Dominic said Ben's direction had ruined his play. Ben – who had got far more drunk than usual, perhaps out of guilt feelings towards the adoring actress – said at least he (Ben) had the grace to have a conscience about the people who cared for him, instead of simply making use of them. Dominic said he couldn't even pronounce 'conscience'. They went home in separate taxis and passed out on their separate beds without speaking to each other.

The following morning – rather late the following morning – Ben made coffee and took a cup into Dominic, who was still in bed, along with the relevant newspapers. It was an olive branch, a kind of apology – although strictly speaking Ben had less for which to apologise. But then, Dominic reflected bitterly, Ben was always ready to put himself in the wrong, even when they both knew the fault was Dominic's. He didn't know quite why he felt bitter about it; he ought to be merely contemptuous, but still, he felt bitter. He almost hated Ben for so debasing himself.

He took the coffee and read the reviews but he did not say anything.

'They're bloody good,' Ben said. 'You should be pleased. It's all you. A passing nod to the cast and a paean for the playwright.' And he repeated, awkwardly: 'You should be pleased.'

'Yes.'

One or two critics also had a good word for Ben's direction. Ben saw it, and Dominic saw it, but neither of them made any comment.

Presently, Ben said: 'I'm going round to the Attic shortly. Are you coming?'

'What for?'

'Well . . . you might like to thank the cast. They all worked very hard.'

'You thank them. You probably already have.'

'Sulking in your tent?' Ben said, with an unhappy grin.

For the first time, Dominic looked at him. 'Take care,' he said sweetly. 'Patroclus came to a bad end, didn't he?'

Ben went out.

Once he had gone, Dominic began to relax. He re-read the reviews, drank his coffee, contemplated his navel. So this was success. Outside, a pale sun was doing its best in the dusty city air. Assorted traffic whined, purred, or rattled according to horsepower and tuning. A bird sang somewhere nearby. Success. A feeling of emptiness – like someone who has come through the crisis in a severe illness and feels drained and tired and happy merely to be alive. A feeling of *being there* – no need to struggle, to work, to wring new ideas from an exhausted imagination. Take a break. Listen to the traffic. Listen to the birds. No need to write about it – just listen. Don't think. Be.

Dominic lay on his bed, and was. *Non cogito; ergo sum.* I do not think; I simply am. For a little while. In due course, the telephone rang. He went to answer it. Anne Heywood, with congratulations. Ten minutes later, Zoë with same. He left the 'phone off the hook and ran a bath. In the bathroom, he found Ben obtruding on his thoughts again. Ben *in absentia* – a Ben who picked up Dominic's towels, put the cap back on the toothpaste. The lingering smell of his cologne: something from Liberty's, a rare vanity. Dominic tried a little on his wrist but even on his own skin the scent reminded him so strongly of Ben that it frightened him. He would have to go, he decided. He would have to get Ben out of his life or himself out of Ben's life – he was not sure which came first. Now, while he had a little success, some laurels to rest on. He would like to lease his own flat – perhaps Francis could be persuaded to help out. And he needed a holiday. He needed to get *away*. Not only from Ben but from all those others with whom, in his subconscious, Ben had become somehow involved – ghosts past and present, real and imaginary, Sheila Raikes and Catherine Lavalle and a man he had never met called Marten de Witt.

He made the call in the afternoon, putting it off as long as possible. The switchboard sounded husky and competent. It did not take long to get through.

'De Witt here.'

Dominic spoke rapidly. 'Dominic Hardinge: I'm a playwright. Sheila Raikes gave me your name in connection with some research I'm doing.' And: 'I called at your house the other day. I believe I saw Mrs Lavalle.'

'I know who you are. I've spoken to Sheila.' A *dark* voice, Dominic thought, very dark grey with no colour in it at all. No accent. No intonation. '*I've spoken to Sheila.*' A man who checked.

Dominic plunged into his story. It was a thin story – he had always known that – but it felt a little more convincing every time he told it. He could almost imagine himself writing the play. 'I know it's a long time ago – ' routine words ' – but if you *can* remember anything . . .?'

'Possibly, I was an occasional guest at Gresham.' There was a silence during which Dominic wondered if he was supposed to say something and decided against it. 'I would like to help you,' de Witt pronounced at last. 'But it is difficult. I am very busy . . .'

'Of course.' Dominic's murmur was automatic.

'Let me see. Next Friday I am having a cocktail party – seven o'clock, at my house. Perhaps you would like to come. We may have a moment to talk, and at least I can introduce you to one or two people who might be of more use.'

'I – thank you.' Dominic tried – and failed – to keep the surprise out of his voice. 'I'd like that. It's very kind of you.'

'Not at all,' de Witt dismissed it. 'By the way, I saw your notices in the papers this morning. Congratulations.' He rang off.

So that was it. The side effects of success: a few lines on a conscientious Arts Page and he had become the sort of person whom Company Chairmen invite to cocktail parties. All the same, Dominic decided, he must have looked specially. Big businessmen did not – surely – make a habit of lingering over the Arts Page, at least not on a weekday. Perhaps he had asked his secretary to look for him. 'Dominic Hardinge. Some kind of playwright. Check it out.' Involuntarily, Dominic found himself picturing de Witt as a grey-voiced spider in the centre of a web, picking up telephones. Come into my parlour, said the Spider to the Fly. At seven o'clock. For cocktails.

The party was held in the living room where Dominic had seen Catherine Lavalle. The room was so crowded it seemed both larger and, to Dominic, claustrophobic. Wall-to-wall people, furniture suffocating somewhere underneath, waiters sliding in and out of the mob like jokers from a pack of cards. Dominic stumbled on something that might have been a footstool or a dead body. These were people, he judged, who never travelled on the tube, otherwise they might have recognised the atmosphere for what it was and appreciated it accordingly. Oxford Circus in the rush hour. Somehow, no drink was spilt on designer clothes and no one's hair was singed in the crackle of cigarette lighters. In due course,

Dominic located his host. A big man who could have cleared a space around himself even in the rush hour. Not exceptionally tall – around six foot – nor fat, but massive, as though his very bones were thicker and heavier than the bones of ordinary humans. Giant's bones. Under the charcoal-grey jacket and hand-made silk shirt Dominic imagined enveloping wads of muscle and skin like rhinoceros hide. His face, too, was large and almost totally expressionless, a wide expanse of flesh interrupted here and there with tight little features – button eyes, a lipless mouth, an unexpectedly small nose. There was none of the naked-animal ferocity which Dominic had more than half expected – only a brick wall, a visible brick wall which greeted him with laboured foreign politeness and enquired if he had met anyone useful yet.

Dominic said he had not and then qualified it. 'I can't tell. It's difficult to talk at parties.'

'Of course,' de Witt responded, evidently forgetting that Dominic had been invited supposedly to talk. 'However – it was a party you were interested in, I think you said. A party you – *saw* – as a child.' Was there anything sinister in his insistence, his hesitation?

Dominic said flatly: 'Yes. Were you there?'

'At this moment, naturally, I cannot say. It might be possible for me to find out. If it is really important . . .'

'It could be.' Dominic, looking down into his glass, was no longer a playwright. He was an actor in a particularly significant scene, measuring every inflection in his voice, every breath, every gesture. He felt nervous, reckless, excited. It occurred to him that he was more than a little drunk.

Then he looked up. De Witt's button eyes blinked and then, lizard-like, fixed themselves on his face. He found himself trying to imagine the texture of that lipless mouth, the grinding strength of bone and muscle. Thirteen years ago, perhaps, de Witt had been a little thinner, more supple, less squat about the neck. Briefly, Dominic glanced at his hands. Huge, square hands reminding him vaguely of his mother. 'Do you know,' de Witt was saying, 'the exact date of this party?'

'September,' Dominic said. ''68.'

'September . . .'

'Surely, darling, you can't have been there. Not September '68. Didn't you tell me that was when your father died?' With a slight shock Dominic realised that the female on de Witt's left – a female he had scarcely registered save as a study in black sequins and black swansdown puffballs – was Catherine Lavalle. A Catherine in Vogue 'party' make-up with a 'party' expression on her face, a sort of spurious animation like the sparkle of artificial diamonds. Her curiously forgettable beauty merged into the background like a chameleon.

'He died at Christmas. But it is true that he was ill in September, I spent much of that time in Rotterdam. Yes' – judicially – 'Catherine is right: I do not think I could have been at that particular party. I am sorry to be of so little help.'

Dominic was silent. De Witt did not sound sorry. Nor did he sound pleased. His statements were produced with no emotion whatsoever to back them up. A brick wall.

The audience – so Dominic called it to himself – was over. De Witt introduced him to a property-dealer who had once sold Nevile Raikes an allotment and an ex-model who had been at school with Sheila. He moved from person to person exchanging the usual polite nothings: Hello – what do you do? – have you met so-and-so? He had never really enjoyed cocktail parties. Presently, he found himself talking to an impressario who turned out to be the younger brother of a member of The Group. A tallish, fairish, thirtyish man with bloodshot blue eyes and an expression of chronic disillusionment. A little too young, Dominic decided, to have been partying with Nevile Raikes & Co. in 1968, brother or no brother. They talked theatre. Alisdair – his name was Alisdair – expressed a suitable interest in *Climax*. Dominic complimented him on a T.V. production in which he had been involved and of which Dominic had caught the last five minutes. Alisdair disclaimed and referred glancingly to problems with the director, a well-known neurotic. Dominic had another drink and began to animadvert bitterly on directors as a race. It was a while before he noticed the party was thinning out.

'I'd like to get to see the play,' Alisdair said. 'Maybe next week.'

'Call me,' said Dominic, fumbling in his jacket pockets. 'Shit, no pencil. They'll have my number at the Attic.'

Alisdair produced a business card which looked as if it had seen better days. 'We'll have a drink together,' he murmured automatically. When he had gone, Dominic went to say goodnight to his host.

'It has been a pleasure,' said de Witt. 'I wish you luck with the play.' Whether he referred to *Climax* or the play Dominic was supposed to be writing he did not specify.

Dominic said 'Thanks' and put his hand into the one de Witt had extended. Briefly, he was aware of the grip of huge fingers, of skin as hard and dry as vulcanised rubber. Hardly a human hand at all, he thought. More like the hand of some gigantic ape. King Kong. He played with the fancy on his way home, but it did not amuse him. He tried to imagine himself facing de Witt in his own office, questioning him, accusing. This time in his fantasy the office was dark, with windows tinted into perpetual night and stage lighting on a scarlet carpet. Behind a desk lamp de Witt sat in shadow. 'I do not know what you are talking about.' The voice: flat, uninterested. 'I was not at that party.' The automatic alibi. And beyond the lamp, a knowing look in the small eyes like a dancing microdot of reflected light. Dominic seemed to hear his own voice growing fainter and fainter, accelerated into a high-pitched chittering noise like the buzz of an insect. Vast shoulders swarmed up out of the shadows. An endless arm reached across the desk. A hand fell heavily on his tiny shoulder, crushing him beneath its weight and lifting him up like a feather. 'You are mad. There was no party, no rape. It was all in your imagination. The madness of an unbalanced child. The nightmares of puberty.' And, gloatingly, damningly: 'You have no proof.'

No proof. Dominic had never thought of that before. He found he was leaning against a wall, struggling with a sudden rush of nausea. He knew now he could never question de Witt again, never make an accusation. He could not endure truth or error, denial or admission. All possibilities were impossible. Even if he *knew*, beyond any doubt – even if he listened to some terrible confession with a face thrust too close to his own, a licking of lips, a beading of sweat on the skin – what could he do? He had no proof, no desire to prove, no hatred, no dreams of vengeance. Only the horror of remembered violence, of hands and tongue and touch, of pain forcing him into nirvana. What could he do with the truth, except relive the past, recreate that horror? He pulled himself away from the wall, stumbled into a lamp post. His knees felt weak. Drink. Someone passed on the other side of the street with a brisk tapping of heels. He began to walk, carefully, placing one foot in front of the other with serious deliberation, through the wash of lamplight on the wet pavement and into the dark.

Alisdair Saunders had gone to the party mainly out of habit. He had very little to do with the music business these days, but he still received invitations from people who remembered him vaguely as Charlie Saunders' younger brother and saw him currently transformed into an up-and-coming producer whose acquaintance might always come in useful. De Witt he knew more by repute than personal contact; he was not even sure if they had ever met in the past. He found him large, silent, and over-polite; an unrelaxed, unrelaxing figure. However, de Witt was unquestionably a god among company directors and Alisdair knew it is always wise to propitiate the neighbourhood gods. On this occasion he had been mildly bored, mildly entertained. As he was leaving someone had told him that the woman in pseudo-Jazz Age black was Cathie Lavalle. It had taken him a minute or two to make the connection. Johnny had met her after The Group broke up but Alisdair remembered seeing details of their marriage in the papers and wondering what happened to innocent young girls who married dissolute rock stars. Evidently they ended up at cocktail parties in designer clothes, under the protectorship of company gods. He thought about her on his way home. He had seen her in the news again recently, but he couldn't recall why. She was one of those women who kept marrying people.

He began to speculate about her relationship with Johnny – whether she had loved him, whether she had loathed him, whether he had been the idol of her adolescence or merely a particularly glamorous meal-ticket. Inevitably, his mind wandered back to the Johnny he had known, idol of his own adolescence – an idol, he thought bitterly, with feet not of clay but of shit. He could still remember, word for word, the pearls of wisdom Johnny would occasionally let fall. He did not want to remember, but Johnny was too strong for him. Even in death. To distract himself, he turned his thoughts to the playwright he had met – Dominic Something – who had a play showing at the Attic. *Climax and Anticlimax*. He had a feeling he had read about that, too. He might as well go and see it one day.

Alisdair had first become involved with the theatre at Cambridge, more or less by accident. In pursuit of his teenage ambitions, he was frequently responsible for organising rehearsal premises and equipment for student bands, or arranging suitable venues for concerts. One afternoon a member of the A.D.C. came to see him, wanting to borrow a dragon which had formed part of the special effects at a recent performance by a rather over-ambitious college group. The dragon had a huge head which could be swung from side to side, a spectacular set of foreclaws, eyes and nostrils which lit up, and – with the aid of a few sparklers – was capable of sneezing fire. The A.D.C. wanted it for a pantomime of the George and the Dragon story which they were producing that Christmas, and somehow or other Alisdair ended up in the dragon's mouth, lighting sparklers, switching its eyes and nostrils on and off, and occasionally uttering a few menacing lines over an amplifier in a booming, dragonish voice. Not the most promising start for a brilliant young producer, but he went on to higher things. By the time he left Cambridge he had made up his mind to try a career in the theatre rather than in the music business.

In London, he spent six months on the dole waiting for the right kind of job. When his father began to mumble about 'Ian' and 'the bank' he moved out, living instead in a very up-market squat in Chelsea which he afterwards claimed was the most luxurious home he ever had. Eventually Fate rewarded him for his unfilial persistence and he got work as a runner in the office of a leading impressario. He stayed there for seven years. He made tea, licked stamps, ran errands. In due course, he graduated to reading scripts, running more important errands, accepting morsels of responsibility – becoming, by degrees, a full-time assistant. He progressed from a Cambridge-trained bicycle to a second-hand motorbike which made a noise like an antique rocket and thence to a rusted Mini, a dubious Citroën, and a decrepit Morgan. He moved from the squat to a shared flat to his own flat. He acquired three suits and a selection of ties. He saw his photograph in the *Tatler* wearing one of the suits and largely obscured by the bosom of a well-known actress. He went to first-night parties and last-night parties, musicals and unmusicals, Shakespeare, Ibsen, Alan Ayckbourn, Verdi, Janáček, Andrew Lloyd-Webber. His haircuts grew more frequent and his hangovers less so. His girlfriends came – and went. His expression lost its last trace of ingenuousness and assumed instead that cast of cynicism which he had looked for in vain in his teens. One day, he noticed. Who was it, he wondered, who had said that the tragedy of life was that you always get what you want? He had wanted to be a man with a cynical expression and behold, he was a man with a cynical expression. It did not give him any sense of achievement.

On the day Johnny Sachs was killed he came back from lunch, sat down at his desk, picked up the 'phone. 'You knew him, didn't you?' said a camp columnist known furtively as 'Voice in the Wilderness'. 'My dear. Don't be so sly. After all, your *brother* . . .'

'Did you really know him?' breathed the receptionist, making an entrance with a mug of coffee. 'Isn't it tragic? It must be such a terribly lonely life, being a superstar.'

And his boss: 'Nasty business. Knew him, didn't you? One of the real greats. They haven't said yet but I suppose it was drugs. It always is with these boys. Tragic, really. Everything on a plate and they have to go and smash the plate. Bloody waste.'

Alisdair shrugged. 'It's one arsehole the less pumping shit

into the oceans of the world,' he said cheerfully. He had rehearsed the phrase in his head several times and liked the sound of it. He liked it even more out loud.

The receptionist looked horrified.

His seven years up, Alisdair went into business on his own. A legacy from his godmother gave him some capital to lose and he promptly lost it. After that, he had a little success, a little failure. *Time Out* interviewed him in connection with an avant-garde play which gave him status but not much cash in hand. He began to think rather less about his ideals and rather more about his income. (Under the surface cynicism, he still lusted after ideals.) He was thinking about his income the Monday after de Witt's party, divided from his accountant by a desk strewn with depressing pieces of paper. When the meeting was over he reached for the 'phone, dialled the number of the Attic. He needed distraction. Any distraction. Who knows? He might have discovered a genius. Another flying pig.

The Attic said they were booked up for the next three days. Alisdair raised an eyebrow – a skill it had taken him years to perfect – and said he would go on Friday.

Looking back on his relationship with Dominic, Alisdair always thought it would be fatally easy to read too much into it. That first night, when he went to see *Climax*, there was a speech in it – Dominic's favourite speech – which seemed to him to express a kind of bitterness which he had long felt but never before understood or tried to put into words. But such bitterness is in fashion: it has been for some time, ever since religion went out of style and someone decided it was better poetry to be gloomy about life. It would be an oversimplification to suggest that a single incident had sowed the seed of that bitterness in both men, or that Alisdair recognised, unconsciously, if not a kindred spirit at least a kindred scar. The speech in question came in the second to last scene, when the hero is in jail, in the happy expectation of being condemned to death for a murder he did not commit, philosophising unmercifully at anyone who comes within range. (Alisdair could not help wondering if persons in jail really do philosophise as much as poets and authors would have us believe.)

'Do what you want,' he tells his hapless lawyer. 'It's all useless. Futile. Life itself is futile. We rush through it in a storm wind of hurtling seconds, unable to take hold of a single moment and put it under the microscope and see what it is made of. We do not know why we are here because we are here for nothing. We are scarcely aware of being born before we start ticking off the years, the days, the hours till death. Like mayflies we flutter a moment in the sunlight, frantically reproducing ourselves, and then it's over. If we are lucky, we learn something of good or evil before our time is up. And for what? To pass on our mayfly knowledge to yet another mayfly, who might or might not pass it on in his turn. Why? To what end? For what final, eternal purpose? You cannot look the book over afterwards, re-reading the best parts. You can only write your chapter and begone. And what is the point of a book that goes on and on indefinitely and which no one will ever read? I do not believe in God. But if there *is* a God – if there is Someone, Somewhere for whose passing entertainment the Endless Book of birth and death is being written in the blood of all mankind – then let Him take note. I shall not die yet, Immortal Reader. I shall not die and close this chapter until I have bored the pants off You. What other revenge can I take for my life, my death, the futility of my existence? Let the God who created me for His amusement be bored senseless. Let Him be condemned to read for all eternity the tedious unfolding of His tale. Or let Him close the Book, and be done with it.'

After the play, Alisdair asked for Dominic. 'He's not here,' said the girl in the box office. 'Shall I give him a message?'

'No,' Alisdair said. 'No message. Just give me his number.'

He always remembered walking home that night, seeing the whole world transformed by his own elation: streetlamps sparkling like orangeade, teenagers in exotic make-up bickering outside a takeaway, the headlights of waiting cars gleaming like wolves' eyes beyond a junction – everything simmering with magical possibilities. That was the night when he really believed he had discovered a genius. Perhaps he had. Since his career began he had been looking for a playwright with something to say, nurturing a secret dream for which he had often mocked himself: the theatre as education, the theatre as prophet, the theatre as the voice of an era. He could not have spelt out exactly what it was Dominic had to say; he only knew it was truth. Artistic truth, at any rate. It might not be new but it sounded new – the New Face of Cynicism, or so Alisdair told himself, writing critical headlines, at last a clear look at a world which (though simmering with magical possibilities) was going nowhere. But Alisdair saw no contradiction. He was too busy being dazzled by his own enthusiasm. Briefly, he recalled the years of his apprenticeship: light-hearted musicals, slick thrillers, the changing vogue in comedies – social, political, farcical, lavatorial. And the occasional so-called 'serious' play. Four-letter words when four-letter words came in. Sex when sex came in. Full frontals, buggery, masturbation until the whole scenario was as old as the hills and the playwrights ran out of originality and the audiences ran out of shockability. Now was the time, Alisdair decided rather grandiosely, for *good* plays to come back into fashion, plays that both entertained and communicated. Plays like *Climax and Anticlimax*.

I must have it, he thought, exulting, desperate, greedy. I must have that play. I could sell it – I could sell *him* – anywhere in the world. Daydreaming, he allowed himself to forget for a few moments the caution and detachment which he had always cultivated, and his imagination took off into the future, dragging Dominic haphazardly in its wake.

Three days later, he and Dominic had lunch together. An Italian sort of lunch in the pokiest corner of a poky little restaurant which Alisdair liked (he said) because it was unpretentious. In reality, it always gave him the feeling of being a conspirator. Studying Dominic in the inadequate lighting, he decided he could have been one of his own heroes. A pretty face, almost girlish, but with a *used* look no girl would ever have: little tightenings of the muscles, little hollows around the bones, a single concentration-line on the pale forehead, sharp as a cut. That droop to the mouth, both vulnerable and a little cruel. Possibly gay, possibly not. A face that betrayed curious contradictions: weakness and strength, self-will and inadequacy, awareness and self-absorption. Afterwards, Alisdair wondered if it was hindsight which made him imagine that face looked damaged, in some invisible way, like a piece of antique porcelain, minutely chipped, which has consequently lost all its value. In conversation, Dominic used the same mixture of sarcasm and disillusion which characterised his writing. Alisdair had heard that all the best writers sound like their work, but he did not necessarily believe it. He had once met Pinter, but had counted few meaningful pauses.

They talked about the West End, about potential theatres, actors, money.

'We'll have a new cast,' Alisdair said. 'The same director, of course. I liked his approach. I saw a play he did last year: *Demons in My Garden*. Hopeless play, but the direction was very good.'

Dominic said abruptly: 'No.'

Startled, Alisdair raised both eyebrows instead of one. 'No?'

'I don't want Ben.'

'Can you tell me – why not?' Alisdair trod warily.

'Let's say . . . I *don't* like his approach. Will that do?'

'He's got a reputation,' Alisdair said. 'Oh, I know he's not Peter Hall yet but one or two critics have called him "underrated". That's always good for a start. It means they can't wait to give him rave reviews later on in order to congratulate themselves on their foresight.'

'I don't want him,' Dominic said flatly. It was at that moment that Alisdair decided he looked both wilful and inadequate. For the time being, he let the subject drop.

Dominic did not mention that Ben was his flatmate and it was not until Alisdair came to contact him that he noticed it was the same 'phone number. But Dominic had said nothing so Alisdair, too, said nothing. And when his turn came Ben said nothing as well, at least to Alisdair. It was as if the three of them were involved in a conspiracy of *omertà* to conceal some disreputable secret, although Alisdair could never discover exactly what that secret was. He made discreet enquiries on the grapevine and learnt from various quarters that Ben and Dominic had had an affair, that Ben and Dominic had *not* had an affair, that Dominic had wanted to end it, that Ben had wanted to start it, that they had come to blows over the play. For himself, Alisdair was still uncertain about Dominic's sexual inclinations, although he had seen him at a party becoming more than a little friendly with a hopeful young actress. Later he wondered if the performance had been instigated for his benefit. When Dominic got his advance he moved into another flat in the Covent Garden area with an obscene sculptor and a divorced publisher of evident playboy tendencies. After that, his resistance to Ben directing *Climax* in the West End gradually weakened, rather as if (Alisdair thought) he lost interest in Ben, or the play, or both. 'It isn't my play any more,' he said, almost pettishly. 'You bought it: it's yours. Fuck it up if you like. It's nothing to do with me.'

'Don't be stupid,' Alisdair snapped. And he added, knowing he sounded a fraud: 'I want you to be happy with it.'

'I'm happy,' Dominic said, 'when I get my pay-cheque. Think of me as a kind of dustman. You get the rubbish; I get paid. Happiness.'

Alisdair, interpreting this loosely, decided it was Dominic's way of giving in without being seen to give in, and said no more about it.

When he saw Ben, shortly after, he was more than usually untruthful about the behaviour of the author. 'He doesn't like what I did with it,' Ben said. 'He made that plain enough.'

Alisdair shrugged. 'First-night nerves.'

Ben did not seem to hear. 'He scarcely spoke to me afterwards. He hasn't even called round for the books he left here.'

Revealing, Alisdair thought, wishing he knew what was being revealed. He said: 'I shouldn't worry. After all, he's scarcely speaking to me at the moment.'

'Sulks,' Ben said with an unexpected grin. Even more revealing.

'Artistic temperament,' Alisdair murmured. He went on: 'Dom doesn't like to admit he's in the wrong, that's all. Like the rest of us. If I suggested any other director he'd be furious. I know: I tried it.' Perjury.

It was interesting, he reflected, how a person could look both grateful and slightly sceptical at the same time. 'I couldn't do it if he really didn't want me,' Ben said heavily. More artistic temperament. Alisdair wondered what would happen if the producer was allowed to have a temperament too.

He said with spurious frankness: 'He doesn't know what he wants: you must have realised that by now. The important thing is what he *needs*. He needs you. *I* need you. The play wouldn't work half as well with anyone else. In his guts, Dominic knows that. Satisfied?'

Ben grimaced ruefully. 'I should be, shouldn't I? I've been waiting for this chance long enough.'

Alisdair said: 'We all have.'

Climax and Anticlimax opened in the West End early in 1981. The New Face of Cynicism, said the critical headlines. Alisdair's cup ranneth over. Ben, as prophesied, was praised as a talent all too often underrated in the past. Anne Heywood talked of Broadway and television. Dominic had an interview in *The Times*, a comment in *Vogue*, a picture in the *Stage*. He was invited to another party by Marten de Witt, but he didn't go. (Alisdair went.) He told himself that this was real success – not that moment of peace that he had experienced after opening at the Attic but triumph and neon lights, horns and trumpets. Only when he reached for his triumph the feeling seemed to evaporate, leaving him betrayed. That transformation scene from struggling playwright to recognition and acclaim had come, not in a sudden explosion, with Alisdair waving his wand like an omnipotent wizard, but gradually, even insidiously, week by week, with every hitch, every telephone call, every new delay. And in the end, he did not feel any different. Dominic famous, Dominic successful, was still Dominic. The first night sped away in a whirl of nerves. He waited in the theatre, black suit, black silk shirt, white silk tie, a Hamlet in monochrome only with very much less to say. That was when he started smoking black cigarettes, to match the suit. The curtain rose and fell, rose and fell again. He scarcely registered the play. Afterwards, applause, congratulations. Zoë, down from Cambridge, kissing his cheek; de Witt (an investor?) shaking his hand, complete with a beautiful girl who looked like Catherine Lavalle but wasn't. And then, in the restaurant, that feeling of coming down. As though he had smoked too much dope and been as high as Everest – only he could not remember getting high at all. Just anticipation, suspense, and then this creeping flatness as if all the colours which he had hoped to see were fading out of the world before his eyes. Emptiness had grown in him like a cancer. What more do you want? Alisdair asked, after the reviews. What did you expect? Dominic had no answer. He had written the reviews in his imagination, long ago. Even the bad parts. Sometimes he felt as if the rest of the human race – society, civilisation, war and peace, madness and progress was his own brainchild, the product of his deformed fantasies, given a semblance of life by some supernal and probably malevolent force. And here he was, imprisoned in his own illusions. A trap. A maze with no way out. A huge, God-given joke?

In the summer Dominic decided to acquire his own flat. He had fallen out with both the sculptor and the playboy publisher so he moved in with Alisdair for a few weeks while the leisurely mechanics of flat-buying got under way. He liked Alisdair – as far as he liked anyone. Occasionally, he was aware that Alisdair was handling him with tact, but it was a detached professional tact, devoid of emotion, unlike the over-sensitive, over-concerned tact that he had grown to expect from Ben. Dominic felt increasingly that he and Alisdair had something in common, although he could not have said exactly what. They could talk – get drunk – he could pour out his latest idea – it didn't matter: Alisdair listened, seemed to understand, remained uninvolved. It was a species of comradeship with another man which Dominic had not enjoyed since he had written songs with Ricky Verelst at school. Underneath – in the words of the film – Alisdair didn't give a damn. The basis of their relationship was strictly business. At first, Dominic found this reassuring; later, being inconsistent, it annoyed him. He was working on a new play, and on bad days it became an extra source of irritation that Alisdair was interested solely in his rate of literary productivity. 'How's it going?' Alisdair might ask, unwarily.

'What?'

'The play.'

'That's all you ever ask about, isn't it? The play, the play, the bloody play. As if I was a machine for writing plays. Your tame genius.'

'Not so tame.' And Alisdair would disappear into the kitchen, or pick up the telephone, or switch on the T.V., unruffled, as if even Dominic's anger was unimportant to him.

'What would you do,' Dominic enquired one evening, 'if you came home and found I had committed suicide?'

'Is that a serious question?'

'Of course it is. Imagine it. Let's say – I've cut my wrists in the bath. Like the ancient Romans. You come in and find me lying in a bath full of blood. What do you do?'

Alisdair appeared to give the matter some thought. 'It depends,' he said, 'whether I want to have a bath or not.'

There were times when Dominic's moods bothered him more than he let on, but he felt it would be fatal to show it. He was never sure how deep they went, whether Dominic was really upset or merely trying it on, like a child who wants attention. Either way, a friendly indifference seemed to be the best reaction. It might annoy Dominic but at least it would not drive him to despair. Some people, Alisdair knew, were capable of becoming genuinely distressed over trivia: a fantasy of rejection, an unthinking word, a suicide they had not committed. Imagination could be a burden as well as a pleasure, and the line between sensitivity and over-sensitivity was so fine drawn as to be virtually nonexistent. Alisdair had known actresses who broke their hearts over lovers who were late for lunch and producers who cried if you forgot their birthday. Dominic, thank God, had a sense of humour – when he chose. Still, there was something about his reactions that Alisdair did not quite trust. Occasionally, he would go quiet for no apparent reason, and Alisdair sensed, under the quiet, the presence of something dark and almost frightening.

For instance, when he mentioned Marten de Witt.

'I saw him in Langan's,' he had said once, casually enough. 'He asked about your new play. Seemed to think you were into the Sixties. I gather he was helping you with some research when I met you at that party of his.'

Dominic shrugged. 'I had an idea,' he said. 'It didn't work. I scrapped it.'

'You didn't mention it at the time.'

'Nothing to mention.'

'Besides,' Alisdair went on, 'I thought you hated research.'

'I do.'

'So what was it all about?'

'Nothing.' The irritation was there – maybe more than irritation – but held in check. It was sufficiently unusual for Dominic to hold anything in check. Curious, Alisdair was about to push a little harder, but the telephone rang and the opportunity was lost. He thought about it later but could come to no conclusions, except that it would be a relief when Dominic moved out. He was not an easy person to have around the house.

The purchase of Dominic's new flat fell through in the late summer, something which Alisdair, at least, had anticipated all along. Dominic went back to the estate agents and Alisdair resigned himself. One day not long after, he returned from his office to find Dominic had gone out, presumably in pursuit of some desirable residence. There was a message for him on the answering service: 'This is Sue Holland. I'm a friend of your cousin Terry Preston. I thought you ought to know she's in hospital . . .'

Dominic had never mentioned Terry Preston.

Chapter Seven

Dominic returned in the early evening having seen a flat which (he said) might do. To him, a flat was merely living quarters; questions of furnishing and general decor left him uninspired. He liked colour schemes to be unobtrusive, chairs sufficiently comfortable, mod. cons. to function without hitch or blockage. He was indifferent to room temperature but felt hot or cold according to his state of mind, something for which few forms of central heating can manage to cater. He disliked ornaments and knick-knacks but liked an abundance of ash-trays which he never bothered to empty and a wide space of draining board where he could abandon the washing up. He did not want a garden since it meant mowing the grass. The flat he had seen that day appeared to have a suitable draining board if nothing else. The bedroom was pale pink but that could be painted over in some nondescript shade of natural yoghurt. Anyway, he was going to make an offer.

'Good,' said Alisdair absently, rifling his own draining board for the pieces of the coffee machine. 'There's a message for you on the answering service.'

He heard Dominic, next door, grunt an acknowledgement and switch on the tape. Sue Holland's voice echoed indistinctly through the wall. Then it stopped. Silence.

Alisdair called out: 'I didn't know you had a cousin called Terry.'

A further pause. 'I'm adopted,' Dominic said at length. 'I was born in a shoebox. I haven't any cousins.'

'An adoptive cousin,' Alisdair said, 'if you prefer it.'

'I prefer –' Dominic hesitated, as though on the brink of anger. 'I prefer not to discuss it,' he concluded. 'I was a foundling; I was adopted; I was orphaned. The whole concept of the family is alien to me. You may have the ragged remnants of my legal relations and welcome: I don't want them.'

'Didn't I meet an aunt of yours – correction: *adoptive* aunt – at the opening of *Climax*?'

'Maybe.'

'Come off it, Dom. You told me once she brought you up.'

'She sent me to boarding school. She couldn't be bothered to bring me up.'

That wasn't how you put it last time, Alisdair thought. A different mood, a different angle. Aloud he said: 'Is she Terry's mother?'

No answer. Having set the coffee machine, Alisdair went into the living room. 'Why this sudden interest in my genealogy?' Dominic snapped.

'According to Sue What's-her-name,' Alisdair said, 'your cousin is in hospital. I may be leaping to conclusions, but I assume she isn't too well. Don't you care?'

'No,' said Dominic shortly. 'I don't.'

Alisdair did not say any more.

Unexpectedly, Dominic's next essay in flat-purchasing went through without a hitch. About a month later he moved out of Alisdair's spare room for good. By that time, Alisdair was more than a little relieved to see him go. He had not discussed with Theresa why Dominic would not see her nor had he again attempted to discuss Theresa with Dominic, but conversations between the two men had begun to fill up with silences and the consciousness of some huge and invisible taboo. The more they avoided the subject, the more important it seemed to become. Alisdair never mentioned visiting the hospital but he could tell that Dominic knew or guessed. Where have you been? Dominic would ask, when he came in. And: Was it fun?

'To see a friend,' Alisdair answered; or words to that effect. He could have lied but he chose not to.

A female friend? Dominic's voice would be half mocking, half afraid. Tell me about her. Is she pretty? Is she plain? Tell me.

But Alisdair always said there was nothing to tell, and then he would switch on the television set, or the stereo, to cover the silence, or else he would merely wait, feeling cruel, knowing Dominic would not ask any more. He did not want to quarrel with him outright. Not yet. After all, Dominic was still his own particular genius, his discovery, the star in whose ascendance he wished to own exclusive rights. One day soon Dominic would finish another play, and when he did Alisdair must be the only possible producer. It wasn't just the money, or so he told himself: this was his future, his inmost dream, the way to idealism, the theatre as prophet, and all that jazz. Even when he laughed at himself he couldn't really find it funny. His dream was very dear to him. And Theresa Preston was only another girl, nothing much to look at, no outstanding qualities, hardly the kind for whom a man might forswear ambition – had Alisdair been that sort of man. Nonetheless, when he returned from driving Theresa down to her parents and Dominic asked him *Where have you been?* he found himself answering 'Cambridge' almost without thinking. There was an edge of anger in his voice which startled him. After all, he reasoned, he didn't know all the facts – for either side.

This time, it was for Dominic to fill up the silence. 'Of course,' he said. 'You went there too, didn't you?'

'You lived there,' Alisdair retaliated, 'didn't you?'

'Bloody Cambridge.' To his surprise, Alisdair saw that Theresa had slipped from Dominic's mind, as though some other memory had taken over. 'It was always windy. I remember when I was thirteen – not long after I first went there – lying and listening to the wind. Like . . . souls in torment.'

'Cliché,' Alisdair said. His anger had left him. Suddenly,

Dominic looked too vulnerable, too fragile for anyone to want to hurt him, no matter what he did. Alisdair reflected wryly that it was probably his greatest asset. The flawed statuette, the cracked vessel – the feeling that a careless finger or an insensitive word might cause him to fall to pieces. Some time, Alisdair decided, he would have to ask Terry what had happened between them. He knew he could never ask Dominic. The mere act of asking might break him up.

After Theresa's return, Dominic did not go back to Cambridge any more. In previous years he had paid the occasional flying visit, taking Zoë chocolates and copies of his reviews and being dutifully attentive to Francis' conversational meandering. He did not go to Sandy's wedding but then, weddings bored him, and – so he told Ben Gamble – Sandy bored him even more. He did not send a present – but he was broke. When *Climax* opened in the West End, Zoë came to the first night, shook hands with various members of the cast and talked to one of the critics about the problems of vegetable gardens. That summer, Dominic drove down for her fiftieth birthday with a huge bunch of roses, a cake from Fortnum's, several ounces of her favourite perfume. 'How sweet of you,' she said, really moved, feeling that at last, after so much trying, she had got through to this lonely, difficult, distant boy. (She still thought of him as a boy.) 'How sweet of you . . . ' She never saw him again.

Considering Dominic's behaviour some time later, it was Alisdair who probably came closest to the truth. He had seen Dominic, particularly when they were sharing the flat, with a succession of one-night stands, selected apparently at random from a mixed bag of femininity. Pretty, plain, intellectual, dumb, pretentious or terribly, terribly sincere – it did not seem to matter to Dominic. Alisdair wondered more than once if he was trying to prove his heterosexuality, boost his ego, or simply cure himself of insomnia. But on the morning after Dominic's face never wore the look of libido satisfied or ego boosted, and the shadows under his eyes were always darker than ever. Alisdair himself had learned to take sexual satisfaction, if only on its most superficial level; indeed, he had almost forgotten that the mysteries of pleasure had ever tormented his adolescent soul. But even for him orgasm was always accompanied by a faint self-distaste, as though, in going through the motions of love-making, he was somehow degraded, an unresisting participant in a shameful ritual. He imagined that feeling, in Dominic, doubled, trebled, self-distaste became self-loathing, degradation an abyss of depression whence he was plunged by some hidden deformity of senses, a spastic who was made conscious only in sex of his ugliness and inadequacy. 'You made him happy, didn't you?' Alisdair said to Theresa. 'That's what he can't forgive. I don't believe that he really loved you, not in any grand dramatic way. But you made him happy and after you left he couldn't find anyone to make him feel like that again. Some people have a very small capacity for happiness. Dominic must have expended all of his on you. And so the memory turned sour on him, and he couldn't bear to be reminded of it.'

He did not actually see Theresa very often after her return to Cambridge. In pursuit of the good of humanity she got herself a job in a mental hospital, which she stuck to valiantly for nine months until the daily dosage of heartbreak and hopelessness became too much for her. She was still living at home, conscious not so much of needing her parents, after so long an absence, but of them needing her. When she came to London for an occasional weekend she would stay with a friend (not Sue Holland), call Alisdair at his office, go to a play with him and pick it to bits afterwards in a quiet restaurant. She would tuck her hand through his arm as they walked along the street, leave the print of her lipstick on his cheek when they kissed goodbye, but there was never any more physical side to their relationship than that. He thought about it, and she thought about it, but neither of them did anything. 'If we had sex,' Alisdair told himself, 'she would be just like all the rest.' He had plenty of sex when he wanted it, but not with the girls he thought of as friends. Sex and friendship did not seem to go together.

He tried to picture her face in his mind, a face of strong, definite outlines, warm colours. Or was it that her personality was strong and definite, her expressions warm? He could not recall that her bones were so different from any other bones, or her skin had any richer tincture. Her eyes, maybe – her eyes were special. Tawny-hazel, or grey, or hazel-grey. He imagined them lit up with the vehemence of some transient emotion, bright dark eyes reflecting candlelight. Not very big eyes of course, but very expressive. (How could eyes be expressive? Lips move and lines betray but an eye is just a random-coloured marble a-swivel in a socket.) He resolved to look at her differently next time, to see what (if anything) gave her that illusion of uniqueness. Sex might dispose of that illusion, reducing her to the level of other women. He told himself he did not want to see Theresa reduced. He would not admit – not even to himself – that the idea of sex with her somehow frightened him. 'Besides,' he thought, lapsing ruefully into film dialogue, 'she's been hurt. Better to let it go.'

'I've been hurt,' thought Theresa. 'I couldn't go through that again. It's better to leave things as they are. He's my friend – my very dear friend. A friend is worth much more than a lover.'

Around Christmas 1981 Alisdair went to Cambridge for a couple of days. Eyes, he decided shortly after his arrival, were not expressive, mere ovoids of glassy appearance transmitting light signals to the brain and physically incapable of changing shape or hue. A camera lens might look lustrous, by candlelight. The next day he and Theresa went for a walk and he found himself noticing that the tip of her nose was pink with cold (were noses expressive?), that Zoë's sheepskin jacket was a little too big for her, that her eyebrows met in the middle. In an attempt to distract himself, he said: 'Your parents were expecting Dominic, weren't they?'

'No. No, I don't think so.' She smiled rather hesitantly. 'He isn't the coming-home-for-Christmas type. Mummy might have hoped, I suppose . . . '

'Do they know – you saw him?'

'No.'

'They must think that rather strange. Your not mentioning him, I mean. Particularly with my coming here like this. Your mother must know who I am, after all; I saw her at the opening of *Climax*.'

'She knows. It's just *because* she realises there's something wrong that she won't ask about Dominic. She's waiting for me to tell her. Only I shan't,' Theresa added, with a certain self-conscious nobility, 'because it would hurt her, and she would blame herself. As for Daddy – he wouldn't notice the roof had blown off unless someone pointed it out to him. All the same, if he knew he'd probably manage to blame himself too, in a different kind of way. You don't understand my parents' capacity for feeling guilty.'

'It's inherited,' said Alisdair caustically, 'isn't it?'

'Do I feel guilty?' Theresa did not sound indignant, only questioning.

'Oh yes. About the unspeakable Otis Friedland, about his wife and six kids in Pennsylvania –' ('Philadelphia,' Theresa interposed) '– about Dominic and your parents and the state of the world. You have a great big eager conscience urging you on to unnecessary remorse and useless do-goodery –'

'If you mean my job,' Theresa said hotly, 'it isn't useless do-goodery. Those people need help. I'm not much use but I'm better than nobody. And at least I'm trying, instead of just thinking about making money and keeping up with the trendies.'

'I don't just think about making money –'

'And,' Theresa pursued, ignoring him, 'if I feel guilty about Otis' family I ought to because although I didn't take him away from them I kept him away. I would have kept him away for ever if I could. And if I feel guilty about Otis it's because I let him down: he neglected his family for me and I didn't offer enough in return, I wasn't strong enough, I didn't love him enough –'

'Balls!' Alisdair interjected. Some way ahead, a man walking a golden Labrador turned and stared. Theresa and Alisdair faced each other. He was conscious of a desire to laugh at her, to shake her, to shout at her. By some trick of the cold winter sunlight or his own imagination, her inexpressive eyes looked brilliant and painful.

She said: 'Please don't let's quarrel. It's Christmas, after all. I want us to be friends. I can't help feeling guilty about some things – you said yourself, it's my nature. You can't browbeat me out of it. Don't you *ever* feel guilty about anything?'

'No,' Alisdair said shortly. 'What's the point?'

It was not quite a satisfactory walk but Alisdair thought about it, from time to time, after he went back to London.

He was very busy. *Climax* closed in the West End in March 1982 but was due to open on Broadway in the summer. Dominic had struck lucky: an extremely successful young actor, previously known only for film roles, wanted to try himself out on stage in the star part. A suitable producer, an unsuitable cast and a great deal of money had materialised accordingly and there were already preliminary flutters among the critics. Rumour had it the screen hero could not remember more than one line at a time and was inaudible from anywhere but the front stalls. Alisdair had various other projects under way and was not much interested in the finer points of transatlantic misjudgment, but Dominic, disillusioned with solvency and insecure with success, wasted a good deal of energy in acid complaint. His hero, he pointed out, was supposed to be dark, pale, intense, concave about the chest and with an overall physique that suggested a past spent starving in garrets. Max Guest, film star and would-be adornment of the American stage, was fair, bronzed, a California beachboy with chest and shoulders developed by a daily work-out. 'So what?' Alisdair said. He wasn't feeling sympathetic. 'The girls will come for his classic profile. The gays will come for his tight trousers. The theatre buffs will come to see him fuck it up. We'll make money.'

'Money!' Dominic was scornful. 'What is money? Those little pieces of wrinkled paper for which men lie and cheat and murder, sell their mothers and grandmothers, barter life and liberty. You can't eat it, you can't screw it, and its artistic value is pretty questionable. Yet I – *I*! – am supposed to get excited because I have whole bank accounts full of the garbage. What do I care about *money*?'

'You care,' Alisdair said sharply. 'What paid for that car collecting parking tickets outside? Not to mention the flat, restaurant bills, hangovers, cigarette-ends.' As he spoke he flicked one from the ash-tray in front of him so that it landed in

Dominic's lap. Dominic stared down at it, more startled than angry. It was so unlike Alisdair to make such a gesture. 'Go and practise your big speeches on somebody else. I've got work to do.'

'*I'm* your work,' Dominic said, blazing with sudden hurt. 'Or have your forgotten? I'm your career, your future, your dream. You need me. I don't need you. There are other producers – any number of them – who would be happy with my custom. They might even be ready to listen when I have something to say. Shall I leave now?'

Alisdair shook his head and murmured: 'Sorry,' although whether because of the threat or because he regretted that gesture of contempt he did not know. As an apology, it lacked conviction. After Dominic had gone he abandoned the script he was reading, lit a cigarette, thought for a while. But he did not like where his thoughts were taking him and in the end he went back to the script.

Under the circumstances, the final row was not unexpected. Alisdair did not want it to happen, or so he thought, but he felt himself drawn towards it with a sort of gravitational pull which was beyond resistance. Words he had not meant to say, gestures he had not meant to make, sneers he had not meant to sneer – as if some other power had got hold of his voice, his tongue, his hands and was using them to his own destruction. Perhaps it is necessary in life that your most precious dreams should not be attained. You have to learn to give up dreams for reality, to blow on the cobwebs of your fantasies and watch them fraying into dust, and then to reach for something farther, something higher, or simply something else. Alisdair did not see it as a choice between Dominic and Theresa, between ambition and principle. Rather, he realised that the choices he made would affect himself as an individual, and the self he became would affect everything he touched, everything he tried to do. In the past, even as he had believed you could separate the artist from his work, the writer from his talent, so he had believed – if only by inference – that you could separate the producer from the man. It was a double standard which had been in operation, no doubt, since art was invented: ordinary morals are for ordinary people; artists (and those who handle them) transcend morality. The creative end justifies the means. Giant talent indicates – nay, demands – giant flaws. Or vice versa.

When Dominic's new play was finished Alisdair read it and allowed himself to imagine, for a brief moment, that he might get to produce it. He knew it was far better than *Climax*. Entitled *Tumours*, it was based loosely on the plot of *After Brideshead* which Dominic had used at college – the reclusive homosexual hero, dying this time of cancer, surrounded by clamouring relatives all busily unveiling the murky secrets of their past. 'It's wonderful,' he told Dominic, early one evening in the new flat over cigarettes and gin and tonic. They talked about direction (Ben Gamble), about possible casting, about sets. All the time, underneath, Alisdair knew none of it would ever happen.

It was growing late when they began to talk about the ideology behind the play. It did not occur to Alisdair that the subject might be dangerous. Nowadays, no one went to the stake for ideology.

'Were I a critic,' Dominic said (he was a little drunk), 'a really clever critic always seeing meanings within meanings and symbols within symbols – I think I would draw a parallel between the cancer in the play and Hardinge's view of humanity as a cancer in the universe. A few mutant cells which came down from the trees and grew, slowly, unnoticed by infinity, until they had suffocated a whole planet, scabbing over the surface with cities and factories and wars, burrowing into the crust, befouling the oceans, sprouting secondaries out in space. Left to itself that cancer could claw its way across galaxies and voids, until the last star was consumed. Only it won't happen. The malignancy is too small, the universe too big. In the end, the tumour will be destroyed – amputated, bombarded with gamma rays, burnt out – and the universe will be well and whole again. End of story. Only it won't *be* a story, because no one will be left to tell it, and no one else to listen.'

Alisdair refilled his glass. 'Poetic,' he said. 'Meaningful. Pretentious.'

'Maybe.' Dominic shrugged. 'It doesn't matter. The critic doesn't exist with the imagination to draw such a parallel, or the literary flair to put it into words. I think in future I shall write my own reviews.'

'Is it true?' Alisdair asked him, abruptly. 'Is that what you believe? Humanity As Cancer?'

'I don't believe in anything.'

'Then why write plays about it? Why write at all?'

'Because I must. Because it passes the time. Because that is my own particular disfunction. A cancer within a cancer, mutation with mutation. I am the kind of tumour that gets its own pickle-jar and an article in the *Lancet*. That's art.'

'Art! A convenient excuse for too much talk and not enough action. Tell me, do you ever spare a thought for us lesser mutants or are you too busy contemplating your own genius?'

'I never knew you were such a passionate humanitarian,' Dominic said in a sharpened voice. 'Dear me. Oh very dear me. People before Art: what a beautiful sentiment. Since when did you take up the dog collar and the sociology manual? You remind me – '

'Yes?'

Of my cousin Terry. Dominic didn't say it but the words hung there, between them, as audible as a shout. There was no more pretence at friendly argument. Afterwards, Alisdair wondered if he had done it deliberately, echoing Theresa's ideas if not her words, forcing a quarrel which he had long known would have to come.

'Who are you to sneer at art?' Dominic reverted to his grievance. 'You and all your kind – producers, agents, investors, critics – parasites who batten on those more talented than yourselves, getting fat on our earnings, grovelling for the scraps of fame dropped from our table? You sun yourselves in our reflected glory, smear yourselves in our shit; and all the while you're eaten up inside with common-or-garden envy. You have to despise us because it's the only way you can justify all the boot-licking and the crawling admiration – because otherwise you could not live with the knowledge of your own inferiority.'

'You're so right,' Alisdair said with sudden and heart-felt savagery. 'You're so bloody right. Sometimes I really wanted to hit you, did you know that? I wanted to smash your thick insensitive head against a wall until I knocked some sense into it. But the little voices were there telling me that you were Dominic Francis Hardinge, different, special, uniquely talented, and I mustn't do anything to short-circuit your inspiration or upset the balance of your brilliant brain. Oh – I knew the little voices belonged to little suckers but I listened. I've been listening to them all my professional life, God help me. I should have known better.' Briefly, he found himself remembering Johnny Sachs. 'Talent may be an asset but it isn't a virtue. It isn't courage or compassion or moral strength. It doesn't make you a better human being. It's just something you're born with, like distorted vision or an extra toe. Modern society idolises people because they write well or play world class tennis or bawl into a microphone or simper on a cinema screen. In the Middle Ages, you had to be a warrior or a saint to get that kind of public adulation. We don't seem to have progressed very far, do we? From the divine to the meretricious.' Dominic was staring at him, too stunned, for the moment, to be really angry. 'I know. I should have said all this long ago. I suppose I must have liked you, sometimes.'

Dominic said in a shaken voice: 'You're in the wrong job. You ought to be on a soap box in the foyer of the National Theatre, telling them all to go back to church.'

'Witty.' Alisdair commented. 'It doesn't mean anything, but it's witty. The quickness of the tongue belies the soul. Tell me, Dom, do you honestly believe in your own superiority – you and all the rest of the glitterati? Do you?'

'Honestly . . .' Dominic savoured the word as though he had almost forgotten what it meant. Then: 'No.' He wanted to be angry – it would have been good, to get angry – but for the time being he only felt betrayed.

Alisdair did not notice. 'You're in the wrong world,' he said.

'Witty,' Dominic snapped. 'Witty and specious. Keep practising: you too can talk like a sophist. In the end, the man in the street won't be able to tell the difference. He isn't interested, anyway. Actor, writer, martyr – what does it matter to him? All he ever wanted was the spectacle. *Panem et circenses*. He doesn't care if it's a talent or a principle that puts you in the ring – he just comes to see blood.' He added, inconsequentially: 'I loathe you. You're a procurer – you and the others. Pimps. I always loathed you'

'Fair enough.' Alisdair finished his drink too quickly. 'The play's wonderful.'

'But I'm not? What a shame. Do you seriously expect me to go on working with you?'

'No.'

'Whatever happened to the producer's dream?'

'I woke up.'

'You'll go a long way,' Dominic said sarcastically, 'on your principles.'

'You'll go a long way on talent. Of course you will. No one else will ever care whether or not you behave like a shit.'

There was a silence. Now was the moment, Alisdair thought, for Dominic to mention Terry. Now when it didn't matter anymore. But he didn't.

'Get out,' he said. He sounded violent, petulant, unconvincing. In due course, Alisdair went.

Back at his own flat, he poured himself a drink, drank half of it in two gulps, looked at the other half. Talent, he thought, was nothing special, just something one person had and another didn't. An extra toe. A gift from the gods. Anyway, it would be stupid to sell his soul for one particular play or one particular playwright. Without self-respect, he would – in the end – have nothing. One day there would come another writer – not another Dominic, but someone, something – which would give him that same magical this-is-it feeling. He knew it with his head if not his heart. Had he ever lost a girl he loved he would have realised the sensation was very much the same; but Alisdair had never been really in love. He only knew something had gone for good, a part of himself, of his dream, and although time must bring him other dreams, other chances, he could not yet imagine feeling whole and hopeful again. He wondered about ringing Theresa, the following morning, telling her what he had done. But he couldn't do it.

Not immediately. In a week, maybe; a month; a year. Because of her, at least in part, he had been driven back against his principles – long-held principles eaten up with wet-rot and neglect but still strong enough to brace him. And now the fight was over and victory or defeat or whatever it was tasted suitably bitter. Now, there was time to review the might-have-beens, to inflict his own little torments. He found he could not bear the thought of hearing Theresa thank him, comment, perhaps even gloat. Irrationally – and he knew it was irrational – he felt himself resenting her for something *he* had chosen to do. One day, he supposed, he would tell her about it. One day when none of it mattered any more. In the meantime, lest he be tempted, he would not even call.

Eventually, she called him, after she went back to college (in London), this time to study psychology. But that was over a year later.

Part Three

'Love is when you have sex with the same person for more than one night.'

Dominic Francis Hardinge:
Climax and Anticlimax

Chapter Eight

Dominic first met Faramond Hunter in New York in the summer of 1982. At the time, he didn't notice her particularly. He had come over for the Broadway opening of *Climax and Anticlimax* and was totally preoccupied with the iniquities of Max Guest. Some of the critics had been kinder than might have been expected, probably because they were gay and, as Alisdair had prophesied, were mesmerised by the fit of his trousers. However Dominic, as he pointed out, forcibly, to Anne Heywood, was neither gay nor kind. To make matters worse, so armour-plated was Max Guest's ego (or alternatively so limited his perceptive powers) that Dominic's subtle darts bounced of him like invisible ping-pong balls. He (Max) attributed it all to the well-known moodiness of playwrights, sunnily threw a party for him, and proceeded to cloud what perceptions he possessed with alcohol and hash. Dominic surrounded himself with an audience of people he didn't know and decided to be witty at his host's expense. Faramond Hunter, he remembered later, was the one in pink.

   She had been invited as one of the excess pretty girls who made up the party decor. Physically, she stood out from the rest, despite similarities of dress and the standard riot of tumble-dried curls; it was a mark of Dominic's self-absorption that he did not immediately notice. The other girls had that same plastic quality of agelessness which he had remarked in Catherine Lavalle; triangles of bistre under jutting cheekbones; shiny red lips which they left behind on the rims of their champagne glasses. They all laughed a lot. Faramond Hunter was seventeen and did not laugh at all. Her face was a flat pale oval with a long serious nose and a full serious mouth. She wore an unobtrusive lip gloss and no blusher. Her eyes were large, dark, and leaf-shaped, made to look larger and darker with eyeliner, and her hair was the colour of old mahogany, black in the shadows, brown shot with gold where the light fell on it. Her eyebrows, in defiance of fashion, arched well above her eyes. An El Greco madonna in the making, one producer had commented; but it was too modern a face for El Greco, too young, too bland. Yet it was not an unintelligent face. Behind the opaque dark eyes there was a suggestion of thoughts hidden, depths veiled, which did not, unfortunately, always come across on camera. Later, when she became moderately well-known, one critic wrote of her: 'Too grave, too still, almost hard, the face of a waxwork and the emotional range of an automaton.' When the other girls in Dominic's audience drifted off to circulate, she stayed and listened. She did not look either interested or bored, but she listened; that was enough for Dominic. Asked afterwards what he made of her, he said he found her unfeminine. (Perhaps because she did not laugh.)

'Unfeminine?' Anne Heywood repeated, startled, remembering the curves of the pink lurex dress, the full mouth and sumptuous hair. 'I know she's very young but I would hardly have called her the Greek youth type.'

'Oh no,' Dominic said absently. 'I didn't mean her *looks*.'

After that cryptic comment it is doubtful if Dominic thought about her again. But behind her nightshade eyes, Faramond Hunter thought about him. Occasionally.

She was born Jessica Faramond, daughter of Annalee Faramond and a young man who disappeared from her lifestory some months before she came into it. Her mother, a child of the Sixties, produced Jessica as a gesture to free love, persuaded doting parents to accept their illegitimate grandchild and broke her heart over the defection of the young man for at least a week. She was twenty at the time, an archetypal American beauty with wide mouth and swinging hair, going through college on hash and high ideals. She always seemed to be exploding into laughter or melting into tears, or sometimes both at once. Possibly her daughter's outward serenity was acquired at an early age, a reaction or a defence against so much surface emotion. The Faramonds were 'old money' and Annalee, an only child, had been spoiled from babyhood and knew no restraints. The hapless grandmother, presented with Jessica as if she were a dozen red roses or a box of Milk Tray, would undoubtedly have spoiled her too had Annalee not driven her car into a stationary taxi a week after graduation and fallen violently in love with the occupant, an Englishman named David Hunter. It was Hunter, unable to have children after contracting mumps in his teens, who officially adopted Jessica, providing her with dual nationality, an English nanny (last of a dying breed), and all the love and security essential to a happy childhood. They lived in a little village in Kent, Hunter – a solicitor – commuting to his London office, Annalee commuting to her social life. To the surprise and chagrin of all their friends, it lasted almost twelve years. But in the end Annalee's staying power ran out and she eloped to California with a film producer, leaving David Hunter to lapse into premature retirement and the cultivation of vegetable marrows.

Jessica returned to America with her mother, but she continued to look on Hunter as her father and England as her spiritual home. She dreamed of the big, shabby house in Overbridge, the garden running down to the river, the tree she had climbed up so often at the instigation of the boy-next-door and then been unable to climb down. In the next few years she was only able to make one brief visit, and somehow that made her private dream even more special to her. In America she grew up, as was the fashion, much too quickly, missing out on adolescence and becoming a teenage sophisticate, precocious and self-possessed; but her memories of England still retained a magical aura that had to do, had she but known it, not with a vanished childhood but with love and stability. Not that she was unhappy. She was fond of her feckless mother and did not dislike her new stepfather, although she felt instinctively that he was unreliable as a long-term investment. But Annalee had never been one for long-term investments. 'What will you do,' her daughter asked her one day, 'when you're forty, and he runs off with a girl younger than me?' She had grown used to the spectacle of middle-aged men with very young girls.

Annalee considered the matter with a certain realism which they both shared. 'I shouldn't think he will,' she said at length. 'Darling Sherry, he's so clever, so very *brave*. Always trying new ideas. He'll never be successful enough to interest a Bo Derek or anyone of that calibre. And you're so much prettier than all the other girls I'm sure he'd far rather be seen out with you. He's so proud of you, darling. There's nothing like a beautiful daughter to stop a man having a roving eye. It gives him the ego-boost he needs when his hair starts going grey and he doesn't wake up every morning with a hard-on. I'm so *glad* I had you, Jessie. Do you know, Papa fussed about adoption at the time but I was *quite* sure it was right to keep you. And we *are* very happy together, aren't we?'

'I see,' said Jessica, not bothering to answer the question. She saw. Now David Hunter was no longer around it was up to her to protect her mother from the consequences of her more impulsive actions. Well, it was what he would have wanted. 'Look after your mother,' he had said before she left. She hadn't understood him then but she understood now. That was when she began to work at growing up.

It was because of her stepfather that she became an actress. He saw her in the school production of *Romeo and Juliet* when she was fourteen and promptly told her, with his customary talent for overstatement, that she could be the new Brooke Shields. Possibly he overlooked the fact that Hollywood was currently packed with girls being the new Brooke Shields. Anyway, a year later she was 'introduced' in a T.V. film with a vintage Star whose collapsing face-lift and pink-tinted eyeballs were still held to be attractive, if only out of tradition. That was when she dropped the Jessica and began calling herself Faramond Hunter. Her mother, who was delighted with her new career, said it looked good in the credits. Sherwin Milberg Productions, otherwise 'darling Sherry', promoted her with enthusiasm. Both the film and Faramond received lacklustre reviews but she found she liked acting and determined to try harder. Even the endless takes and re-takes and the sitting around in between did not bore her; she merely waited quietly, thinking her own thoughts behind a face so blank that one sound recordist was heard to ask if Milberg pulled out the plugs when he did not need her in order not to waste the battery. However, on screen her very blankness was sufficiently striking to gain her a few more T.V. roles and eventually the hazy recognition of a square-eyed public. Her voice, perhaps because of her upbringing, was different enough to be distinctive. According to one critic, she spoke English with an American accent and American with an English accent. A good make-up artist had taught her to avoid blusher and coloured eye shadow: 'Keep your face black-and-white, and if you *must* sun-bathe, cover it up. It'll ruin both your skin and your image.' By the time she met Dominic at Max Guest's party she had done a course of acting lessons and had begun to dream of more serious parts. Dominic, she was told, was a playwright. 'Bitter comedy, darling. Tragical-cynical. Topical-comical. Intellectual hero bewildered by Life. Prostitute girlfriend. *Not* really a suitable vehicle for our Maxwell.'

'How interesting,' said Faramond automatically. She was not a particular fan of Max Guest and had missed the first night. The day after the party she went to see the play.

The following January *Tumours* opened in the West End. Directed by Ben Gamble, produced by Nicholas Flack. The critics approved or disapproved according to their nature, but all of them with sufficient enthusiasm to ensure that the audiences would come, if only to see what was wrong with it. Mary Whitehouse objected to a scene of overt homosexuality. Nothing more was needed. After the initial furore had died down Alisdair went to see it, not actually in upturned collar and dark glasses but sliding furtively into a back row seat and disdaining a drink in the interval lest he should be recognised at the bar. It was no use, of course; he met an old friend in the foyer while trying to make his escape.

'So you came after all,' said the old friend, heartily. 'What did you think of it?'

'I'd already seen the script.'

'I didn't know.' Presuming on old friendship, the old friend abandoned tact over a bottle of wine in the restaurant round the corner. 'So why didn't you do it? Hardinge has the makings of a great playwright.'

'We didn't get on.'

'No one gets on with him, or so I hear. Part of his image. He stayed at your flat for a while, didn't he? Was that what did it? Over-great familiarity – and all that – genders dislike.'

'Despite,' Alisdair corrected, absently. 'I didn't dislike him.' Perhaps it was the wine, or the play, or a passing impulse which made him truthful. 'I disliked what he was doing to me. Sometimes his – attitudes – reminded me too much of myself. Sometimes they reminded me of someone else. Anyway, if you overdo success it acts as a depressant. I distrust highs: you have too far to fall. A little failure from time to time is much more comfortable.'

'Do you still speak?' asked the old friend, more interested in the facts than the philosophy.

'We met at a party two weeks ago.' Alisdair said. 'I said hello; he didn't. I wasn't surprised.'

'I see,' said his friend.

Later that year, when Faramond Hunter came to London, *Tumours* was the first play she went to see.

She had what she thought of as a medium-sized part in a film, some of which was being made on location in a Scottish castle, the rest at Pinewood Studios. Sherwin Milberg called it her 'first major screen role' and saw her off with all the vicarious glee of a jockey who has picked a winner for someone else to ride. Her mother, though pleased about the part, was not quite so happy to see her go. 'I'll miss you, darling – we both will. I know how much you like England, but – don't stay too long. California is your *home*, remember.'

'I have to settle Daddy's estate,' Faramond pointed out.

'The lawyers will do everything,' Annalee insisted. 'That's what they're for. If you would just tell them to put the house on the market – '

'I want to see it first,' said Faramond. She had evidently said it many times before. 'It *was* my home.'

David Hunter had died, very suddenly, the preceding winter. With his customary reticence he had said nothing to anyone, even his doctor, of his increasing internal pains, until he collapsed one day in the vegetable garden, was rushed to hospital and died during an exploratory operation twenty-four hours later. Overdoing the British reserve, had said Annalee when she heard the news, bursting unexpectedly into tears. Possibly she had been overdoing Hollywood with Sherwin and felt a pang of loss for boredom and security. Faramond had wanted to fly over for the funeral but had allowed herself to be dissuaded. If there had been any chance of seeing her father alive she would have gone, but he was dead and (as her mother had reiterated) the director of *Skeleton in My Closet* would be at the So-and-So's next week and anyway, she did not really believe his spirit would be hovering over the floral tributes with a checklist, waiting to see who did not turn up. His spirit, she thought desolately, could come to California and see her. If he had a spirit. She had always promised him a long visit when she was eighteen and her exams were over. (David Hunter had been very hot on exams.) If only he had *asked* me, she told herself, thinking how pointless it was to feel guilty; but he had not asked for anything since he asked her mother to marry him the day she crashed her car into his taxi so many years ago.

In due course, the lawyers contacted Faramond to inform her that the house in Kent and a substantial income from private investments were now hers; perhaps she would like them to arrange for the sale of the house? Resisting maternal pressure, Faramond wrote back to say No thank you, not quite yet, and she would be over later that year to sort things out. Owning a house – even one several thousand miles away – made her feel very grown up. In California, despite her superficial sophistication, she still had the status of a child. Her glamorous clothes were bought under her mother's aegis and worn on dinner-dates with Sherwin. She swam, played tennis and drank the occasional ice-cream soda with the approved son of a parental business associate. She knew certain members of the 'movie set' (such as Max Guest) but was rarely permitted to go to their parties; Sherwin himself had taken her to the party where she met Dominic during a business trip to New York, although it was she who had been invited. Her time was divided between school work and out-of-school work, and her social life was vetted. Once, she had played a teenage prostitute in a T.V. serial (not very well, said the critics), but she had never had sex and had hardly come close to it, even with the approvable son.

'I am eighteen years old and I have never done anything,' she informed her reflection the day before her departure for England. It was not a particularly sophisticated reflection since she had no make-up on, most of her hair was in hot rollers, and nervous anticipation had brought out a rare spot on her chin. 'I've made a start on my career, I suppose, but how can I be a great actress when I haven't *lived*?' She felt a pang of envy for Sophia Loren, who had climbed to stardom out of a Naples gutter. Not, she admitted ruefully, that she would have enjoyed a childhood spent in a Naples gutter, but undoubtedly it had given Sophia Loren an advantage. 'I want to have a Past,' she decided, half-serious, exasperated by the blankness of her face, its unmarked freshness (except for the spot), her potentially mysterious eyes which had, as yet, so little to be mysterious about. 'I want – I don't know what I want.' Nobody does, said her other self, the secret self who hid behind her eyes and almost invariably contradicted her, or laughed at her, or gave her advice. They have to learn.

In England, maybe, she would find out.

She had allowed herself two weeks before filming started. Originally, she had planned to stay in London with some cousins of David's, paying only a flying visit to Kent, but the city was in the throes of a heatwave and two days without air-conditioning made her change her mind. She repacked her suitcases, collected an unfamiliar set of keys from the solicitor and caught the train down to Overbridge. After the yawning salons, limitless floor space and panoramic windows of her

Californian home she found the house unexpectedly small and not as old as she had imagined. In the evenings, used to globes and cylinders of glass that lit up at a touch, the coolie-hat lamps and low wattage bulbs seemed inadequate. She sat in her father's study looking out towards the vegetable garden, half expecting to see his ghost walking towards her, tired-looking and slightly reproachful; but he did not come. The house had been kept clean in her absence – almost too clean – and it felt as if much of the atmosphere had been dusted and polished and vacuumed away. She wondered if she would be afraid, sleeping there alone, but although she sat up for a long time reading by the inadequate lamplight the very shadows seemed indifferent. They don't remember me, she thought, conscious for the first time in her life of things changing, vanishing, being lost. She felt awesomely old with all her eighteen years, touched with sadness, with memory – not perhaps a Naples gutter but a Past of sorts after all. She visualised her eyes, on camera, no longer blank but clouded with secret sorrows. When she finally slept she dreamed she was being pursued down a sunlit boulevard by a flock of reporters. 'I want to be alone,' she said, and there she was in England, and David Hunter was smiling down at her from his portrait in the study. There was no portrait in the study, of course, only photographs; but there should have been.

The next day, sunbathing in the garden, she was hailed by the boy-next-door. Two years older than Faramond, he was down from Oxford for the summer vac. She allowed him to take her rowing on the river and noticed he had not entirely outgrown his teenage acne after all. At fourteen, he had looked as if he might be good looking when his spots cleared up, but in the interim the wrong features had grown stronger (or weaker) and a tiny fantasy she had nurtured of falling in love with him died stillborn. She knew it was necessary to fall in love with someone; she was too innocent, too whole of heart, too hopelessly virginal ever to make a great actress. But the boy-next-door had failed to turn into Jeremy Irons and the only interesting man she had ever met was a playwright at a party who probably did not even remember her name. (She was right: he didn't.) Back in California, England had looked small enough on the map, but now she was there again she remembered how many people there were in that small area, twisty roads, cluttered cities, corners around which the one person you wished to meet might for ever elude you. When her two weeks were nearly over she returned to London and told the estate agents they could sell the house. She felt defeated; but what was the point of hanging on to it? It had not given her anything. Up in Scotland, she made friends with a young man called Ricky Verelst, son of Sir Max Verelst, who was working on the musical score for the film. It was only quite by chance that she discovered he had been at school with Dominic Hardinge.

Faramond and Dominic met for the second time at Ricky Verelst's birthday party in a Soho nightclub. On this occasion Faramond had not curled her hair and wore sea-green taffeta instead of pink lurex; Dominic was vaguely aware they had met before but he could not remember where. Faramond adopted the tactics of Desdemona: she positioned herself near to him throughout the evening and listened. Few men can resist a woman who listens. She did not laugh at his witticisms very often, since excessive laughter did not come naturally to her, but she smiled once or twice. The following day, Dominic rang Ricky to fit a name to the telephone number scrawled on the back of one of Anne Heywood's business cards.

'Ravishing, of course,' said Ricky, 'but isn't she a bit young for you? Anyway, she's a virgin. I found that out in Scotland.'

A virgin. Dominic found the idea somehow reassuring. He said: 'I think I've asked her out to dinner.'

They spent their first date in a restaurant of the expensively discreet variety where famous faces cannot be seen in the bad light and the size of the portions suggests that everyone is watching their weight. Faramond wore black, a colour which should only be worn by redheads and blondes, because she had chosen it herself; her mother never bought black for her. Dominic was reminded of a novice in a convent, and then wondered if novices wore white. Despite his Catholic upbringing, he was not sure. The candlelight transformed her blankness into an inscrutability which intrigued him, not as a man but as a writer; he found himself building plays around her, a modern Galatea, the statue of a beautiful child brought terribly to life, retaining still the heart and emotions of a stone. He imagined her the bride who poisons her husband, the virgin who plunges into perversion and degeneracy, the angel who turns her face away from pity. Afterwards, due possibly to a form of artistic wishful thinking, he could not remember seeing the candle flame or any other spark of light reflected in her eyes: they were dark with their own darkness, sombre and mysterious as a moonless night. He noted the way she answered questions with silence, thinking before she spoke, the rarity of her smiles, the misleading softness of her voice. All a part of the character he had created. So do statues behave, or so he decided, when they have just been brought to life, tentatively essaying their new vocal chords, learning conversation, occasionally remembering to imitate human laughter. Over coffee and his second Grand Marnier, he told her so.

'When did you stop being a statue?' he went on to ask. 'It can't have been very long ago; you're obviously not used to behaving like a human being. I'm not even sure the transformation is complete yet.'

Faramond, uncertain if he was mocking her, did not smile. All evening she had been concealing her nerves behind a façade of quietness, thought-out responses, careful words. She had never before dined alone with a young man like this (ice-cream sodas with mere boys did not count). In the past, her stepfather had always been there, both protecting her and showing her off, her mother's laughter filling up the conversational pauses. All that had been required of her was to look beautiful and be polite. No one had ever asked her what she thought about Greenpeace, or Ronald Reagan, or the Bomb, or even the film industry. She had been, as at Max Guest's party, a professional asset, a well-behaved child, a part of the decor. And now here she was in England, unprotected, unchaperoned, sitting opposite a young man who talked fluently and bitterly about the state of humanity and told her she was a statue come to life. (Dominic, had she but known it, always talked fluently and bitterly about the state of humanity: it was his favourite subject.) She felt naked without her protectors, a nakedness of the mind or heart which was both frightening and exciting. This was living at last. This was experience. Mesmerised by circumstances, she felt as if Dominic's eyes looked into places in her soul which she had not even known were there.

'When did I stop being a statue?' she repeated, slowly. 'I think – yes, tonight. I think it was tonight.' She said it, not flirtatiously or knowingly, but as if it was a mystery which she did not quite understand. She was, after all, an actress, and he had given her a cue. She responded instinctively

Dominic stared at her, startled and a little afraid. Her answer was so perfectly in accord with his fantasy. Suddenly, he found himself thinking not of Pygmalion and Galatea but of Frankenstein and his home-made monster, of beautiful girls with hands of marble, of god-like dreams distorted into nightmares. He had heard of writers terrorised by their own creations, of witches calling up demons who destroyed them. He looked at Faramond through the candle flame and knew it was all nonsense, a game where he had not expected her to know the rules, but the tiny thrill of fear remained. It was the fear, as always, which fascinated him.

Chapter Nine

It was the considered opinion of almost everyone they knew that few relationships could have been more unsuitable than that of Dominic Hardinge and Faramond Hunter. She was too young, too quiet, too innocent, too ignorant of the world outside her own shielded existence. He was too weak, too temperamental, too cruel, too complex, too everything. She ought to find herself a nice boy her own age, thought Zoë Preston with unspecified horror, reading of the affair in a copy of the *Mail* shown to her by an avid daily help. She needs a father-figure, Anne Heywood diagnosed (Faramond could have told her that she had had more than enough of father-figures). 'He'll tire of her,' opined Ricky Verelst, 'when he gets her into bed. It's my fault: I should never have told him she was a virgin. Poor kid.' As for Dominic, what he needed (again, according to Anne Heywood) was someone sensible, maternal, infinitely patient, chronically unruffled, not too glamorous and at least ten years his senior. 'He needs a mother-figure, she needs a father-figure, and there they both are playing at Babes in the Wood,' Anne concluded caustically. 'Disaster.'

In a way, she was right. Dominic, like most people, had both strengths and weaknesses, but his weaknesses were with him always, whereas his strength was more of an erratic force, a lightning flicker which came and went impervious to the demands of the moment. And, as with all weaker characters, true strength was something he sensed and to which he was drawn. He had sensed it in Faramond the first time they met, when he labelled her 'unfeminine'. He sensed it behind the unformed curves of her face and the rather more formed curves of her figure, something untried perhaps and unappreciated, but hard and changeless as the core of a stone. In his imagination, that power made her at times monstrous and fascinating, a cold goddess, an incorruptible killer, a virginal maenad – yet all these things were merely reflections or distortions of the real Faramond, a Faramond who existed and grew the more he needed her, drawn to his weakness even as he was drawn to her strength. Not that she knew it. Had anyone asked her, she would have spoken of him as handsome, talented, successful, forgetting that these were qualities she had met before, if in different men and under different circumstances. She was too inexperienced to realise that it was his vulnerability which attracted her, that germ of failure which endured despite all his talent and success, a deep hurt or capacity for hurt more compelling than any machismo. A strong man would have crushed her; with Dominic, she had room to develop. She was conscious of her personality expanding in his company like a pot-plant after the five-drop difference. She knew this was growing up; she thought it must be love. It did not occur to her that one day, when she was no longer so immature and uncertain, she would be too strong for him.

The day after their first dinner-date, she wrote to her mother. It was the kind of letter Annalee had been dreading: I-have-met-this-wonderful-man and I-am-not-coming-back-yet. 'Let her alone,' recommended Sherwin, unexpectedly philosophical. 'I guess something like this had to happen sooner or later. Best let her get it out of her system. She'll be home in a month or so. She's a bright girl and she's going to be a big star. Big stars don't happen in *London*, do they?' His voice had the same inflection that he would have used for Timbuctoo, or Piddletrenthyde – or anywhere except

Hollywood. For once, Annalee said nothing. Her social life had been London-based for twelve years and she was thinking of the West End. And wasn't this Dominic Hardinge supposed to be a playwright?

The second letter came three weeks later. This time, Sherwin was not so philosophical. 'I am going to live in England,' wrote Faramond, 'with Dominic. We have decided to keep the house at Overbridge and live there, since Dom has had enough of London and thinks he will work better in the country. He is going to write a play with a part for me . . .' 'She can't do this!' stormed Sherwin. 'She's only a kid! Her whole career down the drain!' and 'What does she mean by it, shacking up with this guy? He's old enough to be her – '

'Brother,' supplied Annalee. She was wearing a face pack, which precluded her either storming or shedding maternal tears with any degree of style. In any case, she had always been able to face unpleasant realities when she knew there was no alternative. 'Sherry darling – '

'That new script,' moaned Sherry darling, wearing a swathe in the shag pile. 'Could have been written for her!'

'Of *course*,' said Annalee warmly. 'I'm sure she'll realise all that when – when I get a chance to discuss it with her. We have to be very careful about this. *We* know she's just a child but under law she's an adult. She's eighteen years old. She can vote. It would be *fatal* to try and force her into anything. We've got to handle this very, very gently – '

'I'm catching the next 'plane out of here,' stated Sherwin, reaching, metaphorically speaking, for telephone, secretary, boarding card, overnight bag, and handcuffs, 'and I'm going to fetch her home. I've always loved her like my own daughter. It's time she loved me like a father in return.'

'But darling, of *course* she loves you!' gasped Annalee in horror, with an expression which cracked her face pack from brow to chin. 'Sherry, *please* – !'

In the end, after the removal of the face pack and the consumption of large drinks, it was Annalee who flew to England. In her heart, she knew it would not do any good. She had always sensed her daughter was stronger than her: she had leaned on that strength while she was able and now she knew it would defeat her. It seemed inappropriate to speak of obstinacy in connection with that sable-and magnolia beauty, but nonetheless, under the quiet manners and apparent docility there had always been something immovable, almost implacable, resolution, determination, call it what you will. Faramond, Annalee reflected, would be all right. She would fight for what she wanted and whether she succeeded or failed she would survive. She was a survivor at eighteen and she would be a survivor at thirty-eight. Annalee herself was not so resilient, or maybe her resilience, like her complexion, had corroded a little with time: she needed to live in an atmosphere of adoration, entertainment, change, and without those things she had a sudden panicky feeling she might scarcely exist. And in Sherwin, regrettably, she had found a kindred spirit. She worried about the twenty-one-year-old hopeful whom she had seen all too frequently in Sherwin's offices that summer, but she did not worry about Faramond. There was no need to worry about Faramond.

Dominic, she thought, was charming, reminding her vaguely of Faramond's real father (or was it another one?). Charming, elusive, undependable. She said as much, over a tête-à-tête lunch, bringing up the question of Faramond's film career almost as an afterthought. She already knew the answers. 'I thought I told you,' Faramond said. 'He's doing a part for me in his new play. It's for television – a sort of Gothic horror, I think, with special effects. It's called *Chickamungus* at the moment, but that's just a working title. He says he'll probably change it.'

'*Chickamungus?*' murmured Annalee, bewildered. As a child, she had been given very little nonsense poetry. 'Oh well . . . When will it be finished?'

'I don't know,' Faramond said with a little constraint. 'He's just finished another stage play which I gather the National Theatre may do next year, but it's going to need a lot more work first. Everything depends on that.'

There was a short silence. Then Annalee said: '*Darling*' and Faramond said: 'Mommy' at the same moment. In the end, surprisingly, it was Faramond who spoke. 'I'm eighteen years old,' she said, and it was not clear from her manner whether she considered this a lot or a little. Possibly it was not clear even to her. 'There's lots of time for my career. I don't want to get caught up in the rat-race yet. I need to live a little. I'll never be a really good actress if I don't know anything about life.'

Annalee sighed almost nostalgically. 'Sometimes,' she remarked, 'you sound exactly like me. I never used to think so, but maybe we're a bit alike after all. Darling, believe me, I *do* understand. You have to live your life the way *you* want. How could I ever try and stand in your way?' Since she had no influence, either legal or financial, over her daughter this question was peculiarly relevant. Faramond, however, was beginning to feel guilty. She had expected her rebellion to meet with authoritarian resistance, not surrender and martyrdom. If only she had brought Sherry, Faramond reflected. And then, with sudden determination: She needn't think she can get me that way.

As it happened, Annalee was merely running a forlorn hope. She knew only too well the power of sex. 'I shall miss you,' she said at length. 'So will Sherry. He did enjoy having a pretty young girl to fuss over.'

'You'll manage,' Faramond retorted grimly – the grimness being a sign of her own resolve rather than her attitude to her mother. And, with a rare glimpse of cynicism: 'Make sure he backs a loser next film.'

'I wonder if that would answer?' Annalee said seriously. 'He'd be depressed of course, poor darling, but it would put *her* off. Nobody screws a loser. And I could make a great show of selling my diamonds. I've never been mad about diamonds, anyway. You have to have them for the look of it but I can't really see what the excitement's all about. Jessie, you're so clever! Always so *sensible*, too. What *will* I do without you? You must come for Christmas. With Dominic, of course.'

'We'll see,' Faramond was tactful. 'He may be busy. There's his play at the National . . .'

'What's this one about?' asked Annalee, remembering to sound interested.

'The holocaust,' said Faramond, baldly. 'It's called *Ragnarok*.'

'*Ragnarok*,' repeated her mother. She knew even less Norse mythology than nonsense verse. '*Chickamungus*.' And she added, inconsequently: 'Don't marry him, will you?'

Two days later, when Annalee had left, Faramond dreamed of her saying that.

The last afternoon of the visit was rendered hideous by Annalee's desire to talk about sex. It was so lovely, she declared, to be able to discuss these things with her daughter at last. Of course, she had always believed in total frankness but Faramond had led such a *sheltered* life – not like teenagers back in the Sixties and Seventies. Now, they would be able to have the most delicious private chats, just like sisters. (Faramond, whose natural pallor made it difficult for her to blench, blenched.) Sleeping in a spare room on the first floor, Annalee did not realise that her daughter and supposed lover, on the top floor, had separate bedrooms. Faramond, in the name of rebellion (or so she told herself), did not mention it. There was, she felt, something badly wrong with a state of affairs where the daughter is forced to conceal from her mother the fact that she is *not* sleeping with her boyfriend. Naturally, it was with her mother that the something – whatever it might be – was obviously wrong. Had Annalee not suffered from the Sixties syndrome – i.e. the belief that any couple who do not have instant sex are inhibited, perverted, and actively opposed to World Peace – it would have been quite easy to explain. Dominic, she thought, was *afraid*: that was the problem. Afraid to rush her, to force her, to hurt her, afraid of his experience and her inexperience, afraid, perhaps, of being happy.

He had not said he loved her but sometimes she had caught him looking at her with a curious air of astonishment, almost as though he were unnerved by some reaction of hers, or by his own pleasure in her company. Once, he told her: 'I quite like you, do you know that? I've always wanted a statue of my own to bring to life.' She did not entirely follow his concept of the statue, but 'quite like' and 'my own' meant more to her than all the expressions of love she had ever heard on screen. She did not really believe Dominic would ever say 'I love you'; the words did not belong in his vocabulary, formed no part of the aloof, sarcastic façade which she sensed was so essential to him. Behind that façade, she thought, he must have been terribly hurt, when he was immature and defenceless, probably by some bright, hard, glamour girl who did not know or did not care that artists were sensitive and could suffer. Faramond pictured the scene, usually when she was in the bath, supplying a second-rate Hollywood film script and dramatic background music. The girl always had bleached hair, and Dominic's face, in the final close-up, wore a look of supressed pain which twisted her heart. One day, maybe, he would tell her about it. He would rest his head on her shoulder and say that he liked her very much. Anyway, she could afford to wait. Patience, she discovered, came easily to her. For the moment, Dominic saw her as a cool, remote sort of creature (hence the statue), untouchable because he feared to touch, delicate because he feared to break. There had been one occasion – the second or third time he kissed her – when things had gone out of control. She had panicked and struggled, he had released her abruptly, and that was that. Afterwards, when she undressed and took off her make-up for bed, she found there was a bruise on her breast below the nipple and the skin round her mouth was red and angry where he had bitten her. It had frightened her, but later, when the bruise faded, she wondered what would have happened if she had not resisted him. After all, she told herself, virgins were supposed to be nervous: it was only natural. Next time she would let him do what he wanted, without panicking. Everyone said your first sexual experience was painful and traumatic and best out of the way.

But Dominic had not tried to hurt her again.

Dominic and Faramond did not go to California for Christmas, of course. They stayed in Overbridge, where, as usual, it did not snow, watching television and the video and playing computer games. Dominic's computer was recently acquired and he had become a fanatical computer-gamester. Sometimes Faramond thought that for him the computer, too, was a species of living statue, a cubist robot with a small square screen that winked and blinked at him in primary colours and a keyboard that chattered with more animation than she would ever achieve. Whenever something upset or irritated him he would turn, not to her, but to the little machine, neglecting his work to pick his way through intricate mazes, or fight space-age battles, or swim in shark-ridden seas. Christmas Day, Faramond reflected somewhat bitterly, was no different from any other day. She had wanted to try cooking the turkey herself but Dominic said he did not like turkey and paid the housekeeper treble to come in and prepare venison and chestnut soup. Neither of them ate much. The only decorations were some holly Faramond had collected at the last minute and a wreath which the housekeeper hung on the front door and Dominic did not notice.

'I'm a pagan,' he said. 'What does Christmas mean to me? The official birthday of the Son of a God in whom I do not believe by an early form of surrogate motherhood! And yet I'm supposed to celebrate it by sending my friends endearing picturettes of snow-struck lambkins and buying a great many presents that nobody wants or needs. I think I shall hire a video nasty.' In fact, he hired a suspense thriller which Faramond quite enjoyed and an old-fashioned horror film which proved more funny than frightening. In the evening, they drank Château Margaux and ate chocolates and Dominic, with an air of gêne that suggested he was rather ashamed of the gesture, produced a small box which proved to contain a pair of antique ear-rings.

'*Dom* – !' gasped Faramond in the approved manner, actually speechless with pleasure and surprise.

'Look, I've been meaning to get you something for ages, that's all. I thought I might as well give them to you now as at any other time. And at least you needn't wear those hideous chunks of plastic any more.'

(Faramond obediently removed the plastic.) 'But – '

'And for God's sake don't say *you shouldn't have*. It always sounds so phoney and it's such a bloody cliché.'

Later, admiring the ear-rings in her bedroom mirror, Faramond thought: 'I would have liked a turkey, and decorations, and all that, but it doesn't really matter. Those things aren't important. It isn't as if I believed in it, either.' When they were sitting downstairs on the sofa Dominic had put his arm round her, kissing her in a leisurely way which might have been merely tentative, moving his hands through her hair, exploring her face with the tips of his fingers like a blind man learning an unfamiliar object. While he was kissing her she put her hand on his thigh, wondering if she dared move it any higher, half wishing he would do it for her, carrying her hand to his crotch and curling her fingers around the bulge which she imagined must be there. She had never touched a man so intimately in her life, but endless modern novels had taught her what to expect. But he did not encourage her, and she did not dare.

They went to Scotland for the New Year, to stay with a singer-turned-actor whom Faramond had met while working on her film. He lived in a haunted castle which he had bought from the last scion of some decayed aristocratic family and equipped, at enormous expense, with numerous bathrooms, central heating, and quadrophonic stereo in every room. Pipes skirled on the battlements at night, thanks to still more stereo, probably terrorising any genuine ghost out of existence. The surrounding countryside consisted of a sheet-steel lake, piled-up mountains and impassable roads, the whole blanched out of existence by repeated falls of snow. Add a house party of some twenty people and various decrepit servants with accents as thick as porridge and the result, as Dominic remarked, was straight out of Agatha Christie or Ngaio Marsh. The next thing would be the discovery of the corpse. 'Probably mine,' he added. Faramond laughed.

Downstairs, in a sumptuously-furnished room implausibly hung with swords and claymores and with the obligatory stag's head over the fireplace, he came face to face with Marten de Witt. Dominic had known he would be there, of course – had known it with the same fatalistic certainty that you know it will rain on the day of a long-planned picnic or the baggage-handlers will strike when you are supposed to fly to the Carribean. In any case, the singer-turned-actor had begun his career with Phebus Records, so it was natural that he and de Witt should be well acquainted. Not for the first time, Dominic wondered why he had come, why he had not avoided this particular house party as he had avoided so many others, what fear or fascination had compelled him to be there. He did not like to think of possible answers.

'I saw your latest play,' de Witt said. 'Naturally.'

Naturally? Why *naturally*? What obscene motive (Dominic wondered) could make it *natural* for a man like de Witt to go to the theatre? In Dominic's eyes, he looked more than ever inhuman, a clean-shaven grizzly bear thinly disguised in the suits and ties of civilisation.

'It was most interesting,' de Witt continued. 'A highly original view of the world.' In fact, Dominic's view of the world was fashionable rather than original, but de Witt had picked the adjective more out of courtesy than a desire to be accurate. He was a conventional man who saw the right plays and collected the right people because his position demanded it, and his listeners invariably assumed that the less he said the deeper he thought. Possibly he was aware of this; at any rate he normally had little to say. 'Highly original,' he repeated, after an unhurried pause. He never hurried, even over pauses. And: 'I was glad to be able to help you with some of the research.'

Dominic was silent. For a moment, he could not even remember what *Tumours* was about. But he knew quite well the 'research' did not match the play. De Witt was toying with him, subtly threatening or merely taking pleasure in his discomfiture – the secret pleasure of a satisfied malevolence which Dominic imagined as almost sexual. Or was it only his imagination? Was it, maybe, that de Witt spoke out of politeness, unable to recall what either the research or the play had involved? Briefly, Dominic knew a familiar sensation of imminent madness, as though he clung with his fingertips to the edge of a precipice and beneath him was a dark and dreadful whirlpool. One wrong word, one wrong gesture, and he would lose his hold, and fall . . . He found Faramond was beside him and his hand closed over her wrist so tightly the flesh was bruised. (Later she looked at the bruise, surreptitiously, wondering.) Presently, he remembered to introduce her.

De Witt introduced Catherine Lavalle.

Apparently, Catherine was staying with him again after an abortive and much-publicised attempt to return to her husband. She was now applying to the Pope to get the marriage annulled (Edmond Lavalle was a Catholic), reputedly on the grounds that it had never been consummated. Twice widowed and with a prospective annullment, one gossip columnist had commented aptly that she seemed incapable of getting divorced like everyone else. Rumour had cast de Witt for the role of Captain Dobbin, with or without reason. (At the castle it was known that they had separate rooms.) Perhaps because of the publicity, Faramond was intrigued by Catherine. Thinking of that unconsummated marriage, she had once wondered if they could ever become friends, confiding secrets as girls are supposed to do, even – she had always thought – comparing notes, only of course the circumstances were quite different. For one thing, there was no Paul Derigueur in Dominic's life. But now, meeting Catherine, she saw it was impossible. Mrs Lavalle, she thought, was armour-plated in her perfect make-up, her designer clothes, her party manners and mannerisms – too old and too sophisticated ever to suffer or wish to confide. She would progress swimmingly through her problems, never losing sight of her face in the mirror, uncertain of nothing except what to wear for dinner or the time of her next manicure. It was ludicrous to suppose that she and Faramond could ever talk about anything but the weather.

As for de Witt, Faramond thought him stolid, middle-aged and dull. It was only afterwards, contemplating the bruise on her wrist, that she began to find him frightening.

That night, Faramond and Dominic slept in the same bed for the first time since they had been together. Dominic had had a lot to drink and curled up against her, falling asleep or passing out almost immediately. Faramond lay wakeful for more than an hour, listening to her heartbeat and the noise of the wind scouring the castle walls.

The next day was New Year's Eve. More guests arrived

despite the impassable roads, leaving Range Rovers, sledges and snow-ploughs blocking the forecourt. Their host had stipulated historical costume, and soon the Great Hall (or whatever it was called) heaved and glittered with padded skirts and pushed-up bosoms, masks from Liberty's and fans from the King's Road, and a plethora of diamonds not all of which were paste. Some of the men wore lurex waistcoats and David Bowie make-up; others wore kilts and tried to look like Bonnie Prince Charlie. Dominic had declared earlier that he was sick of this glorification of an effete aristocracy and he at least would go as a peasant, but in the end he looked more like a runaway Jacobite after a bad day at Culloden, elaborately tattered shirt tucked into elaborately patched knee-breeches and a strip of Stewart tartan knotted round his head in the style of John McEnroe. Faramond caught herself thinking how sexy he was and longed passionately and disloyally for him to wrench her into his arms and kiss her with the brutal intensity favoured by heroes in the trashiest historical novels. And then a wave of shame swept over her, partly at having read the novels, mostly at her own treacherous lust – although why such lust should be so treacherous she could not bring herself to work out. She was sitting in front of the mirror at the time with Dominic looking over her shoulder, and she saw the faintest hint of a blush rise under her make-up, but he did not notice.

Earlier that day she had washed her hair and dried it in plaits, and now it stood out around her head in a myriad of tiny artificial waves. With her stiff silver skirts arranged over paniers and her solemn, long-oval face she looked, Dominic thought, like a painting of a Spanish Infanta, formal, decorative, unapproachable, with no more emotions than a doll. With a sudden sense of alienation he wondered why on earth he was living with her. There were times when he believed she almost understood him, but perhaps that was only a trick of the light, an actress's knack of giving the right response to the right cue. Would he want her to understand him anyway, even if she could? That morning, waking beside her, he thought she had come too close, dangerously close; he had wanted, in a confusion of conflicting emotion, to take her, break into her, destroy her – to climb out of bed and run, though he did not know where. He had willed himself into a mood of resignation, remembering without desire the other girls he had screwed, violently and pointlessly, unable to climax, finding no relief and no peace. He was never sure whether he feared to hurt Faramond or to betray himself to her, whether he longed to find her different from the rest or endlessly the same. In bed, he had resented her because she was too close; now, illogically, he resented her for appearing too distant. He knew he was unreasonable and wrong-headed but he told himself it was useless trying to overcome these defects or, indeed, any others. Faramond wanted him; therefore, like everyone else, she would have to endure him as he was.

'I'm going to the party,' he said, letting his mood colour his voice. 'Come down when you're ready.'

She half turned but her face, as usual, gave nothing away. 'All right,' she said quietly. That was all. If she had looked hurt he would have felt even more resentful; as it was, determined not to be cheated of his resentment, he decided she was too stupid to know when someone meant to hurt her and she obviously didn't understand him after all. Statues – he concluded – are stone between the ears. And on the way downstairs he resolved to end the affair, to screw her, to get drunk – anything to break the taboo that her physical presence always inflicted on him. He started to fulfil the last resolve as soon as he reached the party. It was a bad beginning.

How Dominic ended up in another room tête-à-tête with Marten de Witt was something he could never remember. Faramond entered the Great Hall about half an hour later and looked for him in vain. She was still young enough to feel slightly shy among so many strangers but she knew if she searched for him he would only be annoyed at her childishness. An hour or two passed during which she circulated conscientiously, listening to other people's conversations with an air of abstracted courtesy and trying not to let her gaze wander round the room. Then came a lull in the background music when she thought she heard Dominic's voice. She excused herself from the kilted Old Etonian who was telling her how to shoot grouse by computer and slipped through a side door into a species of anteroom. Beyond, a second door, half open, showed a glimpse of another room and a section of leg in patched knee-breech and high boot. Faramond went in.

Dominic and de Witt were sitting round a low table, both unmistakably drunk. Dominic's drunkenness invariably took the form of long rambling speeches where he frequently lost track of his initial subject matter, violent gestures, brooding silences, seismic changes of mood. He was in the middle of one of his speeches when Faramond came in and paid her no attention whatsoever. De Witt's drunkenness was less obvious, manifesting itself in an increased stolidity, a heaviness of movement, a glazed look about the eyes. He seemed to be behaving with deliberate over-restraint, as if he made himself concentrate even before blinking or moving his head. He wore neither kilt nor fancy dress, and his black dinner jacket looked both inappropriate and (to Faramond) sinister, like the Official Receiver at the wedding of a future bankrupt. Remembering the bruise on her wrist, the shadow of antipathy or fear that she had sensed between the two men, she was at first startled and then appalled. It seemed to her somehow ominous that they should be here, drinking together in apparent comradeship. The previous evening, when she had asked about de Witt, Dominic had said little and explained nothing. 'A King Kong of the business world,' was his sole comment, and 'I don't like him.' Now, here was Dominic in full spate, holding forth, as always, on Man's futility and the general uselessness of civilisation, sitting opposite King Kong and looking, despite his period tatters, like a perfect product of civilisation and futility. No claws, no fangs, soft-bodied, delicate, easily crushed. Suddenly, she felt afraid. She said: 'Dominic – '

He did not even turn his head.

Behind her, the noises of the party intruded abruptly. A laugh was broken off and a voice said: 'What *are* you all doing in here?'

Faramond found herself moving aside for Catherine Lavalle. De Witt said: 'Talking' and: 'Hello' and, after further concentration, heaved himself to his feet. Even drunk there was a suggestion of laborious power in his movements. Faramond went to help Dominic, who did not appear capable of getting to his feet without assistance; but he pushed her away. Catherine said something about giving him a hand and de Witt, with slow purpose, wrapped a huge arm about his shoulders and hauled him out of the chair. For the first time since Faramond entered the room, she saw Dominic lift his eyes and look straight at de Witt. Their faces were only inches apart. Briefly, fantastically, she thought they were going to kiss. The colour drained from Dominic's skin, leaving him absolutely white. He said: 'Oh my God' and tried to pull himself free. For a moment, he seemed to struggle in de Witt's grasp. Then he broke away and blundered past them out of the room.

Faramond tried to follow but she was hindered by her paniers and by the time she reached the Great Hall he had gone. An illogical panic rose inside her: without knowing quite why she made for the double doors into the entrance hall. She knew it was imagination but the crowd of guests seemed to be fighting against her, consciously impeding her passage. When she reached the doors they were still creaking a little on their hinges as though someone had just passed through.

In the entrance hall, a draught of ice-cold air struck her bare shoulders: the front door stood ajar and beyond she could see a whirl of snowflakes and a deep blue night. The sound of the party was cut off and instead there was the cough of an engine struggling to come to life. She ran to the door, thrust it open, called: 'Dominic! Dominic!' – but the snow muffled her and the reverberate hills let her down. She saw one of the guests' cars reverse abruptly and stick in a drift. The wheels spun, gripped, spun and gripped again. Then the car jerked forwards and swerved into the driveway heading for the road. About three hundred yards further on it seemed to go out of control, careering off the bank and colliding with a shadow that might have been a tree. The engine screamed, metal crunched, headlamps arced across the sky. And Faramond, stumbling down the frozen steps in a tangle of skirts, slipped, fell and rolled over and over in a cocoon of silver brocade down into the snow.

London. In the early hours of New Year's Day, Alisdair Saunders and Theresa Preston were in bed. It was, as Alisdair said, about time. They had shared a bottle of champagne and stood in Trafalgar Square awaiting the stroke of midnight in the midst of a genial swaying mob. On the way back to Alisdair's flat they had talked about Orwell and discussed whether Mrs Thatcher or Ronald Reagan would be better cast as Big Brother. And somewhere along the line Alisdair had kissed her on the cheek, and then on the lips, and had put his arms around her and kissed her again, slowly, almost thoughtfully, putting his tongue in her mouth and liking it and wondering why the hell he hadn't done it before.

Theresa had moved to London in September to take a degree in psychology and had called him in October. 'I have no qualifications,' she had told him, with the air of someone confessing to a particularly sensational crime. 'I thought if I could get a degree in something really *useful* I might be able to make a more valuable contribution to humanity.'

And Alisdair had smiled and murmured: 'Something useful. Yes, of course,' and had thought how idiotically pleasant it was to hear her, after more than a year, still coming out with the same clichés in the same accents of mistaken sincerity.

Now, in bed with her, he felt a similar afterglow of idiotic pleasure. He did not know quite why it was idiotic; only that, in the past, his post-coital relaxation had always been tainted with that faint suggestion of self-distaste, and now it was gone. In his role as professional cynic, he knew that to feel totally content, totally at peace was the blissful delusion of an imbecile; but nonetheless the delusion persisted. He lay there and enjoyed it.

Presently, Theresa lit two cigarettes and gave one to him. She had been watching old Bette Davis films. 'It's funny,' she remarked. 'The first time I came here, it was to see Dominic. I never thought – '

'Tonight,' Alisdair interjected, 'we won't talk about Dominic.'

'No,' said Theresa. 'Anyway, I hope he's happy with his Faramond. Poor Dom.'

'We won't talk about him,' Alisdair reiterated. 'Why "poor" Dom, anyhow? Why do you think of him as "poor"? For that matter, why do I think of him as "poor"? What is it about Dominic that's so irresistably pathetic?'

'Are you jealous?' asked Theresa, suddenly distressed. 'Because I slept with him?'

'No I am not jealous. Just fed up of the subject. Are you jealous of all the women I've slept with?'

Theresa considered the question. 'I don't think so.'

'Good. There are so many it would be a full time job.'

'Why?'

'Why what?'

'Why so many?'

'Oh – I don't know. Because they didn't mean anything. Because I didn't want them to mean anything. Safety in numbers.'

'Notches on your bedstead?' Theresa suggested lightly.

'Riddled with them.'

'As long as I'm not just another notch,' she said. 'I'm not, am I?'

In the dark, Alisdair smiled invisibly. 'It depends,' he said, 'on your behaviour tonight. For example, if you were to place your hand – just there, and squeeze, very gently – *there* – lovely – then maybe –' He broke off, pulling her against him in a muddle of awkward limbs, pushing his face into her hair, filling his senses with the taste and feel and smell of her. 'If you're good,' he whispered, somewhere in the vicinity of her ear, 'you can move in.'

He felt her begin to respond and then hesitate, holding back for a moment. 'Don't tease,' she said, on a queer note of desperation. 'Love me. Please. I'm not secure enough yet to be teased.'

Love me. He could not say it but his arms tightened around her, pressing her closer and closer until she gasped in pain or pleasure, and in the fury of desire or eagerness to reassure her body seemed at the last to be crushed, enveloped, absorbed in his.

Dominic and Faramond spent New Year's Day in hospital. Faramond had a broken arm; Dominic had severe bruising, slight concussion, and a hangover. When she was allowed to sit at his bedside Faramond found him semi-conscious and vague about the events of the preceding night. 'I drive badly when I'm drunk,' he murmured. 'You shouldn't have come with me.' Later, thought Faramond. I'll tell him later. It'll keep.

On the train south she composed a long-deferred letter to her mother. 'Dear Mommy' (she began) 'I am unable to write this myself since I have a broken arm, so Dominic is writing it for me. The doctor says it is a clean break and will mend quickly. Please do not worry about it as I am perfectly okay and my career will *not* be permanently affected. (Underline "not".) I did it falling down a flight of steps at a New Year's Eve party in a castle in Scotland . . . '

'Who does she think she's kidding?' Sherwin said scornfully. 'Fell down a flight of steps my ass! It's all your fault. You should have brought her home when you had the chance. God knows what she's getting up to over there – wild parties – orgies – satanic rites in ruined castles. Broke her arm did she? The mind boggles at what she was really doing. You wait. When she comes back – *if* she comes back – she'll have a punk haircut and an illegitimate baby and be snorting coke every five minutes. You just wait.'

Annalee forebore to mention that Sherwin himself used coke from time to time. 'I'm sure she wouldn't do anything like that,' she responded vaguely. 'Jess – *Faramond* – has always been so sensible.' It was a phrase, had she but noticed, with which she frequently reassured herself. 'Tell me about the new film. How's it going?'

'Oh – problems. I think we're going to need another writer. The dialogue in those early scenes just isn't right. Boo' – the twenty-one-year-old hopeful, real name unknown – 'says she isn't feeling too creative about it. It's a great idea, but the script – '

'Never mind, darling,' Annalee said liquidly, 'I'm sure it's going to be wonderful in the end.'

Back in Overbridge, their cook-housekeeper was down with 'flu and Faramond attempted to prepare dinner one-handed while Dominic peeled and sliced things for her and argued about the oven temperature and whether the mushrooms should go in before or after the courgettes. Eventually, a species of combined chicken casserole and ratatouille was produced, amidst a good deal of companionable incompetence and an impressive backlog of washing up. Faramond, indicating her arm, said Dominic would have to do it, and Dominic left it for the housekeeper and went to look for another bottle of the Château Margaux they had had on Christmas Day. 'You aren't supposed to have any alcohol,' Faramond pointed out. 'The doctor said – '

Dominic consigned the doctor to perpetual fornication and opened the bottle.

Over dinner, Faramond found herself thinking it was one of the best evenings they had ever spent together. 'I suppose,' she said, surveying their culinary efforts, 'we should really have had potatoes. All the dieticians say they're terribly good for you.'

'Don't talk like an American,' said Dominic. 'I hate potatoes. I would have had to peel them. Mushrooms are all right but potatoes are always covered in earth and shit. This is fine.'

'We could have gone out,' Faramond suggested, evidently determined to catalogue anything she might have done wrong.

'Looking like *this*?' Dominic enquired indignantly. Due to a peculiar system of body gravity the bruises on his forehead had dropped to his eyes, and he looked (he had remarked bitterly) as if he had just lost a violent disagreement with Frank Bruno. 'Anyway, I'm too ill to go out. I've been told to rest.'

He refilled both glasses, drank unhurriedly, toyed with the chicken. He never ate much. How comfortable this is,

Faramond thought. And, with a flicker of realisation instantly dismissed: If I tell him the truth about the accident, we won't be comfortable any more. But it was no good. She had to tell him. Now. This moment of comfort – their whole relationship – was founded on too many mysteries. She responded to his moods but she did not understand them. She sensed, in his deepest Self, a sort of integral darkness, a part of him which she thought perhaps he did not want revealed even to his own eyes. But Faramond, though she did not yet know it, was the kind of person who would always choose truth in preference to comfort. And she was too young, too confident, too unself-conscious ever to consider the cost. She said: 'About the accident –'

'What about it? Did you see the estimate for the repairs to that bloody car? Must have arrived this morning. He didn't exactly waste any time did he? If we'd both been killed he'd have been tapping on our coffin lids before the corpses were cold. He must have had the breakdown truck on the scene even before the ambulance. I always thought the Scots went very dour and inscrutable about working on official holidays but evidently the national reputation for meanness comes first. That bastard obviously thinks he's going to have the seats re-upholstered in silver mink at my expense. It's enough to cure you of smashing up other people's cars for life.'

'I do hope so,' Faramond said. She did not continue immediately, but the atmosphere of comfort had already seeped away, destroyed by the mere mention of the incident, or by Dominic's too-voluble response. 'Dom –'

'What's the matter?'

'The accident –'

He was silent.

'It didn't happen the way you thought.'

Dominic said: 'Oh,' and: 'Why don't you tell that bugger with his estimate? Maybe I can avoid the silver mink seats after all.'

It was a forlorn attempt and Faramond knew it. She said: 'I wasn't with you. I told you that. I broke my arm falling down the steps when I tried to run after you. You drove away. I don't think you saw me.'

Her account was detached, factual, but Dominic apparently sensed an implicit accusation. 'I'm a shit, aren't I?' he said, in accents that were meant to sound bored. 'I can't imagine why you put up with it.'

'Don't you want to know,' she asked him, '*why* you drove away like that? In the middle of a party?'

He shrugged.

'You were with that man de Witt,' she said. 'You'd disappeared. I went to look for you. You were with de Witt.'

In the soft light – candlelight – which had helped to make the atmosphere so comfortable it was difficult to read his face. But his voice betrayed him totally. '*What was I doing?*'

'Getting drunk,' she said. His tension frightened her. It was both a relief and a surprise when he appeared to relax a little. 'You were both pretty far gone. Catherine Lavalle was there too. He – de Witt – went to help you up. That was when it happened. You seemed to be – kind of fighting him. Then you ran out.' And she added, reluctantly, relentlessly, driven by her own particular demon: 'I thought he was going to kiss you.'

Dominic said: 'Perhaps he was.'

Faramond opened her mouth to speak, to protest, to question, to try and laugh it off; but her vocal chords let her down. A chaos of images flashed across the back of her mind with the speed of subliminal advertising: Dominic touching her, Dominic failing to touch her; Dominic staring into her eyes across a dinner-table, a candle-flame, a space of room, always behind barriers; Dominic turning away from her, night after night, for his own solitary bed. And Marten de Witt, huge and inexorable as a steam-roller, grasping a monstrous arm around Dominic's shoulders. Thin shoulders, crushable bones. Catherine Lavalle, some time in the future, making headlines again: The Girl Who Always Gets It Wrong. Herself, in the past, thinking with pitiable superiority: At least there's no Paul Derigueur in Dominic's life . . .

At last, when she could speak, she said: 'Please. Explain.'

'I can't explain,' Dominic said. 'I don't know. I was only – guessing.'

'Guessing?'

He didn't answer. He didn't look at her. The bruises around his eyes were like shadows, the shadows under his cheekbones like bruises. His face seemed to be all smudged and puckered with shadow-bruises, moving and changing in the tremulous candlelight. An unstable face. Like something half-made, half-destroyed, the work of an amateur god who had tired of his creation because he could not make it perfect. When he eventually spoke his voice, too, was flawed. 'It isn't anything. Nothing at all.' And, mouth twitching, thinking of Hamlet: 'I had bad dreams.'

'Tell me.' Her hand moved involuntarily towards him, drew back. As always, by some instinct or telepathy, she found the right words, the right cue. 'Tell me your dreams.'

'Dreams are – personal. Especially bad dreams. I've never told anyone.' But then, no one else had ever asked. Not even Theresa, who had been too tactful to touch his wounds, too certain of her own understanding. Strange, that he should think of Theresa. (He did not think of Dr Glauber.)

Faramond did not understand. She did not know if this thing he had never told was real or imagined. It didn't matter. All she had to do was give the prompt, so gently, so unobtrusively that he would scarcely realise she had spoken. In the effort of concentration she found she had been holding her breath, and she exhaled as softly as a sigh.

'No one?' A meaningless question, little more than a nudge to keep him going. Surprisingly, he answered it.

'Only my mother. At least – I didn't *tell* her. I didn't have to. I came in and she – she saw what they had done. Poor mother. I probably thought she would make me better. I was twelve at the time and I still believed in parental omnipotence. Mothers like to keep their children morons; did you know that? Sweet, trusting, adoring, endearing morons.' His face contracted; the shadows seemed to drag at his mouth. 'She didn't make me better. She just sat there and died.' And, on a note of self-discovery: 'I've never forgiven her.'

Or yourself, thought Faramond. But she didn't say it. He had told her once before how his mother died, when she asked him why he visited an analyst. ('For fun,' he had said. 'Just for fun.') She didn't know what his mother's death had to do with de Witt, if anything; but it wasn't important. She was feeling her way, inch by inch, like someone who treads barefoot among broken glass. She whispered: 'What happened?' She was afraid to speak above a whisper lest the atmosphere should shatter, and his trance of self-revelation be ended for ever.

He hardly seemed to hear her. 'It's terrible,' he said, 'to be a child. To be innocent, ignorant, defenceless. All children should be shown compulsory video nasties at school to prepare them for the nastiness of life. A sort of insurance against the psychological cosseting of besotted parents.' He took a mouthful of wine, moved his plate with a sudden violent clatter of crockery on china. 'I was twelve,' he said, 'did I tell you? *Twelve.*'

'What happened,' asked Faramond, 'when you were twelve?' She sensed that he was trying to be detached and clever, but he only sounded brittle. A brittle wit, a brittle resentment. Even his anger had long gone cold on him, leaving little more than an after-taste.

There was a pause while he stared into his wine glass as if it were a crystal ball. After a while, he said: 'It was September. 1968. The swinging Sixties. Shit. I'd been with a friend for the evening. I used to take a short cut home, down a lane which ran behind some houses. Big country houses with big gardens. Rich people's houses. You know the type.'

'Like this one?'

'Bigger.' The bigness of the houses appeared to be important to him. He went on: 'There was a party in one of the houses. A loud, Sixties sort of party – I could her the music some way off. I stopped to look. It must have been quite late – for a twelve-year-old. Anyway, it was dark. I could see the party going on behind the windows. Black figures on red. And the music, roaring. It was almost magical. Like a peepshow. To a child.'

'Go on,' whispered Faramond.

'I don't know where they came from,' he said. 'Out of the party – out of the night – out of the air. Like phantoms and like giants. Three men. I should have run away, but I didn't. I couldn't move. I couldn't speak. I suppose they were drunk –'

once again, there was a note of discovery '– they smelt hot and strong, like animals. One of them . . . one of them was bigger than the rest. Or just tougher. It was his idea.' There was another pause in which the shadows seemed to reach out of the corners and the candle flame burned thin and tall. Faramond heard the gas bubbling in their artificial fire, the distant growl of a motorbike, the creaks and whispers of a house at night, half asleep, half awake, listening. This time, she did not prompt. It was not necessary. 'They raped me.' Still the wonder. 'There in the lane. The earth got in my mouth.'

She couldn't say anything. Instinct and telepathy failed her. She felt as if she was breaking into pieces. She knew an impulse to go to him, put her arms around him, press him against her, until he gave way and cried into her shoulder with the anguished gusto of a child. But that was in films, in fantasy. Reality was Dominic sitting opposite her, isolated in his own memories, fragile and unreachable. The table came between them, scattered with the debris of their meal. Another barrier. She saw him as if from a great distance. The desire to touch him and the impossibility of touching him were twisted up inside her like a physical pain.

Ages later, or so it seemed, she asked him: 'Why didn't you tell the police?' She knew even as she spoke that it was a stupid question.

'The police?' He appeared to drag himself back with difficulty from wherever he had been. 'I told my mother. She died. I couldn't tell anyone else.'

He picked up his wine glass, drank, put it down, resumed his crystal-gazing into the wine. He had not looked at Faramond at all. A droplet of wax, translucent as a tear, welled from the top of the candle and trickled down the side, clouding over as it began to solidify. For the first time that evening, Dominic wondered what she felt, *if* she felt, whether she had understood him at all. He was afraid to look at her in case she might be crying. He told himself he had a horror of compassion, of kindness, of women's tears.

'What about – de Witt? Did he know?' He could tell from her voice that she wasn't crying. She was trying to work things out, to solve the puzzle, analysing, calculating. Like a machine. Like a statue. When he looked up, the shadows in her eyes hid any compassion she might feel.

'Maybe. I'm not sure. I went back there once, a few years ago. To the lane. There was a girl . . . Anyway, I got hold of the woman who gave the party. She made out a list of names – people who might have been there. I didn't tell her what it was about. I called one or two of them. That was how I met de Witt. He invited me to his house.'

'And then?'

'Nothing. I couldn't ask him, could I? Imagine it – facing him across a desk in some private office thirty storeys above the rest of London. Filing cabinets. Telephones ringing. Secretaries darting in and out. "Excuse me, did you once get your kicks raping a twelve-year-old boy? Yes, 1968 actually. You don't remember?"' He broke off abruptly, as if his own words – or the tone in which they were spoken – had frightened him. 'Anyhow,' he concluded, after a few moments, 'he told me he wasn't there.'

But you didn't believe him, thought Faramond.

'Funny,' Dominic added lightly, as though in an attempt to divert himself, 'that's where I met Alisdair Saunders. At de Witt's house. He took my first play to the West End. What you might call a lucky break.'

Faramond said: 'You don't think Alisdair – ?'

'Don't be silly. He's much too young. When I was twelve he would have been – fifteen, sixteen. Too young.'

'Of course.'

Another teardrop of wax slithered down the side of the candle. What next? Faramond wondered. What can I say that won't destroy him – destroy *us*? She felt helpless, frustrated, gauche, hindered both physically and mentally by her broken arm, her hitherto sheltered life. An actress who has forgotten her lines for all time and stands in the glare of the spot-light, staring at her fellow actor in idiotic dumbness.

'You ought to get out,' Dominic said. 'I have nothing to give you. I've never had anything to give.'

'*No.*' She shook her head. 'I'll teach you to give. I won't lose you to – to a ghost from the past.' I'll be strong for you. I'll love you. I'll make you love me. She didn't say it because she didn't have to. Now, she was crying. Crying not in compassion but in fury and determination. He saw her set, trembling mouth, the clenching of her uninjured hand. He read her thoughts in her face. Strong thoughts. A strong face. Tears blurred her beauty but in ugliness he saw a vision of something crude and almost savage – the naked force which he had always imagined behind her smooth exterior. He found her naive, pathetic, terrifying, indomitable. 'I won't leave you,' she said. 'It doesn't matter about – about anything. I won't let you down.'

'How moving.' He struggled for sarcasm – for any way out of this confusion. 'Too sweet of you.' He knew it did not have his usual edge.

'Oh shut up.' She snapped. 'You can't hurt me. Not any more. Don't you *see*?'

They stared at each other across the table. Presently, almost without realising it, he reached for her hand. Her fist unclenched; he gripped her slackened fingers until she winced with pain. But she did not attempt to draw them away.

'I love you.' This time, she said it.

Perhaps because it was easier, he did not let go of her hand.

Chapter Ten

'I've never told anyone before,' Alisdair said.

It was the first week in February. Theresa's suitcases were piled in the living room, her clothes hung in the wardrobe. Her collection of wholewheat pasta fell out of one of the kitchen cupboards every time you opened the door. The fridge, so long empty or inhabited only by bottles of tonic and occasional cultures of penicillin, was newly stocked with cottage cheese, St Ivel Gold, skimmed milk, unsweetened orange juice. In the bathroom, further health food concoctions in decorative jars testified to beauty-conscious femininity. Alisdair had never lived with a girl before and he was not yet sure if he liked it. Perhaps that was why he had started to drink – 'To celebrate,' he said – and in due course to talk. The presence of Theresa, not as an old friend or an overnight lover but as a part of his environment, little bits of Theresa scattered all over the flat, her ornaments on his mantelpiece (he had no ornaments), her Eysenck and Popper on his bookshelves, her voice on his answering machine, all this threw him off balance, leaving him disorientated and somehow vulnerable. He knew that even if she left a week later the safe shell of his isolation had been fractured for good. Once, inspired by a sort of contained panic, he might have tried to repair the damage, using little gestures of withdrawal, silences, monosyllables; but not this time. He had invited her into his life and now, having begun, he felt suddenly that it would be folly not to go on. The situation (or the alcohol) induced in him a kind of recklessness; he found himself telling her about other girls he had known, ships that bumped in the night, commitments he had not made. Actresses and would-be actresses, fellow students at college, fellow hippies at school. And somewhere along the line, Elaine Gisborne. Odd how clearly he could still visualise her, with her speckled-egg complexion and her boyish sexy body and her daunting reputation. He told Theresa about the night he had not visited her and – with a sort of wry contempt for the Grand Tragedies of adolescence – about standing on the bridge contemplating suicide. And, one drink and two cigarettes later, he told her why.

She was lying on her stomach beside him, with the pillow under her breasts. She half turned towards him, and he sensed rather than saw the expression of vivid horror on her face. He could not look at her directly. 'But – what did you *do*?'

Do. The operative word. Theresa, he thought, would have stood up and screamed, charged in like Lassie on the warpath, run back to the party yelling Rape! and Murder! and anything else that came to mind. She would not have lain there and watched. He must have been drunk or mad to tell her. Perhaps that was why he had never told anyone, because in the telling he relived to the full the shame of that resolute inertia. Time had not healed or dulled it, only covered it up. He wondered if it would change her feelings for him, if she would decide not to stay after all, and he realised – belatedly – that although he was not happy or settled he did not want her to go just yet.

'Do?' There was no point in dressing it up. 'Nothing. I suppose I was paralysed – petrified – rooted to the spot. There are plenty of convenient phrases, aren't there? I did nothing. I didn't try to stop it and I didn't go for help. I just – lay there.' He paused, glanced at her, continued with harsh flippancy: 'I could always plead drunkenness, couldn't I? Maybe that would get me off. "The witness was incapacitated by an excessive intake of alcohol and illegal substances." All bullshit, but it might pass in court. A whitewash for cowardice and inaction. I did nothing because – I did nothing. I lay in the grass like a cow-pat and watched Johnny Sachs having fun.'

Theresa said, awkwardly: 'You mustn't blame yourself.' (I might have known she would come up with that line, Alisdair thought.) 'You were only seventeen, weren't you? I expect you were in shock. There's probably a medical explanation for it. Anyway, you couldn't have done much against three of them.' And: 'Even if you'd gone back to the party I daresay everyone would have been too smashed to understand what you were talking about.'

She looked, Alisdair thought, muddled, earnest, not quite comfortable with herself or with him. He ought to have been relieved at her attitude, but he wasn't. 'You've explained everything nicely, haven't you?' he said. 'Don't make excuses for me. I've tried that myself often enough. I should have *done* something. The next day, I should have told my brother, gone to the police, made a statement. I couldn't – no, not couldn't. Didn't. I felt as if I'd been living in a sewer without noticing it. And then one day I woke up and smelled the shit. Johnny stank. I stank. Everything stank. I'd been such a fool, trailing around after him like a groupie, thinking him so bloody wonderful. I felt like an accomplice.'

'But he *was* wonderful,' Theresa said unexpectedly, 'in a ghastly sort of way. I remember seeing him on stage when I was fourteen or fifteen. He was incredibly wild and sexy and magnetic. When you're that age, you're very susceptible to that sort of thing. Glamour and charisma. You know. And being close to him, seeing him so often, it must have been that much worse. You don't have to feel stupid. Getting starstruck in your teens is only natural. And after – after the rape – it must have been frightfully traumatic for you. It's a miracle you didn't become a pervert or something.'

'You're looking at me,' said Alisdair, 'as if I was an interesting case out of one of your bloody textbooks.'

'Sorry,' said Theresa. But the atmosphere had lightened. Suddenly, it was not so difficult to go on.

'I used to think I *was* a pervert; that was the trouble. I

agonised about fancying Elaine Gisborne because she had no tits.' ('Nor have I,' commented Theresa.) 'I even dreamed about *him*, once or twice. The Boy. That was how I thought of him – just the Boy. I suppose it was what you and your psychologists might call a morbid fascination. I wasn't a homosexual but I was so desperately afraid I might be. I used to catch myself looking at other boys and worry that I was beginning to find them attractive. Ludicrous, isn't it? Ludicrous and pathetic.'

'Youth,' said Theresa profoundly, 'generally is ludicrous and pathetic.' There was a pause while she thought visibly. 'What do you suppose happened to him? The Boy, I mean.'

'I don't know. I've always wondered. I used to read the papers from cover to cover looking for anything that might connect. Not just sexual assaults – children gone missing or playing truant from school or even dead. None of them seemed to fit. It was difficult because I wasn't sure how old he was – maybe ten or eleven, maybe in his early teens. Girls of fourteen are definitely women, but fourteen-year-old boys can still look like kids. And – I hadn't seen him properly. It was very dark in the lane.'

'Perhaps,' Theresa suggested tentatively, 'it wasn't – I mean, they didn't actually . . . perhaps he wasn't as badly hurt as – as you thought?'

'No,' Alisdair said. 'There was some moonlight. I couldn't see *him* – he was lying on his face – but what they were doing was . . . sufficiently clear. Anyway, I could hear them talking. Encouraging each other. Johnny's voice was distinctive. There was no chance of a mistake.'

'When you think about it,' said Theresa after a few moments, 'it really is extraordinary. Even if his parents were out, he couldn't – *surely* – just sneak in and have a bath and be more or less normal when they got back? Nobody could.'

'I know.'

'There must have been something in the papers that you missed. Maybe it was attributed to someone else. If there was a child molested in the area –'

'There wasn't. I thought of that. I used to fantasise that he wasn't real, that he was some paranormal manifestation – a projection of their lust. My own late-night horror film. Idiotic, wasn't it? He was real enough. They say you can smell fear. I never believed it before but I smelt fear that night, human fear. It's a very unghostly smell.'

'Strange,' Theresa said, musing. And she added, inevitably, 'I wonder where he is now.'

Thinking it over afterwards, Alisdair came to the conclusion that, clichéd though it might be, he did feel marginally easier for having unburdened himself. Bringing his memories out into the open could not change their ugliness, but ugliness seen and faced is always less terrible than a hidden ugliness which preys on the imagination via the subconscious. And although he was not freed from guilt he found that now he could accept it and try to place it in perspective. He dreamed of the Boy, one night not long after, but the immediacy of violence and terror had gone; it was a dreamlike dream, a slow-motion action replay of something long over, where he floated just outside the ring of darkness and moonlight, disembodied, uninvolved. Then the Boy got up and came towards him and Alisdair saw he was no longer a boy but a girl with a freckled confident face and pale unshapely limbs. Suddenly he knew he was dreaming. He struggled to wake up, feeling himself sinking, drowning, suffocating under endless layers of sleep. The dream vanished and he fought for consciousness for a millionth of a second that lasted a small eternity. And then with a final, gigantic effort that seemed to drain all his strength he broke through into real darkness. Sleep and struggle drained away; his pulse was slow and even; he opened his eyes. Beside him, Theresa lay sleeping deeply. In the past, he had always disliked waking in the night to find a stranger in his bed; but Theresa was not a stranger and he registered her presence with a pleasure that was close to relief. He turned towards her, putting his arms around her. She stirred, mumbled, resettled herself in his embrace; but she did not wake. Alisdair lay for some time, feeling unexpectedly peaceful, before he slid back into unconsciousness.

Perhaps it was because of this new level of acceptance that, meeting Sheila Raikes at a party a few weeks later, he did not try to avoid her. He had been meeting and avoiding Sheila Raikes at parties on and off for years; given their circle of acquaintance, it was inevitable. She and Nevile had involved themselves (and their money) in the music business, the theatre – anywhere they would meet people whom they regarded as artistic and glamorous. Nevile Raikes's more dubious activities had caused him to drop out of sight but had given Sheila a certain glamour of her own, only slightly tarnished by time and a prolonged association with Alec the roadie. Her past, after all, included big business, big names, crime – the Real Thing. When she dropped Alec, lifted her face, put on padded shoulders and began dating a successful divorce lawyer twelve years her junior nothing more was required. Alisdair had known who she was since the Nevile Raikes scandal hit the newspapers and Charlie Saunders had commented with his usual brevity: 'Remember him. Went to a party there once – some place in the country. So did you. Must have been . . . '68.' Sheila had even spoken to him, over the champagne and cocktail olives, and he had backed off into the crowd with some polite comment of no particular significance. But that was in the past. Now, he found himself agreeing with someone else that Sheila was Looking Marvellous and, when she approached, he did not slip away. He told himself he had done enough slipping away in his lifetime.

Long after he wondered if it was chance, or Fate, or mere inevitability which guided the conversation. Truth, like murder, will out. 'A producer,' Sheila said. 'Of course. I've always been fascinated by the theatre. My ex-husband put a small fortune into that follow-up to *Hair* which folded in a fortnight.'

'It happens,' Alisdair murmured. 'To all of us.'

'He was a crook,' Sheila went on (once, this forthright statement had been daring; now, it was merely automatic). 'In the ordinary way of business, he was as sharp as a needle and as bent as a corkscrew. But when it came to the Arts, I think the stardust got in his eyes.'

'It happens,' Alisdair repeated. He even thought of adding: To all of us. It occurred to him that his side of the conversation lacked sparkle. You spend years avoiding someone, he reflected, and now, when you've finally summoned up the courage to talk to her, you can't find anything to say. There was a moral there somewhere.

'Tell me,' said Sheila with spurious enthusiasm, 'is there anything of yours I should have seen? I'm afraid I don't always remember who produced what.'

'Nobody does,' Alisdair responded. He named a T.V. film which she assured him she had seen and liked and went on to a comedy thriller which was opening in a month or two. Conversation became more animated. And in due course, inevitably, he mentioned Dominic.

'We're going to see his new play at the National next week,' Sheila said ('we' presumably encompassed the divorce lawyer). 'Brilliant, isn't he? Do you know, I met him once.'

'Did you?' Alisdair was polite.

'It was a few years ago now – before he was well-known. He came to see me. I remember, he looked like something the dustmen had left behind: shabby jeans, old sweatshirt, a hole in his shoe. Back in the Sixties, mind you, the effect would have been deliberate, but not these days. Artistic poverty has rather gone out of fashion, hasn't it? Now, it's all black tie and designer casuals. He didn't smoke black cigarettes then, either; just ordinary common-or-garden white ones.' Showing off, thought Alisdair, amused, that she knows he smokes black cigarettes. She had produced a packet of her own, as though the subject reminded her of a basic need; Alisdair accepted one. 'I keep meaning to give up,' she said. 'Thirty a day since I was eighteen. I ought to be dead. A friend of mine went to a hypnotist . . .'

Lung cancer. Hypnotism. In seconds Dominic would be forgotten. But Alisdair was curious. 'Why did Dominic go to see you?'

'Oh – he had an idea for a play, he said. Apparently when he was a kid he'd lived in this village – Gresham – Nevile and I had a place there, I only sold it recently. We used to have big parties . . . He said he'd seen one of them – peered through a window or something. It must have made a big impression on him.' She laughed rather self-consciously, perhaps remembering some of the things a curious child might have seen: 'He may be a genius, but I daresay he was once a nosey brat just like all the rest. Anyway, he told me he wanted to use this party as the basis for a play. A group of people at a rave-up in the Sixties; the same people fifteen years later. Married, divorced, disillusioned. You know the sort of thing. Would you believe it, he actually expected me to remember which party it was and who might have been there? *Fifteen* years ago!'

Alisdair found his cigarette had accumulated two inches of ash and tipped it carefully into a bowl of cashews. He heard his own voice asking with surprising naturalness: 'And did you?'

'I did my best. I gave him a list of the people who came to our parties regularly. Don't know if it was any use to him. Coming to think of it, it must have been just afterwards that I read about his piece at the Attic. Were you anything to do with that?'

'*Climax*,' Alisdair said automatically. 'I took it to the West End. I don't suppose –' He hesitated. 'Who – who was on that list?'

'Lord knows. Old friends. Various rock stars he had probably never heard of. Groups ditto. Kingmakers like Solloway and Ginsberg. Moneymen like de Witt.' And, eyebrows raised: 'Why?'

'I – met him at de Witt's.'

'Well,' said Sheila, with a smile that reminded him inexplicably of Lewis Carroll's crocodile, 'maybe you have me to thank.'

'Maybe.'

He could not think at all. His body continued to function, hands raising and lowering his glass, liquid wetting his lips, but inside his brain had stopped. He felt as if the ground, formerly quite solid, had suddenly disappeared from beneath his feet, and he was falling, falling, his mind spinning dizzily in space. He tried to pull himself together, to make sense of what he had heard; but he went on falling.

Sheila Raikes did not seem to notice.

'I suppose he must have scrapped the idea eventually,' she was saying. 'I daresay writers start a lot of things they don't finish. Like the rest of us. Life – real life – is full of loose ends.'

Alisdair opened his mouth, shut it again. On the facing wall, a picture came into focus. A nude lying in a field of what appeared to be phallic macaroni. It was quite irrelevant.

'Tell me,' he said at last, 'how did Dominic find you?'

'I'm sorry?'

'I just wondered – how he knew – who you were? Whose party. Whose house.'

'Oh . . . the Forders, I think. They used to rent Wellesley Court. I sold it to Jack outright last year. *She* had a baby . . . Yes, I'm sure Dominic said he'd met her. It seems likely, doesn't it? He'd have gone back to the house.'

'Yes,' Alisdair echoed. 'He'd have gone back to the house.'

Sheila Raikes looked at him strangely, almost (he thought) with suspicion. The light gleamed on her silvered cheekbones and capped teeth. She said: 'Are you all right? You sound – odd.'

'I'm all right.'

Somehow he got away.

Outside, in the car, his brain went back into action, freewheeling in a hundred different directions at once. He seemed to see a whirling mass of jigsaw-pieces, a kaleidoscope of images, incidents, memories dancing crazily in his head. Fragments of information shuffled and re-shuffled themselves and tumbled haphazardly into the pattern. Dominic and Theresa. Dominic and Ben Gamble. All those one-night stands, all those mornings-after, never fulfilled, never contented, never at peace. Dominic – smoking black cigarettes and talking about a cancer of the soul. And Dominic, growing up in the village where the Raikes had lived – what was it called? Gresham? – returning, years later, asking questions about a party. A party in the Sixties. And finally, meeting Alisdair at de Witt's, working together, becoming – briefly – friends. A feeling of shared cynicism, shared experience. Chance. Coincidence. Fate. Or was it? Sheila Raikes had sent Dominic to de Witt, to track down the original party guests. And he found – me, Alisdair thought, seeing another piece of the jigsaw fall into place. He came to look for me, and he found me. Why did he never ask the right questions? What else did he find? Who could have told him? He must have learned, in the end, that the trail was old and cold, and the phantom he pursued had gone up to Heaven in a fireball nearly a decade earlier. Alisdair could never imagine him leaving the search until he was sure of the truth. Perhaps Johnny or Bryan had told someone (as an afterthought, Alisdair remembered that Rafe was still alive). Perhaps – but it was no good. The possibilities multiplied themselves without conscious assistance from his brain, carrying him away into the realms of fantasy. He told himself that it was all impossible, that none of it could ever have happened. Dominic had had a besotted and forceful mother into whose arms he would undoubtedly have rushed, sobbing out his dreadful tale. Even had he said nothing, she could hardly have overlooked his distress or the state of his clothes. The Boy – whoever he was – had disappeared into eternity, unnoticed and unloved. Theresa had always accused Dominic's mother of too much love rather than too little. When had she died? Surely it was – 1968. Yes – 1968. And Dominic – Dominic had sat a night and a day beside the corpse, and had been found at last by a neighbour, silent and shocked.

At home, he asked Theresa again for the date of Joan Hardinge's death, making some excuse. He didn't want to confide in her. Not now. Not yet. She looked, he thought, so clean and straightforward – rather like the wholemeal bread with no additives for which she scoured London's health food shops. You are what you eat. Wholesome wholemeal Terry. She was currently having Doubts about psychology. Doubts which were clearly visible in her creased forehead and anguished eyes. Was psychology really *important*? Was it relevant? Could Freud – sacrilege – possibly be wrong? Was sex honestly the prime cause of everything?

'Everything,' Alisdair said firmly. He lay down on the sofa with his feet up on the arm and switched on the television for some late news. He was not ready for revelations. He needed to think.

There were some things he could check. A couple of days later he drove down to Gresham to revisit the house. As he went through the village he was startled and a little disquieted to find it so familiar. Children playing on the green. A clutter of little shops. A 'picturesque' pub. He remembered driving through with Charlie, the morning after the party, looking at the children, and the queasy suspension in Charlie's Citroën and Charlie himself, outlined against the window, asking no questions. Alisdair was so lost in thought he almost overshot the house.

Wellesley Court. That was it. He had forgotten the name, but it sounded right. Sufficiently pretentious. There was a short driveway and a gravel sweep on to which he duly swept. The house – or the front part, at least – looked for some reason less familiar than the village. Maybe he had never really noticed it. A large house, conservative, neither modern nor old. Virginia creeper here, clematis there. Urns. There were urns, too, at the back, he remembered. He rang the doorbell. Inside, he could hear a baby crying enthusiastically and the crash of something breaking. Presently the door opened to reveal the baby and a girl with a ski-tan and lots of hair who asked him in American what he wanted. The baby stopped crying to fix him with a baleful glare.

'Mrs Forder?'

The girl called over her shoulder 'Mrs Forder!' and the baby hesitated and then began to cry again. Alisdair was trying to recognise the entrance hall and failing. A young woman emerged from another room looking scarcely older than the girl but far less healthy, with the sort of deathly pallor that some women have before they put their make-up on. Her jeans hung loosely from twiglet hips and dyed blonde hair drooped over her face, showing about two inches of dark brown at the roots. She said: 'Can't you shut him up somehow?' and 'Take him upstairs, anyway. Give him a bottle. Change his bloody nappy. I can't stand much more of this row.'

When girl and baby had gone she turned to Alisdair with something of the candour she had once shown to Dominic. 'Babies are hell,' she confided. 'They just don't tell you. I thought it would be all right with a nanny but it isn't. I haven't even had a bath yet. How can I help you?'

He had been so preoccupied with his own emotions he hadn't thought of a story. It hadn't even occurred to him that it would be necessary. He thought wildly and pointlessly for a few seconds and then in desperation opted for the direct approach.

'Do you know – have you ever met Dominic Hardinge?'

Karen Forder looked slightly bewildered but unsuspicious. 'Dominic Hardinge. I don't think . . . '

'The playwright.'

A frown, indicating concentration. Then light dawned. 'Oh, yes! How very odd – I mean, how funny you should ask. He came here a few years ago – I forget exactly when but some friends took us to see one of his plays a year or so later. It was terribly depressing. Anyway, I remembered about him then. I'd been sitting in the garden – it was quite warm – and we sort of got chatting.'

'In the garden?'

'He was in the lane at the back, looking over the hedge. At first I wasn't quite sure what he was doing there but then he told me he used to know the people who lived in this house. Nevile and Sheila Raikes. At least – I *think* that's what he said. I can't really remember. We talked for a bit and I gave him some coffee. Was he – is he a friend of yours?'

'I knew him, Horatio,' Alisdair said.

His subsequent silence evidently gave Karen pause. She fidgeted with the door handle and looked around vaguely for assistance. Eventually she said: 'Look – please — what is all this about?'

'I'm afraid I can't tell you that.' Alisdair still hadn't thought of a story. He felt that, for Karen at any rate, it was scarcely worth the trouble. He took refuge in the language of spy thrillers. 'It's all rather confidential.'

'Confidential?' Karen, it was obvious, never read spy thrillers. 'Why is it confidential?'

'I'm afraid I can't tell you that either. Can you remember anything – *peculiar* about your conversation with Dominic?' (Now, he sounded merely theatrical – or idiotic. He decided to get away before the American nanny, or worse still the absent husband, put in an appearance. Either of them were certain to be less manageable than Karen.)

'No. No, I can't. Look –'

'He didn't mention a *party*, by any chance?'

'I don't remember. I told you, it was years ago. I want to know –'

'Thank you,' Alisdair interrupted. 'You've been very helpful.'

He got into the car and drove away, more shaken than he liked and ruefully convinced he would never make a private detective.

His other visit was to a small recording studio in South London. It was joint-owned by a tasselled Rastafarian who chain-smoked cannabis and an ageing hippy who had once played the guitar for a well-known rock group. Rafe Dunston. In the Sixties he had been tall and rakishly skinny, with high cheekbones that diverted attention from a weak chin, a full mouth and soulful spaniel eyes. Now, he was merely a thin man with thinning hair (still worn long) and a face that seemed to have no flesh on it at all except in the lips. His eyes, his chin, even his Adam's apple appeared to droop. His wife Sue was also there: Alisdair dimly recalled a slim girl hiding behind her hair, but time and marriage had given her a certain resemblance to her husband, except that in her case the intervening years had added a bottom. As for the studio, it had an air of subsisting precariously on Arts Council grants, although actually it didn't. After the depressing preliminaries required by courtesy – 'How are you? What are you doing? How's So-and-So?' – Alisdair asked, this time with rather more caution, if Dominic Hardinge had been to see them. About three years ago, he added, peering through Rafe's wispy hair to catch any trace of expression on his face.

But Rafe and Sue both looked blank – a reaction which provoked little external change. Rafe said, as if it explained everything, that neither of them were really into the theatre. Presently, in their turn, they asked him what it was all about.

'I don't know,' Alisdair said untruthfully. He wondered why, assuming he had learned the truth, Dominic had done nothing about it. Perhaps, even long dead, Johnny had stolen the scene as usual. Rafe had always been unimportant.

On the way out, he said: 'If Dominic *should* come round, let me know.' He didn't expect it. Not after three years. Unless he chose to confront Dominic himself, this was the end. And confrontation, Alisdair reflected with familiar bitterness, had never been his strong point. So that was that. He might, one day, discuss it with Theresa. One day . . .

Outside, it was raining. South London drizzle. Alisdair drove home.

Meanwhile, down in Overbridge, Faramond Hunter waited for things to change. They didn't. She slept in her room and Dominic slept in his. The bruises round his eyes went from red to purple to yellow and then disappeared and, rather more slowly, Faramond's fractured humerus mended itself. 'My arm is much better,' she pointed out one day. 'Good,' said Dominic. 'I'm fed up of writing your letters.' Which was unfair, since she had only asked him to write for her twice. He never mentioned either the accident or their subsequent conversation; indeed, sometimes she almost imagined he shrank from her. In the American magazines she had read, ideal couples always claimed the only way to solve problems was to Discuss Everything, but Dominic's soul-baring avoided danger zones and Faramond had never learnt to bare her soul at all. Their moments of true intimacy had always rested on her finding the right words at the right time; she could not risk groping for the wrong ones. She said nothing, he said nothing, and the wall that separated them at night might have been a fortress. But the more he seemed to recede from her the more she loved him, sharing in secret the fantasy of his pain and aching almost unbearably to lie with him, to give herself to him, to make him whole.

As for Dominic, he did not know which troubled him the most, his self-revelation or her declaration of love. The outward serenity which was a part of her physical make-up, something in her bone-structure rather than her spirit, defeated him: behind it he imagined not only strength but the patience of an angel and the inexorability of Nemesis. He could not resist her, could not go to her, and so he ran away – to London, to work, to another room, another bed. *Ragnarok*, opening at the National, took a good deal of his time; having once objected violently to Ben Gamble's direction he now objected violently to any other director, and spent long hours in the theatre making himself unpopular.

On the first night the critics proclaimed Dominic a major talent but said the play was not one of his major works. Set in a luxurious subterranean retreat during a nuclear war, it showed a small group of the super-privileged watching the destruction of the world upstairs on bomb-proof camera equipment while eating their way through six months' supply of caviare and champagne. They are joined at the last minute by a stranger, who turns out to be someone's long-lost brother. The play ends with everyone dead except the long-lost brother, who sits amidst the débâcle drinking champagne, wondering whether to open the ventilators and let in the radioactive fall-out since he cannot see any meaningful reason for continuing to stay alive. The comedy element, according to one critic, was not so much black as grey. Faramond, in common with most of the audience, left the theatre feeling unutterably depressed.

With *Ragnarok* left to its own devices Dominic spent a week raging over the reviews, turned the whole play into a computer game, rewrote the beginning of *Chickamungus*, tore it all up, and got drunk. After the hangover he shut himself in his study – the study that had once belonged to David Hunter – in search of inspiration. He wanted, he told Faramond in the language of Garbo, to be alone.

At Easter, Faramond flew to California. Alone. Dominic had a new idea and was working unusually fast, with (so far) no breaks for depression and no revisions. He would not tell her so much as the title (presumably he hadn't thought of one) but he said there was a part for her. However, he could not possibly go away. Not at this stage. Faramond said No, of course not, and packed her bags.

* * *

Three weeks later Faramond returned from California with a sun-tan which did not reach her face, a suitcase full of new clothes and a grim determination that this time she was going to make things work. Her parental visit had given her a sense of infinite maturity: California was the same, her mother and Sherwin were more or less the same, but she had realised on the very first evening that she herself was indefinably different. She had left a child who did as she was told and come back a grown woman whom no one told to do anything (Annalee was very careful about that). She owned a house, lived with a man, she was in love, she had problems. Maturity. She had routed Boo without effort at a breakfast party where the latter had appeared over-made-up, overdressed, dripping jewellery and dropping names. Faramond wore no jewellery (not even her antique ear-rings), refused to curl her hair, underdressed by Bruce Oldfield and mentioned Laurence Olivier only in passing. ('That serious look kind of suits her,' Sherwin commented afterwards. 'We've got to get her into something as a nun.') It was only a little victory, won for her mother, but it was the first time she had even been conscious of competing. She knew a feeling of limitless power and potential out of all proportion to the circumstances, as though the whole unknown unimaginable future was a ball of plasticine between her hands, waiting to be shaped according to her will – a feeling that comes only when you are very young, or stoned out of your mind on hallucinatory drugs. Back in England, she believed she could manage anything. Even Dominic.

He met her at the airport with the news that he had had his licence endorsed for drunk driving and protested only automatically when she insisted on taking the wheel on the grounds of legality. Victory number one. That night, they went out to dinner and came home in a taxi. He kissed her at the bedroom door and although he drew away she knew he was shivering from the contact. Inside her own room she undressed slowly in front of the long mirror, studying herself with all the solemnity of a bride on the eve of her wedding. Her sun-tan disappeared in the soft light and her body looked pale and almost colourless. Not the body of a virgin, narrow-hipped and small-breasted, but a woman's body, suitably curved and, had she but known it, a little incongruous beneath her grave young face and schoolgirl hair. For a moment she cupped her right breast, exploring, felt the nipple soft and then hard under her fingers. Her expression did not change. Then she wrapped herself in the negligée which she had bought on Rodeo Drive, observed with faint satisfaction that it concealed nothing, and switched off the light. Outside, some animal – she thought it was a hedgehog – called shrilly. She waited in the darkness, counting her heartbeats, before moving towards the door.

Dominic was thinking about her coming to him when she came. He imagined her materialising at his bedside, naked and deadly: a siren without a voice, a succubus with silken muscles who would wind him in her arms and strangle him. The image filled him with a fearful desire. In her absence the Faramond he was writing about – the character in his play – had merged with the reality until the two could no longer be separated, and when he saw her standing there it was like the fulfilment of every twisted dream. Moonlight through the open curtains caught the silver threads in the negligée, clinging to her like a spider's web. Slowly she took it off, slowly she climbed in beside him. The shadows of her hair hid her face. Don't speak, he prayed, feeling her breath on his cheek. Kiss. Touch. Feel. But don't speak. Don't even sigh. Drink me with your mouth, tangle me in your limbs, absorb me in your body. But don't whisper. Don't mention love. Don't break the spell.

But Faramond was neither siren nor succubus. There was a moment – a perfect moment – when they lay together, breast to breast, thigh to thigh, his erection hard and strong between them. And then inexperience betrayed her: she faltered, fumbled, lost momentum; he sensed uncertainty and the magic died. She did not speak but it hardly mattered. The hair slid off her face, showing too much of her expression. And with the glimpse of her vulnerability came the terrible understanding of his own. Inadequacy and the fear of inadequacy, the obscenity of desire, the blood-guilt of love. He remembered Sandy, and suddenly the body pressed against his became flesh, soft and clammy. He pushed her off almost violently, turned away from her. Faramond lay on her back, shaking. Neither of them spoke. Neither of them slept. Hours later the first drab glimmer of dawn came through the window and found them there, unmoving.

Afterwards Faramond was to wonder if she was a little mad the next day. She was in a state of ice-cold, clear-headed, conscious sanity which is almost always a sign of incipient madness. Her body functioned on automatic pilot; her emotions were in suspension. She knew it was important to think, to resolve, to be practical and constructive – above all not to feel, lest the agony and humiliation which must surely be just beneath the surface proved too much for her. If she had been able to break down, to sob herself into oblivion, better still, if she had been as patient as Dominic feared or hoped, perhaps things might have been different. Perhaps. But Faramond was young and desperate, with all the patience of a Romeo rushing eagerly into suicide. She was filled with a terrible determination, with shamelessness, with the courage of lemmings.

When she saw the magazine the article leaped into her ice-cold mind like a message direct from fate. The magazine was one of several she had brought from the States and the article was about the treatment of rape victims. A new organisation was confronting them with their attackers, encouraging them to unburden themselves of pent-up hatred and despair, to insult, abuse, condemn, ideally, to work things out. Therapy. A magic word for which her California background had given Faramond a proper reverence. She would have to try therapy. Had she known herself a little better, she would have realised that she was the gambler who has lost all but his shirt, staking his whole life on the turn of a card. Win or die. But she did not know.

Despite her initial resolution, it was over a week before she had decided exactly what to do. Dominic shut himself in the study and worked furiously at his play. They met at meal-times and spoke like strangers. It was worse than a nightmare because there was no dreamlike fade-out, only a grey reality that impressed itself upon Faramond in ugly detail. What Dominic thought or felt she did not try to find out. When the moment came she was aiming for shock tactics – a dreadful gamble that the barriers would come down and behind them she would find the Dominic she wanted. She did not think of failure. The gambler never does.

She went to see Marten de Witt the day after Dominic told her he had finished the play. It seemed like the right moment. Although she was only semi-conscious of his feelings, she sensed vaguely that to break the thread of his concentration, even for necessary therapy, would be – in his eyes – unforgiveable. But now the play was completed and he had immersed himself in computer games. Another form of running away. She took the car and drove to London.

It had not occurred to her that de Witt might be away. She had neither written nor 'phoned, preferring – that phrase again – shock tactics, so filled with the totality of her obsession that the possible absence of a vital participant had never crossed her mind. She stood on the doorstep, staring blankly at the maid who had answered the bell. She was suddenly aware that she was trembling, though whether from tension or cold she did not know. The maid – Spanish this time – said Mr de Witt would be back tomorrow and would she like to see the Señora?

'The Señora?' Faramond murmured automatically, further bewildered by assorted linguistic titles.

Señora Lavalle.

Faramond, panicking, said No, no, she wouldn't see Señora Lavalle, and she would come back tomorrow without fail. She got into the car and made her way to the home of her Hunter relations, who (fortunately) were in residence. At least their company would be a distraction. She had tried to rehearse the scene with de Witt in her mind several times but imagination failed her; she had no idea what she would say, what he would say, whether he would respond to pleading or threats – or, as seemed increasingly probable, merely turn away in stolid disinterest. Another day to wait was another day of speculation, nail-biting, suspense. And with her arrival in London had come the first faint glimmering of returning sanity. Perhaps it was the crowds – turbulent crowds of happy, unhappy, more or less normal people, busy with their own private comedies and tragedies, effectually reducing her little life and all its problems to those of a termite in a hill teeming with a million other termites. Whatever the reason, a still, small voice inside her had begun to whisper that this was obsession, possession, madness; she must abandon the directives of a demon fate and go back to Overbridge. But the mere mention of Overbridge brought her thoughts to an abrupt halt. In Overbridge there were no rushing, hustling, reassuring crowds. In Overbridge there was Dominic, bent over the computer with a pale, closed-in face, separate bedrooms, loneliness, a negligée, worn once, that she would never wear again. She could not go back. Besides, to turn aside now savoured of cowardice, and Faramond was brave beyond fear, and beyond sanity.

The following afternoon around four o'clock she presented herself at the house again. De Witt, she was told, was not back yet; apparently his 'plane had been delayed. Señora Lavalle was out but would return shortly. Faramond considered for a few moments. She had no desire to see Catherine but the thought of having to go away and come back yet again was unbearable. Somehow, she was convinced that if she did not find de Witt this time she would never find him at all; she visualised herself returning fruitlessly to a house where he was always denied, until her nerve eroded and her determination sagged, and in the end she gave up altogether. And Catherine, despite her superficial glamour, had generally impressed her as a curiously negative personality; being polite to her for a little while would be possible if not easy. Faramond said she would wait.

Catherine came in about half an hour later. She had evidently been indulging in some form of physical exercise – squash, Faramond guessed, or maybe aerobics – since she was wearing a dark green velour tracksuit and little or no make-up. Without her usual warpaint her eyes appeared unemphatic, her lips blurred. She looked much younger and less sophisticated than she had seemed in Scotland. When she greeted Faramond her manner was civil but hesitant, as though she was not sure whether the unexpected visitor should be welcomed or ignored. 'Concepcion told me,' she said, 'you wanted to see Marten?'

Faramond said: 'Yes' and waited for the inevitable questions.

But Catherine's curiosity was obviously little more than an afterthought. She wandered about the room, glimpsed her profile in a mirror, lit herself a cigarette. Her 'Why?', when it came, sounded purely automatic.

'It's business,' Faramond said firmly, having prepared her excuse. 'I hope you don't mind my waiting. It's very urgent.'

What business Faramond might have with de Witt Catherine evidently neither knew nor cared. She said: 'I suppose it's all right,' and then, recollecting her social formula, switched on a smile and made suitable enquiries about Faramond's arm, Dominic, the success of *Ragnarok*. 'I'm afraid I missed it,' she murmured (it was still on), 'but I heard the reviews were wonderful.'

'Actually,' said Faramond ruthlessly, 'they weren't. But you can go and see for yourself if you want to. It's at the National.'

Catherine said: 'Oh, the *National*,' as if this explained everything. Possibly it did.

Faramond, realising that it was her turn, tried to think of something about which she could make polite enquiries and came up against the unmentionable barrier of Catherine's marital problems.

In due course Catherine ordered tea.

The tea, when it arrived, was Lapsang Soochong, with a choice of milk or lemon and silver tongs protruding from a bowl of lump sugar. Faramond took a slice of lemon and two sugars since she felt that, mentally if not physically, she was going to need the energy. Catherine also had lemon and a lacing of the latest natural sweetener. A small plate of biscuits put in a belated appearance, presumably for the benefit of the visitor since, Faramond now remembered, Catherine watched her weight with the devoted absorption of a financier monitoring the Share Index. The tea-cups were very elegant –

the sort that seem to be standing on tiptoe in an attempt to get out of the saucer – and the spoons were silver and Faramond felt that cucumber sandwiches were present in spirit if not in fact. She tried to drink her tea quietly and failed. So did Catherine. Perhaps to cover up, they both started to speak at once.

'After you,' said Faramond, thinking that with anyone else the incident would have broken the ice. But with Catherine there seemed to be no ice to break. No humour, no reserve, no persona at all. She wondered how much longer it would be before de Witt returned.

'Did you – ' Catherine paused ' – did you call yesterday?'

'Yes,' Faramond said. 'I didn't ask to come in. The maid said Mr de Witt – Marten – wasn't back till today so I didn't see any point in troubling you.'

Catherine murmured something noncommittal which might have been meant for a disclaimer. 'I thought it was another reporter,' she volunteered unexpectedly. 'We've had them on the door-step incessantly ever since we announced the engagement. Only usually it's me they want to see.'

'Engagement?'

'Oh yes. Marten and I are engaged. Didn't you know? It was in Dempster's column last week.'

Faramond said nothing. The rumours about Catherine and de Witt had been going on so long without supporting evidence that she had come to believe them groundless. She had even wondered, once or twice, if de Witt *chose* to play the role of devoted friend, in order to keep the gossip-mongers from any inkling of the truth. Using Catherine – Catherine with her beautiful face and her dramatic past and her media coverage – as a shield against the world, against himself. And now – he was going to marry her. Catherine who never got it right. Had she lain all night beside Edmond Lavalle, as Faramond had lain with Dominic, humiliated and untouched? Had she turned to de Witt for security or love? Surely not love, thought Faramond, in whose youthful eyes de Witt had no looks and less charm. She glanced up, and found her hostess was watching her with an air of expectation. She's waiting for me to congratulate her, Faramond realised in horror. Suddenly, her secret knowledge had become a huge and terrifying responsibility, something which affected not only herself and Dominic but other lives and other futures. But she could not tell Catherine. Sophisticated, characterless, unapproachable Catherine. Even without her make-up, it was impossible to talk to Catherine.

Faramond said, playing for time: 'Your annulment worked out okay, then?' *Could* an annulment work out okay?

Catherine, her eyes roving round the room as they always did, even when it was empty, as if in search of someone more interesting, murmured a vague affirmative.

'When – when are you and Marten going to get married?' Faramond asked desperately.

'Oh, six months or so. No hurry.'

'In a church?'

'Of course,' said Catherine. 'I always get married in church.'

It was impossible to tell if there was any irony intended, Faramond reflected. Catherine's face was as devoid of humour as of all other qualities. But it was no use: Faramond could not convince herself that it would be all right just to let it go. With a horrible premonition of impending embarrassment, she said in an unsteady voice: 'Are you – do you – *love* him?'

Catherine stared at her. For once, her reaction was everything Faramond had expected: incredulity, distaste, an innate British shrinking from the discussion of vulgar emotion. 'I beg your pardon?'

'Do you love him?' Faramond repeated staunchly. For all David Hunter's influence, she was not truly British.

Catherine said: 'What an extraordinary question.' The words were suitably off-putting, but the tone was blank, as though she suddenly found herself at a loss, and some of her poise appeared to have deserted her. For the first time Faramond realised she must be little more than thirty, not really a sophisticated woman but a girl who went on making the same mistakes over and over again. It came to her abruptly that *she* was the strong character; Catherine, under the surface, was defensive and unsure.

She said: 'You must tell me. Please. I wouldn't ask if it wasn't important.'

'I'm afraid I – '

'*Please*.'

Catherine hesitated, looked down at her lap, where her hands toyed automatically with a huge ruby which was presumably her latest engagement ring. When she looked up again, her face was quite different. All her outward responses – politeness, surprise, restraint – seemed to have shredded away like petals from a dying flowerhead: what remained was another being, naked, hard and defenceless. 'No,' she said in another voice, a voice edged with broken glass, 'I *don't* love him. Does it matter? And what the hell has it to do with you?'

'If you don't love him,' Faramond persisted, ignoring the question, 'why are you marrying him?'

'Because he loves me. That's why I married Jonas Virgo, and he made me very happy.' She paused, briefly, as though taking a deep breath. Then she went on: 'I married Edmond because I loved him. When I was seventeen, I married Johnny Sachs because I loved him. As far as I'm concerned, falling in love is always – bad judgment. I want to be happy again. I want to feel *safe*. I've known Marten since my marriage to Johnny: he adores me, he always has. He's rich and successful and sensible. He won't hurt me, he won't let anyone else hurt me. All I really want – *all* I want – is never to be hurt again.'

It was an extraordinary speech for Catherine who only spoke small talk, but Faramond was past noticing. Too agonised to think, she said the first thing that came into her head. 'You can't do it.'

'Of course I can. What do you mean?'

Faramond explained what she meant.

Chapter Eleven

Faramond had gone before Marten de Witt returned.

'You'd better leave now,' Catherine had said. 'I must fix my face. I look all blotchy and swollen – like one of those posters about battered wives. Damn you, why did you have to catch me with no make-up on? I never cry with my make-up on.'

'Never?' Faramond asked, fascinated.

'Not since Johnny's funeral. I managed to shed a tear or two at the graveside – you know, elegantly, without smudging. Then when I got home I shut myself in my room and sobbed and sobbed. We were still wearing false eyelashes in those days and I cried mine halfway down my face. You can't imagine the mess.'

'You must have loved him a lot,' Faramond said rather blankly.

'I loathed him.' Catherine was still in her mood of brutal frankness. 'I was crying because I was so bloody thankful to be out of it all.'

'You loved him once.'

'Yes. Once. Maybe you have to love somebody once, in order to loathe them properly. Anyway, he spoiled me for loving anybody else. I tried with Edmond – I thought he was gentle and different. *Different!* Like hell! I should have known it would't be any good. Johnny spoiled everything he touched. He was like that.'

Yes, he was like that, thought Faramond. He touched Dominic, too, and Dominic was – spoiled. But I won't let it end that way. Johnny Sachs is dead. I'm alive, alive and strong. I can fight. She looked at Catherine – polite, perfect Catherine – and saw red angry eyes, smeared cheeks, a tremulous hand holding a cigarette. It seemed to her that in the last half-hour the world had turned inside out.

She said: 'Describe him to me.'

'You must go.' Catherine hardly heard. 'You don't want to see Marten any more. I need to fix my face.'

'I'll go when I'm ready.' Faramond stayed put. 'Describe Johnny to me. I want – to picture him.'

'Hell, how can I? Look at a photo. There are enough of them. He was ugly. He was beautiful. He had a big mouth and a big cock. When he overdid the drugs and the drink they both went flabby. He liked hurting people. When I fell in love with him I thought he did it because he was vulnerable. Underneath the toughness and the sex appeal and the superstar image I thought he was just a sweet defenceless little boy. It was my own special discovery – as if I had found the key to something secret and infinitely precious. I daresay you think the same about your Dominic, don't you? He's so vulnerable *underneath*. Shall I tell you something? We're *all* vulnerable. You and me and Johnny and Dominic and everyone on this earth. We're all weak and defenceless and frightened. It's no big deal. When you're very young and stupid you find a hidden weakness in some guy and you think it's magical. It isn't. We're all the bloody same.'

'Even Marten de Witt?'

'I daresay. What does it matter? I'm not in love with him. I shan't find out.' She lit another cigarette from the first. 'Please go.'

At the door, she told Faramond: 'Marten might ask you to the wedding – I don't know. Don't come. I don't want to see you again.'

Faramond nodded. So it was true, she thought: Catherine could not really confide in anyone. No friendships, no real relationships, just ceaseless concealment behind an immaculate façade. What else had Johnny done, to destroy her so utterly?

But she couldn't help Catherine. She had enough to do, helping Dominic. She got into the car and drove slowly back to her cousins' house.

Later, she rang Dominic. It was impossible, of course, to say anything over the 'phone. 'I'll be back tomorrow,' she told him. 'I'm not sure when.' He didn't say he missed her but she thought he sounded a little desolate, as though he had not been quite certain whether she was coming back at all. But maybe that was just wishful thinking on her part. She wondered why, without any real evidence, Dominic had been so eager to believe that it was de Witt he was looking for. He had gone to de Witt's house, surely, to find out the truth – and the truth had been there, if he had only spoken to the right people, asked the right questions. Dimly, she was aware of danger, of shadows behind shadows, of a darkness in Dominic's soul which no light would ever penetrate. But Faramond was a believer in the power of light; she still had faith that the Truth would solve all things. Resolutely – she was always resolute – she pushed any doubts to the back of her mind. She did not understand that for Dominic it was not the fact behind the fantasy which mattered but the fantasy behind the fact, the shadow behind the substance – a core of chaos and darkness at the heart of all reason, the dream that underlies all reality. In Marten de Witt he had found a figure he could fit to the shape of his nightmares – of dullness, he had made inscrutability, of heavy courtesy, silent threat. He was a writer, a fantasiser, a spinner of imaginary webs. What he would make of Johnny Sachs, dead and cold and out of reach, Faramond could not have guessed and never thought to try. Their whole relationship, the very love with which she hoped to save him, was merely another product of his fantasy, another dream out of disorder – and like the worst of dreams it was about to come true.

But Faramond was blind to any warning signs. After calling Dominic she made herself a cup of coffee, declined to go out with her cousins, and settled down to think. Johnny Sachs was dead. Bryan Solloway was dead. Who was the third man? Ralph something, Catherine had said. A former member of The Group. She hadn't known his surname. Faramond cast round in her mind for an acquaintance in England who might be an expert on the music of the Sixties. Eventually, she thought of Ricky Verelst. At least he knew about music, even if it wasn't the right kind. She caught him on his way out.

'No idea,' he said cheerfully. 'Yes, of course I've heard of The Group. Charlie Saunders was the drummer. God knows what happened to any of them. It's like the elephants: you know – where do rock musicians go to die? Anyway, whence the interest? You're far too young to remember the Sixties scene. Even I'm too young to remember it properly . . . Damn; here's the taxi. Look, why don't you try – '

The next morning, three 'phone calls later, Faramond had found what she wanted. Rafe Dunston. Married – possibly still married. Running a recording studio south of the river. The last call had given her the address.

It was past noon when she got there.

Around three, Sue Dunston arrived at the recording studio to be greeted with the information that her husband had driven off just after lunch with a beautiful girl. He hadn't said where he was going or when he would be back. He looked agitated.

'But he doesn't know any beautiful girls,' said Sue Dunston, bewildered. 'Who was she?'

The bespectacled young woman who made coffee and occasionally manned the reception desk said she talked like an American and had a funny name.

'We don't know any Americans,' said Sue. 'At least, only Jack Rotweiler, and he's a man. He might have a daughter, I suppose . . . are you *sure* Rafe didn't leave any message? I'm giving a supper party tonight, and . . . '

No, said the receptionist with relish, no message. 'He was very upset,' she reiterated. 'Very upset. I couldn't help overhearing – ' she hesitated, but Sue merely looked anxious so she went on ' – they were talking in the office you see, and the door wasn't shut properly. Anyway, they were talking pretty loudly. *He* said he wouldn't go with her, and *she* said he must go, he owed it to someone or other. I think it was . . . Dominic. Yes, that was it. Dominic. I think it was this Dominic they were going to see.'

'We don't know any Dominic,' said Sue, with slightly less certainty this time. Somewhere, recently, she had heard the name Dominic. If only she could remember . . .

'Rafe was very upset,' repeated the receptionist, evidently seeing herself as a sort of Greek chorus. She added, rather more practically: 'Why don't you go into the office and sit down for a bit and I'll bring you some coffee?'

Over coffee, Sue remembered. She consulted the office telephone book which, as a result of his visit, contained Alisdair's number, and then agonised for some time over whether or not to make the call. In the end she rang, only to be answered by a polite but unresponsive machine with a bleep. She left a message after the bleep and rang off.

Faramond reached Overbridge in the late afternoon. It was one of those days with white colourless sky and no sun, a day of bland light and pale shadows. There was no wind and the air was neither cold nor warm. A nothing kind of day. The English spring – not to mention summer, autumn, and winter – is full of such days. Overbridge looked innocuous and civilised, polite well-kept houses sitting behind box-hedge and privet-hedge, hiding no secrets. It was a place, thought Faramond without originality, where – surely – nothing dreadful or dramatic could ever happen. She had lived there for twelve years as a child, going to school in a big town nearby, making friends with most of whom she had since effortlessly lost touch. Nothing had happened then. Picnics and children's parties and country walks but nothing out of the ordinary. Once, when she was ten, she and some other girls had seen a flasher in a neighbouring wood. They had laughed and pointed and the flasher had run away in horror. Sometimes, she had had nightmares (the worst ones had been about wolves), but she had always woken in the end and her nanny or her father – occasionally even her mother – had been there if she needed reassurance.

And now – now she had come back, seeking peace and security again, bringing her dread and drama with her. Only somehow, despite everything she had learnt, it was difficult to believe in dread and drama here in Overbridge. She stole a glance at Rafe's profile, the sunken jaw and frightened eyes, and was reminded suddenly of the flasher who had run away. A petty, scared, rabbit-like man racked, not by enormous guilt and searing remorse, but by cowardice and embarrassment. Maybe both dread and drama had vanished years ago, with the ideals and orgies of the Sixties, with Johnny Sachs, with Bryan Solloway, exploding into eternity or seeping out of a whisky bottle, leaving only the dregs, cold ashes, the scrapings of the past. When Dominic knows the truth, Faramond thought, when he sees Rafe, then he will realise that it is finished. We will be able to start again.

At the house, she put the car in the garage and Rafe in the sitting room. Dominic, as she had known he would be, was in the study. He had fixed up his computer on David Hunter's desk and was engaged in watching little pink men jumping over walls pursued by bright green Martians. He scarcely glanced up when Faramond came in.

'Dominic, switch that thing off. I have to talk to you.'

He glanced up at that, startled. She had not said 'Hello' or 'I'm back' or any of the things he had expected. She was leaning on top of the computer and her whole attitude, even her voice was different. There was no more serenity, no quiet self-containment – none of the qualities he had invented for his own private Galatea. This Faramond was eager, determined, desperate, vivid. Even her pallor was intensified. She had always seemed to him the kind of girl who would never make a scene, never scream or rail at him; but this bright-eyed creature was a stranger and inwardly he shrank.

She said: 'Dominic, you must listen to me.'

'I'm listening.' But his eyes strayed back to the blank computer screen as though he were still far away. She did not understand that he was afraid of what he had seen in her face.

'I've been thinking a lot lately. About us, and everything. I've known, ever since that night when – when –' inwardly she cursed herself for her hesitation, her incoherence, the fluent lines she had rehearsed and forgotten '– ever since that night we didn't make love, I've known we can't go on like this. Living in the same house but not touching, not talking to each other, not *communicating*.'

Dominic snapped: 'I'll leave.'

'*No*. You can't just run away all the time. Don't you see, it won't solve anything. Wherever you go, you'll still take yourself with you.' (Where had she read that?) 'Anyway, I won't let you run away any more. I love you. You can't just walk out on that. You've got to face things. You've got to look at what happened – take it out of the shadows – see it in the daylight. Because you've always tried to repress the memory it's grown and grown the way things do in the dark – got all out of proportion. You remember huge bogeymen – monsters of superhuman strength and cruelty – but they were only *men*, Dominic. They were stronger than you because you were a child, they were cruel because they were drunk, but they were also human and – and weak and maybe even pathetic. You're a man now. You're as strong as they are. You have to look at them in the *light*. Hate them if it makes you feel better. Get all the hate and fear and darkness out of your system. Then –'

'Then what?' His voice was bitter and hard but underneath she terrified him. 'Then everything will be all right? Then we'll all live happily ever after? Is that it?'

Faramond looked down, shaking her head, hot tears stinging her eyes like acid. 'I don't know. I don't know. But we have to *try*.' She said 'we' because it sounded less accusing than 'you'. 'All you've done, ever since it happened, is run away. You didn't even make any real effort to find out the truth. You got halfway there and came up against Marten de Witt, looming in your path like – like King Kong in a business suit, and you turned and ran away again. But it wasn't de Witt. He's nothing but a big lump of stocks and shares. Anyway, he's going to marry Catherine – '

'What do you mean: *it wasn't de Witt*? How do you know?' And, no longer bitter and hard, the voice of naked horror: '*What have you done?*'

She faced him, defiant, hardly aware of his fear. 'I went to see him. De Witt. I had to.'

'You *saw* him? You mean, you actually *asked* – '

'I didn't ask him anything. He wasn't there.' She went on, speaking very quickly to get it all out in a rush: 'I went to see him and I sat down to wait and Catherine Lavalle came in. And we had tea and then she said she was going to marry him. I had to tell her, don't you understand? I couldn't let her marry him without telling her. Not after Edmond Lavalle and Paul Derigueur and everything. And she said it wasn't true. I thought she was just being stubborn but she said she *knew* it wasn't true. She looked – I can't describe how she looked. A bit like somebody seeing a ghost, only – no, more like a ghost seeing a live human. Kind of pale and shocked. She said she knew it wasn't true because she knew what had really happened. She said her husband had boasted of it to her on their wedding night. *Boasted* of raping a boy. Her first husband – the pop star. Johnny Sachs.' And then, when he didn't say anything: 'Johnny Sachs. You know, The Group. Do you remember . . .?'

His face was averted; he gave a strange little shiver. 'I remember.'

There was a silence while he seemed to try and take it in. She wondered whether the shadows in his mind were shifting, thinning out at last or merely re-grouping, forming different shapes, different memories. She waited for him to speak and when he didn't she hurried on, determined to get the whole story over and done with. 'The other two were Bryan Solloway – his manager – and one of the guitarists. Catherine said, they wouldn't have done it without Johnny. She said he used to go crazy sometimes and he made other people crazy too. I suppose – that was how he affected audiences. He must have been a little mad. Too much success, too much dope, too much everything. They were all on drugs in those days. It was the Sixties.' In the Sixties, her tone implied, anything was possible. An era of pop festivals and peace demos, of long hair and free love and irresponsibility. To Faramond, it was literally a lifetime ago. History.

Still Dominic said nothing. He said nothing for so long she began to wonder if he had understood her. She did not realise how tense she was until she saw the white knuckles on her fingers, gripping his arm. She must be hurting him but he did not react. At last he whispered something. It sounded like 'dead'.

'Dominic? *Dominic*?'

'He's dead.'

'Johnny Sachs . . .? Yes, he's dead. They said it was an accident. Bryan Solloway's dead – drink and heart. What they did was terrible but they were just men and men die. You're *alive*. You have to start living – living with your whole self, not just on paper – in plays – in fantasies. You can't go on hiding from reality. Life is wonderful! Come out of the dark. *Live.* Live – with *me*.' Urgency filled her like rage: her body trembled from the strength of it. Words she had half-practised, ideas she had half-formed, scraps of magazine articles, film scripts, T.V. soaps all came tumbling out together, jumbled with eagerness, incoherent with sincerity. Tears brimmed her eyes and ran down her face, disfiguring her. Her pallor was gone; angry blotches smeared her cheeks. Dominic stared at her as if she was scarcely human. 'Come out of the dark!' she repeated, furious, desperate. And then: 'Dom – say something. Please. *Say* something . . .'

His face was still pale and tearless. Shut in. There was light in his eyes but it was reflected light, the limpid daylight from beyond the window. She did not know that he was seeing before him yet another monster – a monster of his own creation – a statue-come-to-life with its bleeding heart and sinews of stone. But reality, as always, was infinitely more traumatic than imagination. Reality clutched at him, cried over him, begging, demanding, reaching out inexorably for something he could not give. 'Say something,' she implored; but he could find nothing to say. No cool gentleness to console her, no sarcasm to set her at a distance. In his mind's eye there was a picture – the album he had stolen from Ben Gamble. He couldn't remember what it was called. On the cover, Johnny Sachs, red lit, arms outstretched, mouth open in a tiger's snarl, sweat poured like petrol over his naked torso, liquid shadows delineating every muscle. The Group at Wembley – Radio City – wherever it was. He had been still at school when he read of Johnny Sachs' death . . .

With an effort he dragged himself back to the present. The problem of the moment. Faramond. She had stopped crying but she was still ugly with emotion, lips and eyelids swollen, nose red. She looked very young. Her shamelessness horrified him but in her youth and ugliness he found her pitiful. In his imagination there had been no pity and he did not know how to handle it.

He said: 'So they're all dead . . . How easily people die these days. A turn of the wheel – a tremor of the heart – and it's over. I didn't know you could die so easily. I remember . . . strength. Physical strength. *Power* . . .'

'They aren't all dead.' Faramond's voice was suddenly devoid of emotion.

He didn't seem to hear. 'Come out of the dark!' he mimicked. 'You can't run away from things! Live – breathe – fuck. What a script! I've done you a better one than that. Only you mustn't cry so much for mine. I don't *think* you have to cry at all . . .'

'They aren't all dead,' Faramond said again, this time with more emphasis. 'The guitarist – Rafe Dunston – he's still around.'

Dominic had been drifting rather aimlessly towards the window; now, he stopped. She sensed rather than saw the shiver that ran through him.

'Checked everything, didn't you?' he said after a pause. 'How very thorough.'

'I went to see him.'

'Did you?' He kept his back to her, gazing out of the window at the white daylight in the garden.

'He has a recording studio in London,' Faramond said, inexplicably compelled to offer detail. 'It didn't look very successful.'

'Fascinating.'

'I – think – you should see him too.'

'*See* him?' This time, he turned round, but his face was dark against the window and she could not make out his expression. 'You think – I should – see him?'

'Yes.'

'You seem to have done a hell of a lot of thinking lately!' His tone was meant to be spiteful, but it sounded almost like bluster. 'Why should I see him? To accuse? To forgive? Or is it all part of Facing Up to things? Don't run away, Dominic. Don't hide. Be a Man. Stand up – face up – look life straight in the eye. I am the Captain of my Soul.' He added, abruptly: 'You make me sick.'

He hurt her, but she didn't show it. Somewhere at the back of her thought she knew that cliché and therapy had failed her, she was destroying herself, destroying him, their relationship was falling into pieces and no power in the universe could ever make it whole again. But it was too late now to turn back.

She said: 'You have to see him.' And: 'I brought him. He's here now. Downstairs.'

Dominic said nothing at all.

She came towards him, seized his wrists. He might have fled from her but there was nowhere to go: wall and window were at his back. In her face he saw fear and courage and an unshakeable purpose.

'You *have* to see him,' she said passionately. 'You have to realise – He's nothing. An ageing hippy –' Rafe was in his late thirties '– a failure, a cowardly little rat of a man. The kind of guy who runs after a big star like Johnny Sachs doing anything he says and then spends the rest of his life trying to forget it ever happened. You can't – you *can't* – ruin our whole future for a man like that!'

Who was she trying to convince, Dominic wondered, with the part of his brain that was still able to wonder.

She was pulling at him now, pulling him towards the door, towards the stairs, towards whatever was waiting at the bottom of the stairs. He said: 'You're mad. I won't see him – I can't –'

She saw the panic in his eyes, hesitated – remembered that glimpse of Rafe's profile in the car and the flasher in the woods who had run away. She went on hoping although she knew there was no hope, struggling with all her reason against all her instinct.

On the stairs, Dominic said suddenly: 'I'll never forgive

you. You know that, don't you? Whatever happens, I'll never forgive you.'

In the living room, Rafe was standing by the French windows looking out at the garden. He had tried to open them but either they were locked or the handle was too stiff. His hand shook and the window rattled. He thought of creeping out of the front door, borrowing Faramond's car – but he had seen her take the keys from the ignition and he didn't know where she had put them. He thought of the station (there must be a station), of catching a train. But there might be no trains for ages and he would be there on the platform when Faramond came after him . . . His imagination quailed at the scene. He knew it was ridiculous but he felt trapped – trapped in that ordinary innocuous living room with its watercolour-hung walls and Victorian furniture and the neatly stacked logs in the cold fireplace. The room itself seemed to shut him in, without bolts or bars, like an animal in a snare waiting to be killed . . .

He heard footsteps on the stairs, Faramond's voice – 'He's in here.' The door from the hall was thrust open.

Dominic and Rafe Dunston looked at each other.

Neither of them spoke. The bland daylight showed them to each other in merciless detail. Dominic's face was pinched with tension and almost bloodless. Rafe looked wretched and afraid.

The silence was like a little piece of eternity.

Then Dominic said: 'You.' It might have been an accusation or an affirmation. It might have expressed anger or contempt or disappointment or all three. Perhaps, in his mind, time had kaleidoscoped – the past was scarcely a week old – the giants who had tormented him grew huger and darker until they filled his memory. But the giants had disappeared long ago and there in front of him was all that remained – Rafe Dunston, a puny, miserable-looking man, more hunted than haunted, apparently bewildered by the events of the afternoon. Out of the dark into the daylight. He did not look either evil or good, triumphant or remorseful.

Only uncomfortable and frightened. *Frightened.*

Dominic moved so quickly his very speed was a kind of violence. He caught Rafe by the hair, forcing his head back, dragging the skin taut against his skull. His mouth gaped and the Adam's apple jerked up and down in his neck. 'You!' Dominic repeated. 'You. *You.*' He began to shake the head to and fro, banging it against the French windows. Rafe hardly struggled and suddenly Dominic felt strong. He let go the hair and took hold of the throat, squeezing, digging in his thumbs. The touch of the bare skin disgusted him, like the skin of an uncooked chicken. Rafe was gasping now and his eyes bulged. Dominic felt strong – strong. He gloated with strength . . .

It was Faramond who stopped it, pulling Dominic away, only half sure she was right to interfere. She had no concern for Rafe.

'If you kill him,' she said, 'they'll send you to prison.'

'You brought him here,' said Dominic. He was shaking with leftover rage and he looked at Rafe as if he was a thing, not a person. 'What do you expect me to do with him? Give him tea?'

But Faramond had no expectations any more. 'Talk,' she whispered hopelessly. 'Talk.'

Dominic went over to the sideboard and poured himself a large gin, knocking the bottle against the glass as he did so. 'Get out,' he said, without turning round. 'How the hell can we talk with you here? Go for a walk. Go for a drive. Drown yourself. Leave – *me* – alone.'

Faramond went. She had done enough – too much. There was nothing more she could do.

Rafe sank cautiously into a chair, rubbing his throat. No one had offered him a drink. He badly needed a joint.

Dominic stood looking down at him, his expression unreadable. There was a long pause while Rafe's eyes shifted round the room and he fidgeted with his shirt collar. Dominic just looked at him.

At last he said: 'Let's talk then. It's been a long time – hasn't it? Let's – ' he picked his word '– reminisce.'

He shivered as he said it, but Rafe did not notice. 'Reminisce?' The word seemed to baffle him, as though he needed to look it up. He was having problems with his vocal chords.

Dominic said: 'You'd better have a drink too,' and fetched another, even larger gin. Rafe gulped too eagerly and choked.

Dominic waited while he got his breath back, watching him like a hyaena.

'Let's talk,' he resumed when the fit was over. 'Talk.'

And: 'Tell me about Johnny Sachs.'

It was already late when Alisdair returned to his office. He had been out all afternoon at a meeting which had stretched on into five o'clock drinks and it was only on the way home that he remembered his secretary had the day off and he ought to check his answering machine. He rang the recording studio as soon as he had heard Sue Dunston's message but there was nobody there. He scrabbled through notebooks and directories before finding her home number, filled with an irrational urgency. A child answered the 'phone, evidently sucking a sweet. Presently the child was replaced by its mother. Sue Dunston had no sweet but she was confused and inattentive.

'I don't know what he can have been thinking of – just going off like that – he hasn't called or anything and the Barretts'll be here in half an hour. Perhaps I ought to put them off but I've made a large quiche – I don't know what to do – the receptionist said an American girl but we don't know any Americans. Except Jack Rotweiler . . .'

Alisdair asked a question which was interrupted by the clatter of a dropped receiver. 'I'm so sorry – what did you say? Boris, don't give sweets to the cat – he doesn't want it – yes, she said they mentioned a Dominic – I think she was listening at the door. We don't know anyone called Dominic.' And: 'No, I don't know where they were going. An American girl with a funny name. A *beautiful* American girl.' Clearly she found it difficult to believe that Rafe could have anything to do with a beautiful girl. 'I don't know why I called you really – only you *did* say Dominic, didn't you? – I knew I'd heard the name somewhere. I daresay Rafe could've forgotten – he forgets names – but I thought – do leave the cat alone, Boris – I'm so worried –'

Alisdair murmured something soothing and rang off. He did not feel soothing. He sat for some time staring into space and trying to think. An American girl . . . Faramond Hunter? Presumably, but – That was just it. But. Various possibilities flickered through his mind, each increasingly grotesque. He remembered that Faramond and Dominic were supposed to be living together, somewhere in the country. Kent – Sussex – somewhere like that. Who would know?

After a moment's hesitation he picked up the 'phone again and rang the Heywood Starr Agency. Everyone had gone home.

He rang Anne Heywood's home number. No answer.

He rang an assortment of theatrical friends.

He even rang Nicholas Flack.

It took him three quarters of an hour to find out the address.

Faramond sat at the bottom of the garden looking at the river. She did not know how long she had been sitting there. One hour, two hours; maybe more. From time to time memories of her childhood filled her empty mind – the fence David Hunter had built when she was very young to keep her away from the water – Nanny telling her stories about the troll who lived under the riverbank waiting to catch little girls. She could still see the troll quite clearly, as she had always pictured him, a huge pumpkin head on a disproportionately small body and a wide grinning mouth with warty lips. Now, she was grown up. The fence had gone. The troll had gone. Still, she had a feeling of belonging, here in the garden. Her garden.

She didn't belong in the house any more. The house was a stranger to her. Somehow, without repapering the walls or shifting the furniture, Dominic had taken it over. It was not just the black cigarette ends mouldering in the ashtrays or the computer equipment sprawled across the study desk. Some element in his personality had infiltrated the very atmosphere, so that comfortable memories were dimmed and her father's retiring ghost had long ago effaced itself. In every room Dominic seemed to linger, brooding, silent, suffering and afraid. She tried to imagine the house without him, but she could not. She could not imagine him leaving or staying, rejecting or reaching out to her. Her imagination had run dry and she could not visualise anything any more, either good or bad. It was as if Time had shrunken in upon itself, imprisoning her in this one moment, this hour, like a fly in amber. She could look back, timidly, into the safety of a vanished past; but forward there was nothing. A blank wall, doorless and windowless. She was no longer even sure day would follow night.

It was growing dark now: shadows were creeping up out of the river and welling from the boles of trees. A little wind came from nowhere in particular and began to blow the clouds away, exposing what might have been the evening star. Suddenly, Faramond was aware that she was cold. She got up and began to walk towards the house. There was a light in the living room, a single light, yellow in the dusk. She stood outside the French windows, peering in. Almost, she had raised her hand to knock. The lines of a poem she had read sometime came into her head:

> *Who knocks? I, who was beautiful*
> *beyond all dreams to restore,*
> *I, from the roots of the dark thorn am hither*
> *and knock on your door.*

She didn't knock. They were together in the small circle of the light; she was outside, shut out in the dark like a phantom, unnoticed. She thought: he has forgotten me. Their heads were bent together like conspirators, whispering secrets. They were sharing a joint: she could see the caterpillar of ash on the end and the tiny glow as Rafe inhaled. Then he passed it to Dominic and his lips began to move but she could not hear what he was saying. They were talking, communicating, just as she had wanted, but she did not feel either relief or hope. They seemed to her to be trapped in that ring of light, just as she was trapped, no longer Dominic the victim and

Rafe the fallen enemy but both victims, both enemies, bound by some unspoken allegiance, disagreeably akin. Faramond withdrew from the window, unseen, and went round to the kitchen.

In the hallway, she paused for a minute. The living room door was shut. She had not been particularly quiet but no one had heard her. No one called to her. She felt as if she had ceased to exist. She went upstairs slowly. The stairs hardly troubled to creak.

In her bedroom, she sat down on the bed, took off her shoes. It was too much effort to undress any further. She had been through so many emotions in that one afternoon she did not think she would ever be able to feel emotion again. It was two nights since she had slept well and she had reached that point of absolute exhaustion where she did not even know she was tired. Her body slowed; her mind stopped. She sat on the bed and gazed out of the window.

Presently, she fell asleep.

Downstairs, Rafe had been talking for some time. He had drunk a quantity of gin (he hardly ever drank spirits) and shared three or four joints, and he had long forgotten whom he was talking to or what it had once been about. He was remembering the old days – the Good Old Days – days with The Group, when every record was a hit, every girl was available, every fix was a meaningful experience. He came of a generation who idolised Youth, only to discover, to their unending horror, that they too could grow old. He had never really recovered from the shock of reaching thirty. Now, he had a house in Clapham, two point six children, life insurance – a sort of shabby Left Wing respectability. He worried in a mild way about the possibility of his son sniffing glue or his elder daughter having an illegitimate baby. On occasion he even found himself telling Sue that teenagers weren't what they had been in the Sixties, that sex, drugs, rock 'n' roll etc. weren't what they had been.

'Those were the great days,' he maundered wistfully. 'I'm telling you, man. The great days. We changed the world. We were the first with everything. The first to smoke grass, the first to have free love, the first to play rock 'n' roll. We had the first great demos – anti-Vietnam – Grosvenor Square – they don't have demos like that any more. Nowadays it's all dole queues and depression and Princess Di. We didn't think much of princes and princesses in our day. We were the royalty – kings, man, rock 'n' roll kings, kings of the world. The audiences used to howl for us like animals. Once, Johnny lost every stitch of clothing – I saw some girl kissing a piece of his shirt like it had belonged to Jesus Christ. Now, they have designer wardrobes and take care of their shirts. The girls don't scream and cry any more, they just clap like coach parties at the ballet. I tell you, nobody was ever young like us. No one ever will be. We were the only ones who understood what being young meant . . .'

Dominic did not disillusion him. He had listened to the dreary diatribe with a sort of concentrated patience, like an angler waiting for one particular fish to appear before casting his line. Rafe spoke almost totally without emphasis or inflection, words and sentiment coming out in an incessant drone as if from some whining piece of machinery. When the right fish came to the surface, Dominic interrupted.

'Tell me about Johnny.'

Rafe gazed at him through the smoke of his joint, vaguely surprised that there was still somebody there. 'Johnny . . .' he murmured, evidently bewildered at being drawn back from his meditations on Youth. And then: 'Johnny was king. Johnny was *the* king, man, the king of kings. They worshipped him like he was God and the devil all rolled into one. He was the first rock 'n' roll superstar. Do you know, in '62 when The Group started, they were still wearing suits?' (Rafe had joined in '65, but he did not mention it and Dominic did not care.) 'The Beatles and the Stones and all of them – wearing *suits*. Suits and ties and short hair. They made Johnny wear a suit too. You know what he did? He wore the suit all right – but he *didn't wear a shirt*. I'm telling you, man. He was the first rebel. The others were just baby-faced boys out for a good time. Johnny – Johnny was different. He didn't take any shit from anyone. He stuck two fingers up at the whole world.

Mary Whitehouse – all those Tory wives – they made a fuss. Repressed old cows, Johnny called them. He said it in an interview – right out in public. They need a good fuck, he said. He didn't care.'

Possibly Rafe's recollections were distorted with time, but Dominic did not query them. The figure of Johnny Sachs, grown huge with nostalgia, seemed to loom in the shadows – the same figure on the album cover, with its whipcord muscles and feral grimace. A ghost maybe; but somehow that ghost held more reality for Dominic than Rafe or himself. They were flimsy beings, wraiths malingering in a present which was itself only a leftover from some vital moment in the past. That moment endured; Johnny, long dust and ashes, was there in flesh and blood and sweat, not spirit but substance; the heat of his body pressed upon Dominic while his own grew clammy.

But the room was empty. It always would be.

Presently, Dominic got up and went over to the cupboard by the music centre. When he opened it, a tumble of records spilled onto the floor. Rafe went on talking as if he had not moved.

'You're too young, man. You wouldn't remember. You got the world after we'd blown it wide open.' (He might just as well have said: I fought the war for people like you.) 'We kicked out the old traditions – old ideas. We kicked the establishment right up its arse. We grew our hair and took our clothes off. We *fucked*.'

Dominic murmured with only the faintest note of sarcasm: 'I doubt if you were the first generation to do that.'

Rafe was undeterred. 'You don't understand, man. We used the word. We did it in the open. We pulled back the curtains and let it all hang out . . .'

Dominic had found the record he wanted. From the music centre came the roar of a crowd long grown older and wiser, the preliminary twang of a guitar-string, a brief, unintelligible introduction. And then the clamour of the crowd merged into the pounding of the music, and as Dominic turned up the volume the noise seemed to gather itself together like a wave and come crashing into the room, so that the walls shook and ornaments rocked on their shelves. And for a few seconds it was real, it was there: the exulting mob, the arching lights, the relentless cannonade of drum and guitar, and over all the voice of Johnny Sachs, magnified a thousand times, howling like a hyena, hissing like serpent. It seemed to Dominic that he was hearing it for the first time.

He turned the volume down again. Rafe was still staring into the cigarette smoke with unfocused eyes. Johnny Sachs belted out his own particular creed with slightly diminished stridency. *I don't believe in nuclear wars and prison bars and Santa Claus I don't believe in anything no more*. Old words for an old idea. The album cover was propped up against the wall on top of the music centre. Johnny's image was veined with creases and smeared with stains of what might have been wine, relics of some party years ago. On the record, the technology of the Eighties amplified every scratch.

Dominic sat down beside Rafe. There was something in his attitude that was almost affectionate, a kind of invidious gentleness. He removed the joint very tenderly from between Rafe's fingers. Rafe was still muttering 'We fucked the establishment' and 'We fucked them all'.

'Bullshit,' Dominic said softly. 'You became the establishment. Just like in any other revolution. Yesterday's rebels become the barons and bureaucrats of today. Look at the big stars – Paul McCartney, Elton John – bloated with success, idols of wealth and capitalism. You were never a big star, of course. You were one of the nameless ones who fell by the wayside, thrown out of the golden chariot while the chosen few drove off to join the same old party. Poor Rafe. You gave up the fight without even trying. A failure – a cosy, shoddy, half-baked sort of failure, clinging onto society by the tails of its evening coat. Poor Rafe . . . ' And Dominic stroked his cheek, very delicately, with the tip of one finger, his face twisted with a kind of fascinated distaste.

Rafe seemed scarcely aware of the caress. 'Give me the joint,' he said. 'Please.'

'In a minute . . . It's a joke, isn't it? You want so much to be up there with the stars, fat and rich and successful. You want so much to go to the party. Poor Rafe. What a joke. Laugh,

Rafe. Laugh at the joke.'

Obediently, Rafe laughed. A high-pitched, automatic giggle, heh-heh-heh, like the yapping of a miniature dog.

And Dominic remembered. He had not known the voice of Johnny Sachs but he knew that laugh. It was there in his subconscious, buried deep under the years and the shadows. A tiny echo of truth among all the magnificent horrors of his imagination. Suddenly, past and present came together – fell into place. Knowledge became understanding. He saw himself clearly at last, caught in the dragon gaze of invisible eyes, possessed by a demon he could not touch, could not hold, could not exorcise. He wondered if he would ever be free of it, and what freedom meant. He had never been free. He knew now he was afraid of freedom.

Rafe reached for the joint but Dominic had crushed it out on the table. He stood up. He wanted to speak but he was choked with loathing and self-loathing, so that he did not know which was the strongest, or which the hardest to bear. Rafe stared up at him. By some trick of the light his dreary eyes looked almost beseeching.

Meet me in Hell, sang Johnny Sachs. *I'll be waiting for you.*

'Laugh at the joke!' said Dominic, his voice distorted with ill-contained violence. 'Laugh, Dominic. Laugh at the joke!'

Rafe did not understand. He wanted the joint. 'Johnny fucked them,' he insisted, pathetically. 'I'm telling you, man. Johnny never became the establishment. Johnny died.'

'Yes,' said Dominic, and his voice was suddenly quiet again. 'Johnny died.'

And: 'How did he die?'

'In a car,' Rafe said. 'A car accident. He hit a petrol tanker.' He still did not understand. Now, he never would.

'I remember,' Dominic said. 'That must have been – spectacular.' There was a dreadful eagerness in his face, but he still spoke very softly. His eyes were pale and brilliant in the lamplight. 'Tell me about it. Tell me – all – about it.'

Meet me in Hell, sang the record.
I'll be waiting in Hell
Take a shortcut to Hell

All your hopes and your dreams
All your loves and your schemes
Take you down into Hell
Come and catch me in Hell
I'll be waiting in Hell
Baby, meet me in Hell
Hell
Hell . . .

Faramond woke abruptly to find herself sitting bolt upright staring wide-eyed into the darkness. She had a feeling she had been dreaming – dreaming vividly and horribly – and in her dream something had frightened her so much that it had jerked her awake in less than a second. Her heart was thumping so hard that her body shook, and she felt hot and cold as though a sweat of terror had broken out all over her only an instant before. Her fear was so real that it was a few moments before she remembered other things. Rafe. Dominic. Dominic saying, 'I'll never forgive you . . . Whatever happens, I'll never forgive you –'

Memory came rushing back. She had fallen asleep on top of the bed, fully dressed; she had no idea how long she had slept or what time it was now (her travelling clock was still in her bag in the hall). Yet even with her return to reality, Fear remained. It was there in the bedroom with her. She could smell it, taste it, hear it – a faint, acrid smell, sharp as poison, a dryness in the air, an undercurrent of noise both breathless and hungry. A part of her mind was still semi-conscious or she would have known what it was. But all she knew was the presence of Fear. Every nerve in her body tingled with it.

She got up and ran to the door. Already, a tiny coil of smoke was creeping through the crack underneath; but she did not see it. As she opened the door, noise, smell, smoke rushed in on her, filling her ears, her nostrils, her lungs –. She slammed the door again and leant against it, as if the smoke outside might try to batter it down. She was gasping for breath and her eyes stung. When she was able she reached for the light switch and pressed it, but nothing happened: evidently the circuit had been cut. She ran back to the bed, pushed up the window, leaned out into the night.

It was too dark to see clearly, but she was aware of more smoke pouring from somewhere on her right – the direction of the living room – and a ground floor window almost immediately below her flung a red shadow on the grass. For the first time she thought how isolated the house was, on the edge of the village, detached from its neighbours, surrounded by garden . . .

She leaned further out of the window but there was no one in sight. No people, no ladders, no fire engines. Nothing.

She called 'Help!' and even 'Dominic!' – but her voice sounded small and feeble against the voice of the fire and she knew Dominic would not come. Dominic was in the living room with Rafe, heads together like conspirators, whispering secrets . . .

She turned away from the window, fighting a rising panic. Inexplicably, the darkness in her bedroom seemed to have thickened; she realised suddenly the smoke had been creeping in behind her back, under the door, through the keyhole, cornering her against the window like an animal at bay.

She thought: 'I'll have to jump.'

It was a long way down.

This time, when she called for help, she was screaming.

It was very late when Alisdair reached Overbridge. He had wasted some time before he left London trying to get hold of Theresa, who was still at college. He hadn't told her anything, only that it was urgent and he didn't know when he would be back. On the journey down, he got stuck in a traffic jam as a result of a collision between two lorries and was there for over half an hour.

He lost his way twice.

When he finally got to Overbridge, he had no idea where to go and there was no one about to ask. He took a turning at random and saw a young couple coming towards him, a girl in a leather jacket and a boy with spiky hair. Alisdair pulled over and opened the window.

'I'm looking for River Street . . .'

The boy turned and pointed. 'That way.'

'Hey!' His girlfriend nudged him. 'What's that?'

Something in her voice made Alisdair's vague fears grow suddenly sharper. He craned his neck in an attempt to see.

The boy said: 'Looks like a fire.'

Alisdair snapped: 'River Street?'

'Yeah . . . Must be. Haven't heard any engines, though.'

'Get to a 'phone,' Alisdair said. 'Bang on the nearest door. Hurry –'

The girl said uncertainly: 'Someone might have called already' – rather as if she was afraid of committing a social solecism.

The boy was more practical. 'Don't be silly, Shirl. Go up to Aunt Jane's on the corner. Knock and shout. Go on, run.' And, to Alisdair: 'I'm coming with you.'

Alisdair opened the door without further comment and the girl ran off up the road, high heels flying.

The boy said: 'Left here' just short of a turning but it was unnecessary: Alisdair could see the smoke, dim against a black sky, and a flare of red underneath. He knew it made no sense but he kept remembering Johnny Sachs, crashing his car into a petrol tanker and hurtling into hell in a ball of fire – Johnny Sachs, reaching out across the withered years, across the gulf of the grave, a dreadful charismatic spectre, roaring in the night like a dark wind, filled with the power that swayed audiences and wrecked theatres, driving lesser men to acts of violence and madness . . .

They pulled up outside the house on the opposite side of the road. Alisdair got out and the boy followed him. The voice of the fire seemed to be mingled with the crashing of cymbals and the rumble of drums and the howl of a crowd long swallowed up in Time . . . As they drew nearer, smoke poured over them, drifting sparks settled on their clothes. Alisdair cupped his hands over nose and mouth; the boy did the same. The ground floor windows were squares of flame in a dark wall. No one could live in that furnace. Alisdair screwed up his eyes and peered upwards through the smoke.

The fire had not yet reached the higher floors. Even so, he saw Faramond only dimly, one leg over the window sill, her cry for help stifled by the fumes in her lungs . . .

The boy said: 'We need a ladder.'

Alisdair mouthed: No time. He called up: 'Blanket! Throw down – blanket!'

Somehow, Faramond understood. With her last strength she dragged a cover from the bed, tugged and bundled it through the window. The darkness was full of tiny pink and green specks which danced in her vision like fireflies. Bursts of colour exploded in her head. There was no air any more. She clawed her way over the window sill like a drowning man climbing a sand bar . . .

Below, Alisdair and the boy had picked up the blanket.

'Nearer,' Alisdair said, voiceless. 'Must get – nearer . . .'

The heat blistered their skin, scorched clothing, singed hair. Faramond let go the window sill and plunged earthwards, hitting the blanket in a tangle of arms and legs and tumbling, winded, onto the grass . . . From inside the house came a roar as of some baffled god, the thunder of breaking floors and falling beams. Even as they crawled or stumbled to safety a part of the wall burst outwards, fire tore through the gap, and smoke came toppling down on them like a wave . . .

In some remote corner of his mind Alisdair found himself remembering the three people who had died with Johnny Sachs more than a decade ago. Time slipped. Behind him, the burning house became petrol blazing on an open road, and Johnny's ghost, grown monstrous and vengeful from long years of death, reached out towards him with hands of fire . . .

Chapter Twelve

At the inquest, the Coroner suggested it was a suicide pact.
 Forensic evidence revealed that much of the ground floor had been doused in petrol, parrafin, and lavatory cleaner. (David Hunter always kept a spare can of petrol in the car, a habit Faramond had continued.) There was little left of Rafe and Dominic but experts declared Rafe's clothing had also been soaked in paraffin, though Dominic's had not. Dental evidence was produced to tell the corpses apart; Rafe, despite his comparative youth, had had several false teeth.
 Dominic's accident on New Year's Eve was resurrected, and Dr Hieronymous Glauber himself gave evidence of his depressive tendencies.
 Sue Dunston was not well enough to appear, but Rafe's receptionist testified that he was 'very distressed' when he drove off with Faramond.
 Alisdair stated that Sue had called him because he was 'a mutual friend' and she was anxious about Rafe. He managed to imply that Sue had remembered some previous acquaintance between Rafe and Dominic although the receptionst had said she knew of none. He had a dressing on his left arm where it had been burned and a red scar on his cheek which doctors assured him would disappear eventually. The fire

brigade had told him he was Very Lucky. Alisdair had never thought of himself as lucky and he was still getting used to the idea.

Faramond gave her evidence last. She had a bandage on her ankle where it had been sprained in her fall and an assortment of minor burns and bruises. The fire brigade had told her she was Very *Very* Lucky. She wore her hair brushed back off her forehead and coiled in a bun on the nape of her neck, a style that emphasised the gravity of her face. A graze on her temple which the hair might have concealed stood out ugly purple against the whiteness of her skin.

The Coroner asked her why she had gone to find Rafe that day and driven him down to Overbridge.

She said: 'Dominic told me to.' Her voice was not loud but it carried effortlessly in the panelled hall. An actress's voice.

Did she know why Dominic wanted to see Rafe?

'No.'

What happened when she and Rafe arrived at the house?

'I left them together.'

Did she know what they talked about? Had she overheard any of their conversation?

'No.'

What had she been doing?

'I went and sat in the garden.'

For how long?

'I don't know . . . It was dark when I came in.'

The Coroner was trying to be gentle and fatherly with her but something in her manner rebuffed both gentleness and fatherliness. She was, he thought, too self-contained for someone so young who had been through such an ordeal. A sort of desperate calm. He said: 'I understand you told the police that Hardinge and Dunston had been drinking and smoking illegal substances. How did you know this?'

'I saw them,' she explained. 'Through the window. On my way back to the house.'

'Did they seem –' the Coroner sought for a word '– agitated? Violent? Depressed?'

'No . . . ' For the first time, he was aware that she was looking at him, a dark, serious look which seemed to compel or beseech some special understanding. 'They were sitting very close together, sharing a joint. They looked . . . furtive and sly. Like men who are plotting something – something secret and dreadful.'

'Are you sure,' the Coroner said 'that this isn't the wisdom of hindsight? Are you sure that was the impression you received at the time?'

Faramond said firmly: 'I am quite sure.'

'Did you go in and speak to them?'

'No.'

'Why not?'

'They looked too – too private.'

'What did you do?'

'I went upstairs to bed.'

And finally, the question for which she had been waiting: 'Do you know any reason why Dominic Hardinge might have wished to kill himself?'

Faramond hesitated, arranging the words in her head. 'He was like that,' she said at length. 'He was kind of – damaged inside. I loved him very much but I couldn't help him.' And, in a low tone: 'No one could help him.'

The Coroner became gentle and fatherly again. 'You can't think of anything – anything at all – which might have, so to speak, pushed him over the edge?'

'No,' said Faramond. Her voice was neither too loud nor too soft. 'Nothing at all.'

When it was all over, Faramond drove back to London with Alisdair and Theresa.

Outside, the press had photographed Alisdair's scar and Faramond's graze and swept-back hair. Dominic's Mystery Death made a headline in the tabloids and a sideline in the *Telegraph* and *The Times*. The *Guardian* gave him a lengthy obituary, dwelling on his presumed Left Wing sympathies, his symbolic taste in cigarettes, the anti-nuclear protest play as exemplified in *Ragnarok*. Dominic (Alisdair said later) would doubtless have appreciated it all.

In the car, Faramond asked: 'Do you believe it was a suicide pact?'

[222]

Alisdair said: 'Maybe.'

Faramond did not want to think about Rafe, but she could not help it. She could see him in her mind, slumped in a chair, the joint burning away between his fingers, a thin coil of smoke slowly unravelling before his unfocused eyes. He did not seem to notice the paraffin trickling down through his hair and over his clothes. Dominic stood above him, holding the can, pouring the deadly liquid steadily, deliberately, his face still wearing that expression of peculiar concentration which she had seen when she looked through the window . . .

The image in her mind was clearer than any memory. She thought about the lies she had told – unnecessary lies – and the gentle fatherly manner of the Coroner. And she felt guilty, and adult, and empty of all love.

Alisdair wondered a good deal about the things she had not said, but he asked no questions and Theresa, following his lead, was unusually quiet. They had discussed Dominic between themselves; they would not press Faramond. Her face shut out all enquiry.

The journey passed in silence.

It was almost a year later when Dominic's last play, *The Doll*, opened in the West End. It had been sitting on Anne Heywood's desk at the time of the fire, still unread. Legal complications had slowed up production: Dominic had left no Will and it was finally decided that his estate (including the play) was the property of Francis and Zoë Preston as adoptive next-of-kin. Zoë was anxious to see the play staged. In the end, Alisdair produced it, Ben Gamble directed, Faramond Hunter starred.

'What would Dominic have said,' Alisdair speculated, 'if he could see us now? All the people who failed him, battening on his talent like leeches. Yes, that's how he'd have phrased it. Battening on his talent . . .'

He was talking to Theresa over a drink about an hour before Curtain Up.

'We aren't battening,' said Theresa. 'This is his immortality.' And: 'Anyway, you didn't always fail.'

'Didn't I? I lay in the grass, and did nothing. When I learned the truth, I did nothing. Always nothing . . .'

'You drove down to Overbridge,' Theresa pointed out, 'on the night of the fire.'

Alisdair gulped a mouthful of gin. 'So what?' he retorted. 'I was too late.'

Theresa said: 'Not for Faramond.'

Faramond Hunter sat in her dressing room studying the face in her mirror. An oval face thick with make-up, nostrils picked out in scarlet, dark eyes inked in against a topcoat of powder. A doll's face. *The* Doll. She tried to remember her lines, and found that she couldn't. A long time ago there had been someone called Dominic Hardinge whom she thought she had loved. He had written a play for her and then, when it was finished, he had killed himself. In that moment it seemed a curiously natural progression of events. She tried to feel sadness or pain but there was nothing inside her at all, only a horrible sick emptiness. She thought: 'I have a Past,' remembering that a Past was something she had once wanted, but it didn't seem important now. There was only the doll's mask in the mirror, and behind it blankness, panic.

Presently, Alisdair came in. 'How do you feel?'

'Awful,' whispered Faramond. Even her voice seemed to have gone.

'Good,' said Alisdair. 'They always say the real stars feel like that.'

He didn't know if it was true but, as intended, it reassured her.

In the auditorium the theatre-goers were settling themselves in their seats. Among those present, Zoë Preston (not Francis, who was getting rather frail and elderly), Sherwin and Annalee Milberg, Anne Heywood, assorted critics and other vultures of the West End. Everyone was waiting to see if Dominic could live up to his death and produce a really exciting piece of posthumous work. Marten de Witt, though he attended a good many opening nights, was not there. His wife was in Antibes or somewhere equally hot and expensive.

The curtain rose.

The play was drawn loosely from the plot of the ballet *Coppélia*. Set a little way in the future, it centred round a solitary genius who designed and constructed wonderful clockwork toys, prototypes for subsequent mass production. These toys were his whole world: he gave them names and personalities, talked to them in a way he could not do with real people. Every so often, a representative of the Toy Company came and took one of them away to the factory. He suffered as if from a bereavement. When he made the Doll – the lifesize figure of a beautiful girl – he resolved to keep her for himself. He was in love with his own creation. The girl appeared and the audience was left in doubt whether she was the Doll come to life, a cruel practical joke, or merely a figment of the toymaker's imagination. A relationship developed between the two of them, until finally, at the climax of the play, they made love. The toymaker fell asleep, waking later to find beside him not a living woman but only a doll, cold and inanimate. In a fit of rage and despair he tore its head off and threw the broken body into a box.

The stage darkened. A greenish glow touched the box. The toymaker did not see; he was slumped in a chair with his back to it, abandoned to loneliness. The lid of the box opened and a figure climbed out: the girl, whole and perfect again. She crept up behind the toymaker's chair, took his head tenderly in her hands.

Then she wrenched it off.

He gave one hideous cry, and a jet of stage blood shot from what appeared to be a widening rip in his throat. All the lights went out.

In the dark, a faint sigh ran though the audience. Thirty seconds later, the lights came on again. The cast appeared, intact, to take their bows. The audience began to clap, at first out of sheer relief and then with mounting enthusiasm. Faramond, filled with glory, forgot Dominic, forgot everything in the dazzle of success. Already, one of the critics was composing phrases about her 'Sphinx-like features' and 'inexplicable air of mystery'.

'Doesn't she understand?' said Theresa. She had not seen

[225]

or read the play before. 'Doesn't she see what it's *about*?'

'I don't know,' Alsdair admitted. 'She doesn't confide in me. Anyway, Dominic didn't write about truth. He took people – situations – and distorted them in his imagination until they became warped and evil. It was reality and simplicity that he couldn't face.'

It sounded almost like an epitaph.

In the foyer, he heard words like 'grotesque', 'bizarre' and 'crude melodrama' being bandied about with relish. He thought: It'll do. The enigma of Dominic's death was being revived: critics delved deep into the play for hidden meanings and hitherto disregarded clues. A Bright Young Man of journalistic leanings was already planning a biography. He pictured it serialised in one of the Sundays: 'Genius With Death Wish'. – 'A Modern Mayerling' – 'Dramatic New Revelations'. He had no idea what the revelations were to be but he was sure he would think of something. There would be a massive hype, blockbuster sales –

It was only just beginning.

Like James Dean, like Marilyn Monroe – like Jimi Hendrix, Marc Bolan, Johnny Sachs – Dominic Francis Hardinge passed into legend.

[226]